RICHARD ANDERSON

◆

BOXED

Complete and Unabridged

AURORA
Leicester

First published in Great Britain in 2019 by
Scribe Publications

First published in Australia in 2019 by
Scribe Publications

First Aurora Edition
published 2019
by arrangement with
Scribe Publications

A catalogue record for this book is available
from the British Library.

ISBN 978–1–78782–196–5

Published by
F. A. Thorpe (Publishing)
Anstey, Leicestershire

Set by Words & Graphics Ltd.
Anstey, Leicestershire
Printed and bound in Great Britain by
T. J. International Ltd., Padstow, Cornwall

This book is printed on acid-free paper

BOXED

Dave Martin is down on his luck: his wife's left him, his farm is a failure, his house is a mess, he's withdrawn from his community and friends, and tragedy has stolen his capacity to care. He passes the time drinking too much and buying cheap tools online, treating the delivered parcels as gifts from people who care about him. And then boxes begin to arrive in the mail: boxes that he didn't order, but ones that everyone around him seems to want desperately. As he investigates, Dave is drawn into a crazy world of red herrings and wrong turns, good guys and bad, false friends and true, violence, lust, fear, revenge, and a lot, lot more. It's not a world he understands, but is it the only one Dave can live in?

Books by Richard Anderson
Published by Ulverscroft:

RETRIBUTION

To Sue, Issie, and Matt, and the rest of the
G.A.B.s. Every generation.

1

I don't want to be me.

I don't want to be Dave Martin, loser, parked at his mailbox under the river gum: two beers' drive from Stony Creek Pub, half a state from Sarah, and at least eighteen months past useful.

But there's only one way I can stop, and I'm not ready for that.

I step out of my ute into the heat, and notice, again, there is a faint organic stink on the air, like a whiff from a long-dead animal. I can't place it, and don't care to.

I know that summer is supposed to be finished, but no one told the sun and its mate, the wind that blisters off the plain, making me feel like a dry frog stranded between water points. But I see the plains grass is still green, the dust is holding low, and the kurrajong tree leaves are shaking their shiny vigour, so perhaps the last few months haven't been that hot. Can't say I've been paying attention.

To the east, a scattering of large eucalypts prevents me from seeing my running-down homestead, expansive and red-roofed, and its messed-up, park-sized garden, even though it would take a crow less than a minute to flap its ungainly way from here to there.

A police car cruises past on its way towards town, tyres scrabbling for authority in the loose gravel. The driver, a woman I feel I might know,

1

does not wave, or raise a hand or an eyebrow in acknowledgement. That's odd. Everybody around here waves, one way or another — especially strangers. I have only seen a police car on this road once. I hope it doesn't mean someone has died. At least it won't be someone I care about.

But that is not important.

What is important is that the mailman is supposed to deliver three times a week — Monday, Wednesday, Friday — even if there are floods, fires, or public holidays. But our current mailman couldn't give a proverbial. If the weather on the TV says bad storms or even good storms are likely, he stays in the pub, his bedroom, at his gaming desk, or wherever he dwells when he is not delivering the mail. It's not right.

When I was a little fella, we had a mail-lady called Mrs Crowther who talked with a slow Australian drawl that you don't hear anywhere anymore. Mrs Crowther would get the mail to us, no matter what. And not just mail. She delivered groceries, tractor parts, and even messages from friends ten properties away. There wasn't a natural disaster or a government indisposition that could stop her. On our small colour TV, American cartoons had mailmen who said things like, 'Wind nor rain nor sleet nor snow, the mail must get through.' We knew Mrs Crowther watched the same cartoons. Not this bloke. I'm guessing he watches Asian porn and truck-smash videos on his phone, and delivers the mail when he feels like it.

But today I open the lid to find he has bothered to come, and on time, and left me a

2

large box that just fits in my oversized mailbox. Everyone out here has a big mailbox, courtesy of those Mrs Crowther days and before, when everything came by mail. In these parts, we were long-distance shopping well before the internet came about.

My latest thing is buying cheap machinery online (I mean immorally cheap, like $80 chainsaws that even at a local hardware barn would cost $250) just so I can get the parcel in the mail. It's a small pleasure, but these days there aren't many opportunities for pleasure or even distraction. I do not drink anymore, because the morning-tea beers were taking a hold of me. So I hardly ever go to the pub. I no longer have staff. I don't have anyone to talk to or share things with. The only other person here is James.

I lift the parcel out, and place it on the passenger seat. It's like Christmas for losers. A present delivered to my mailbox is thrilling, even though the wrapping paper is brown and without decoration, I know the contents, and the person who sent it is probably an algorithm. Although, given the companies I have been buying from, and the prices I've been paying, what is inside is usually a weird surprise: parts missing, specifications wrong, assembly backwards. This time it is supposed to be a submersible pump: $85, including delivery. A small one (half a horsepower) for a failing bore. At the price, it was worth the risk, even though I knew it might come without something significant like, say, the pump. Anyway, I drive the box home as if it really is a Christmas present from someone who cares about me.

My house is huge and beautiful, but decrepit. My family has owned it for five generations. It has sweeping verandahs, multiple roof angles, and large rooms with high ceilings and wide-board timber floors. It has five bedrooms and three bathrooms, a huge kitchen, a living area, a dining room, and a couple of other rooms that at times had TVs, overflowing bookcases, games, soft couches, and room for people to relax on their own. The only rooms I use are my bedroom, the kitchen, and a bathroom. All this is surrounded by the verandahs broad enough for ping-pong tables, dining tables and chairs, and hammocks. Outside, there is a meat house that is just one room, a cool room, and extra quarters that used to be for maids and cooks.

In earlier times, it featured on glossy pages in fashionable lifestyle magazines: the backdrop for my parents, freshly washed, seated, looking attractive and significant at an artisan's timber table on that verandah above a lush, colour-filled garden. Even though the articles featured the house and the 'flair' that was evident in my mother's decorations, as well as the garden she reinvigorated and toiled in to create effortless beauty, the photos revealed it as no more than a humble offering to my father. Nothing, no matter how beautiful or hard-worked-for, existed without his approval. Once you passed this mailbox and crossed the front ramp, everything was owned by him. That was my father: squattocrat and autocrat.

These days, my house would not grace the pages of a giveaway newspaper or a failing website. The roof needs work. The bathrooms need work. The stumping needs work. I don't have the money, the skill, or the patience to fix these things, and since Sarah left, I don't have the inclination. So if the roof leaks, I put a bucket under it. If the floors lean, I lean back.

I take the box home as if it was long-awaited (four working days for delivery, actually), and put it on the kitchen island. It looks a little worse for wear, as if they had run out of new boxes and had to use a second-hand one. Entirely possible. I get a knife from the drawer, insert it in the top line of the box, then cut, rip, and tear like a birthday-blessed six-year-old. There is probably three times the amount of packing tape these companies normally use, but let's face it: opening is half the fun, right?

A submersible pump is a stainless-steel cylinder that usually comes in two parts, both of which might be mistaken for a silver flask. There are no stainless-steel cylinders in this box. When I finally get the packing removed, I find flat stacks, big bricks of something solid. Six of them. They are wrapped in a type of thick plastic film that seems to be from another era. I have a bit of a chuckle to myself. The ways that these companies come up with to cheat me are ingenious or monumentally lazy, but always entertaining. I guess the bricks contain plain old paper-fill, and it does seem like a kind of justice. I rip back the last film of unneeded protection, and look at what I have paid for. What I see is

$100 notes in stacks, like in the movies, neatly packed and wrapped. Weird green-blue in colour, thirty centimetres high, three wide, two deep. The only time I have seen more than two $100 notes together at one time was at the races with my father when he bet big on a long shot just to show off.

I jump back, curse in rapid fire, and then lean forward and shove the box hard, off the bench, and away from me. It thuds on the floor without losing a note. Is this a nasty trick? I need money. Everyone knows that. Has someone sent these bricks of cash, undoubtedly fake, photocopied, to ridicule me? Could Sarah, my wife, now in the city, have done this? No, never. But who else? A local business? The truth is, I'm not significant enough for people to hate me. I'm no longer a big-enough player for local businesses or any of the other farmers to pay much attention to me. The only time I come up in their conversation is when they ponder how long I might hold out for before selling up. They're greedy buggers.

I take a few steadying breaths, pick up the box, and check the lid and the outsides for letters conveying a prank, or threat, or at least an explanation. There is nothing — no directions, no explanations. If the money is real, I must have received someone else's mail: a drug dealer, a bikie, a crooked cop. Very soon, they will work out that their money has gone missing, and will come looking for it. They will have no trouble finding it or me. I can look forward to being bashed or killed, or both. But I am making assumptions. The only knowledge I have of this sort of carry-on is from the TV.

I check the name and address: Dave Martin, Five Trees. It is mine. It has been sent to me. This makes no sense. Do I have a rich, long-lost, underworld uncle who was looking out for me? Sending me boxes of cash? No chance. I examine the notes. They feel like the right sort of polymer material that bank notes are made from. Maybe 3D printers could do this sort of thing. I unearth my computer from a topsoil of books, magazines, and chip packets, then do a web search on how to identify a $100 note. I find a useful video, and, following its directions, I check the window on the notes for clearness, examine the image in those windows and the micro-print near it, and the raised type, as well as the shadow image of the coat of arms, and everything else they suggest. If these dollars are fake, they are bloody good ones. I try to pick a few notes randomly from the middle of the pile. They seem to be genuine, too. Fuck. What to do? I estimate there is around $250,000 in the box. Not much to an underground criminal, but a bloody fortune to me. I take the box off the bench and place it in the cupboard. It is unnerving me and stopping me thinking clearly.

Should I tape it down and stick it back in the mailbox? Pretend I have never seen it? Or leave a note on it saying 'Wrong address — I didn't order any parcels'?

But this money could make a huge difference to my life. I could reduce some of my bank debt, pay the rates, send an expensive present to Sarah, offer to take her on an overseas trip, and

7

explain that my fortunes have changed, I've got my act together, and I am keen to get her back. Very, very tempting. But, one way or another, it is stealing. And the people I will be stealing from are likely to be very upset. Not much point making a huge improvement to a life that no longer exists.

However, I know I will never get my hands on this sort of money again. Not unless I sell the farm, and I can't do that because James is here. I know the box of cash isn't worth dying for, but nobody would honestly say my recent version of living was worth fighting for either.

And then, out the window, I see a huge, new, white four-wheel-drive ute — shiny, chromed, and tricked-up — come meandering up my driveway, crossing the ramp, and coasting to a halt. Christ, I think, they've come for me already. My rifles are locked in the gun cabinet at the other end of the house. By the time I could get to them, unlock them, and get them out, the bad guys would have a rifle barrel shoved up my arse. I step back from the window, and watch, remembering there's an old set of golf clubs in the garage, and a cricket bat somewhere that might be useful for self-defence.

But the person getting out of the car isn't the tattooed hard man I was expecting. It is a shapely woman with brown, straight hair, slim in tight jeans, and wearing a loose top. She loosens her hair and looks in my direction. It is Elaine Slade, a farmer from two properties down my road towards town. Elaine is the sort of woman who is immaculately, effortlessly turned out,

8

even in work clothes. In my community, it is agreed that she is beautiful, but for me that is academic. I can't see beauty; it only makes me think of Sarah. So when she gets out of her car, shakes her hair back, and stretches her lovely neck, my only emotion is relief. Elaine has not come to heavy me over the money. She's probably come to ask to borrow a piece of machinery; although why she would want to borrow any of my broken-down machinery, I'm not sure. I see her step up to the front door, knock, and step back. She says, 'Hello' to no one, extending the 'o' just a bit, and waits.

When I open the door, she smiles brightly. 'Hi, Dave. How are you?'

I tell her I'm well, and do not mention that I've just received a quarter of a million in cash in the mail.

'I'm glad I caught you. I thought you might be out in the paddock somewhere.'

I say something about lunch, and she nods understandingly. Lunch is one of the few legitimate reasons a farmer can be in the house in daylight hours.

'I am sorry to bother you, but it's just that I've had a parcel go missing in the mail, and it's overdue and very important to me. It's crockery, from my great-aunt. Not really so valuable, but important to me, and *very* breakable. The mailman said he left a parcel in your mailbox, and I wondered if you'd mind checking that it wasn't my missing one?'

What I say without a moment's consideration or reference to the idea of giving the money back to keep myself alive is, 'I'm really sorry, Elaine, but I don't know what the mailman is talking about. I didn't get any parcels in the mail today. Just a few bills, and a couple of farm-machinery catalogues.' I laugh at the paltry nature of my mail.

She looks concerned. 'Are you sure?'

'Absolutely positive. That new mailman is bit of an idiot, though. He probably got confused.'

Elaine is confused.

'Grant? I can't believe that. Why would he say he dropped it here if he didn't?' She's a little scary with her glamorous certitude.

'Maybe he took it.' It is a kind of brave, historical punt: blame the mailman. But she ignores the suggestion.

'Do you think someone else could have got to your mailbox before you?'

'I can't say I pay much attention. But it's possible. Although, why they'd want to . . . I mean, it's not as if there's ever going to be anything in my mail worth stealing.'

She doesn't fall for the self-deprecation.

'Grant said you get boxes all the time. Every few weeks there's something. From overseas. And today there was one that wasn't from overseas.' She looks at me, and even though the look is not unpleasant, there is a steeliness in the way she says the words. She seems surprisingly close to 'Grant'.

Elaine is relatively new to the district. Never been in farming before. Had an uncle on the land she used to visit when she was a little girl. Rode horses, collected eggs. Couldn't get it out of her system, or so the story goes. Can't say I'm close enough to her to have even heard it second-hand. She's lived here three or four years. Her husband was a well-known potter, but died in an accident somewhere, on business, six months ago. A small plane crash in Africa or something. I can't remember, but it made the news at the time. The obituary was significant, or so everyone said. I didn't read it. Apparently, he was quite a big name as far as pottery went (even if she's the one with the money). A 'ceramicist' or something, he was supposed to be. Made all kinds of kooky stuff: weird animals, huge human-like figures, funky kind of urns, and normal-looking plates, and cups and saucers.

I knew him a little bit. Tito was his name. Used to see him round a bit, and one day after he'd been living here for a year or so, he calls me, out of the blue, and says he needs a big favour. He told me he wanted to become 'more a part of our community', and asked could I help him. He wanted to be a local, and not an outsider or the 'artsy, city guy up the road'. So he came and had a beer at my place. Elaine was away somewhere. We chatted about things, and I liked him. He asked me about the community, and maybe I talked it up a bit too much. I told him about my friends, and one friend of James's in particular. I said they were people who cared about other people. I think it was the beer talking. Anyway, I 'took' him to a community meeting, a field day, and to the pub where I tried to introduce him to locals. He was a nice enough bloke, a bit wound-up, but friendly. After that I

11

wasn't much help to him, because I had my own issues. And then he was dead before the locals got to know him.

I guess we're always suspicious of newcomers. What are they up to? Are they going to hang around? Are they going to refuse to pay their bills like other city people? And someone like me needs to hang on to the belief that money won't buy you farming cred. You have to have lived it for a lifetime, or at least a good long while. No matter how much money you've got, you'll never be a real farmer like me. Bullshit, of course.

'It's never anything special,' I say to her. 'Just machinery parts, and small pumps. I'm afraid I can only afford the sweatshop versions.' There's a nasty half-joke there, but she does not laugh or express understanding. She steps up close to me, her skin perfect, her teeth white and untampered with. 'If my parcel turns up, you'll let me know, won't you?' It's not quite menace, but it's a very close cousin. Or is that her version of a come-on? Either the money is hers, or she really likes crockery.

I am unreasonably calm.

When her car is gone, I sit with my head in my hands on the front step. If she's missing a box of crockery, then I've really done no wrong. It would have been wrong to involve her in the knowledge of the cash. That would be incrimination. But if the money is hers, I have stolen it from her. Which means she'll be back, or someone will be back in her stead.

So why was the box addressed to me? A trick to avoid detection, obviously. And why the story about crockery? Because she didn't want to involve me. That would be incrimination.

But without being bothered by conscience, I have possibly created a problem.

I get the box from the cupboard, take the money out, put it in two green garbage bags, and put the bags in one of the guest bathrooms (I never have guests). Then I go to the garage, and find the last present I bought myself: a four-in-one hammer drill, $120, free delivery. At the time, it turned out to be much smaller than I thought. It was supposed to be a jackhammer. But now I know it will fit, in parts, into the box. I put the parts in the box with the packing material, and masterfully add the instruction booklet, then tape it up. If Elaine or one of her minions turns up again, I will say I found the box after all, someone must have picked it up accidentally, realised their mistake, and then replaced it. This seems extraordinarily brilliant to me. If Elaine does own the money, she might believe that the box had been picked up and swapped with the hammer drill by someone who knew what she was up to. I am just a neighbourly fuck-up. There was no way she would suspect me of being that clever or daring. I will present it to her unopened, saying I hadn't ordered anything, so the box has to be hers. Perhaps we will open it together, or maybe I will leave her to it and wait for a response.

And then I hear another engine, and a ute rolls into my driveway and parks in the same spot Elaine had. It is a dirty-yellow, battered tray-back that I know belongs to Ben Ruder, who owns a swag of country at the other end of my road. He's a successful prick, self-serving, hard as nails, and the sort of person never embarrassed into doing anything for his community or his fellow man. Ben has never bothered to hide his feeling that any farmer with my sort of financial troubles is an idiot and a layabout. He makes his way casually to my front door, not limping, but moving with the cautiousness of someone who could. He is in khaki shorts-and-shirt work clothes, a floppy, grease-stained hat, and looks like he might be down to his last dollar. It is a ruse. He is as wealthy as anyone hereabouts.

Ben is the one person I know capable of being involved in illicit deals that might include boxes of large amounts of money. He used to have a piggery on the farm, and everyone knew there was something not quite right about it. He shut it down some years ago. Rumours have it that he owns dodgy real estate ventures, brothels on the coast, and a holiday resort for paedophiles in Asia. Probably not true, but you get the gist of the bloke. No one makes up stories like that about popular, good-natured people.

'Ben. What can I do for you?' I'm not wasting pleasantries, and I know he isn't expecting me to.

But, 'Hey there, Davey boy. How've you been keeping?' My alarm bells are clanging air-raid warnings. Ben is affable and relaxed. He is visiting an old friend he hasn't had a chance to catch up with in a long while. I've not seen this version before.

'Okay. You?' I am suddenly aware that, except for James's area, the lawn is long, and the garden beds are a mess. There are branches down, and leaves in piles everywhere, backed up against walls and tree trunks. The couch and the kikuyu have taken command of the veggie garden, and the timber fence along the north side is rotted and collapsing. Someone only has to drive into my garden to know what state I am in. It makes me sad to think what my mother would feel when she saw this mess. But why do I suddenly give a toss?

'Oh, you know, all right. Getting on a bit, slowing down. Everything seems to hurt first thing in the morning when you're my age.'

I can't think of anything to say except, 'Tell someone who cares.' I refrain from comment.

'But, like they say, it's better than the alternative.'

'What alternative?'

'Being six foot under. Being dead, mate. Being dead.' I think it's meant to be a joke.

'Yeah.' We look at each other for a few seconds, and I guess he decides his approach is a waste of time. He's never actually done anything wrong by me except treat me like someone of no account. Maybe that's enough reason to hate him. And he is basically a shit human being who gets to feel like he is a part of a good community, has people who talk to him and humour him because they believe that is their duty in a small community. If he lived anywhere else, the only reason anyone would have anything to do with him would be money. At least that's what I think.

15

'I'm missing a box. That internet tracking thing says it was supposed to come in the mail today, but it didn't. It's got precious stuff in it. Precious to me, anyway.'

'So how can I help you?' *Or perhaps you could bugger off.*

'The mailman said he dropped a box off here, so I was wondering if there was a mistake, and you had my box.'

'I don't think so.' I respond too quickly, and he reads me easily. He squints, and points past me through a gap between me and the doorway, to the box recently taped up, sitting on the kitchen island. 'I see a box on the bench in there.'

'That's right. It is addressed to me. Nothing to do with you.' His eyes are faintly bloodshot, and I'm thinking he's a man who is used to drinking heavily on his own.

'It looks like it could be mine. Can I have a look?'

I know how this will go. I will deny him entry, he will insult me, accuse me of being a thief, threaten legal action, and say he will get me one way or another. He's that sort of guy. I don't need drama like this when I have quarter of a mill in crisp notes in my bathroom.

'How can it look like it's yours?'

'It just does.'

I take my time examining his face — the thickening weathered skin, the multiple folds around the eyes — knowing I could take all my feelings of rage against the world, the piercing fury of injustice, out on Ben Ruder, and not feel any remorse. I could hit him over the head with

16

a baseball bat, watch him slump, and know that the better people of the world might not be cheering me on, but they would understand. But instead of belting him, I say, 'Have you got a knife?' Cool as.

His hand goes to a pouch on his belt.

'It's not been opened. You're welcome to have a look.' I extend an arm to show him the way. I'm getting good at this. If he's looking for the money, I'm willing to bet he won't want to open the boxes in front of me. But if he declines, how would he ever know, short of having someone steal them from my house?

He removes his hat, takes a pocket knife from his pouch, and steps forward. 'I'd appreciate that.'

We stand on either side of the island, and look at the box. The phone starts to ring, and I let it. Ben is focused on the box. He checks the address panel, and runs his hands expertly over the cardboard and tape surface. Then he stabs the knife into the seam in the top, and cuts backwards the distance of half a hand. He peers into the box, and then pushes a hand in the gap. I can't see what he is finding. He pulls his hand back out, and says, resigned, 'It's not mine. Some sort of hand tool. Did you order one?'

A man's voice on my answering machine says something about boxes.

To block it out, I say loudly, 'I don't think it's any of your business.'

He gives a half nod, and a shrug as if to say *If that's the way it's going to be*, and turns and walks towards the front door. It lights a little fire of rage inside me.

17

'What precious thing are you expecting in the mail? A gimp suit?'

'Fuck off, you loser.' He says it over his shoulder, my insults nothing to him.

'The souls of abused Asian boys?' I am yelling it from the doorway as he gets into his ute and puts the finger up at me.

I walk across the lawn following him, bad-mouthing him all the way out of the garden and down the road.

Then I stride back up to the garden shed, and drag the mower out, fill it, check the oil, and proceed to mow the perimeter of James's area.

After the mowing, I play the message on the answering machine. It says nothing about boxes. It is a man from the Department of Agriculture doing a survey on whether I am baiting foxes.

Exhausted from the mowing and the stress of the day, I decide I will have a drink. I'm not an alcoholic, so it's not like I can never drink. It's just that I choose not to. But when I choose to, it is a serious decision. So instead of dinner I have a beer, and then another one, and another few. I open a bottle of red and drink it, and then manage a couple of scotches, because there is some in the cupboard. I pass out on the couch in my clothes.

2

I'm woken by a rapping on the back door that my half-asleep brain tells me is the rattle of a Thompson gun held by Ben in a three-piece suit backed up by Elaine in full gangster-moll attire, blonde bob included. But then somebody yells, 'Dave!' and I wake properly, and know it is the voice of my brother-in-law Mick, and I think perhaps this really is Armageddon. I open the door for him and manage a 'Hey' before I go to the sink for water.

'Mate, you look rough,' he says, delighted at my poor state and his relative exuberance. 'I thought you might have been dead.'

'I'm not. Just a bit of flu.'

'Flu be buggered. You're hungover. I can smell it.'

'What are you doing here?' The water is cool and clean, and I wish for a bathfull of it.

'I'm here for you.'

Mick is short, fit, and useless. I don't need two useless people in the house.

'Oh good.'

'Seriously. I know how tough things have been for you, so I thought I'd better come and keep you company.'

'Sarah sent you?' Mick is the last person in the universe I want for company. He is the kind of ignorant, self-confident bastard who can't stick at anything, can't finish anything, and yet talks like he is the only competent tool in the shed. And, worse, he never has any money. By comparison, I am a workaholic with a slush fund.

'No.'

'She okay?'

'Within reason. Probably better than you. You're a bit of a mess.' He looks around as if he is thinking of buying my house. 'This place is a bit of a mess.'

'Thanks. I'm loving your company so far.'

He drags a large, soft overnight bag in through the doorway, and drops it on the floor.

'I guess we'll be doing some cleaning up together.' I know Mick has never done any cleaning up in his life.

The box is still open on the kitchen island. Marooned again, in point of fact. He walks over to it, pries it open, and says, 'God, you still buying that shit, are you?'

I put my glass down on the sideboard and look at him square on. 'Mick, I don't want company at the moment. I appreciate you coming, but it's important I'm left on my own.'

'Fine. I get it. I'll stay a couple of nights, and get out of your hair.' He pulls the parts out of the box. 'Whoa. A jackhammer. What would you want with one of these things?' He jiggles it at me.

I don't want Mick around for even a day, but I guess he has driven up from the city, which is over four hours away. He'll have to stay at least one night. And then my mushy brain remembers the money in the guest bathroom. Bloody hell. What made me put it there? I groan like I'm going to be sick, and make quickly for the bathroom — confident, but not certain, that he won't follow me.

I take the garbage bags, jam them in the linen cupboard, go back to the bathroom, and flush the toilet, twice for authenticity.

When I return, Mick has taken a seat, his feet up, and says, 'I thought you'd given up the piss?'

'I have. Just fell off the wagon for one night.'

'Yeah, right.' He looks around the room again. 'So, what's on? What are we up to?'

'If it's Saturday, I'm going to the races.' I knew the races were on in town, but I hadn't known, until I said it, that I was going. Somewhere in my boozy sleep I had decided that I was going to launder the money like every good crook does: on the horses. It needed laundering because TV-crime knowledge tells me the serial numbers would be marked by the banks and the police. And an innate and unpleasant sense of cunning suggested Mick could be very useful in that laundering.

Mick leaps to his feet, and rubs his hands together.

'Bewdy. I love the races.'

The races in Waterglen are an odd affair. There are bookmakers, punters, and usually horses, but most of the action happens elsewhere: on the big-city courses watched on TV screens. The Waterglen racetrack is a pleasant enough place: a well-maintained little grandstand, a bar, plenty of white railings, and a marshalling yard that has green grass, some roses, and other areas of lawn. I guess going to the races, whether you're betting on the local chaff-burners or some bolter on the other side of the country, can be a good day out. The idea is making me sick-nervous because I have no idea what I'm going to do. My barely-thought-through plan is to give money to the bookies in small amounts, and hopefully I'll win some back. I know I'll be worrying that everyone is watching me and that maybe the owner of the cash is in the crowd stalking me.

While Mick is getting himself organised, I take a brick of notes out of a bag in the linen cupboard, remove a fistful of hundreds, shove them in my pocket, and put the rest of the brick in the toolbox in the back of my ute. In the fog of my hangover, I know things are happening too quickly. I'm allowing myself to jump ahead on slim assumptions that will almost certainly lead to trouble. I should have either put the money back in the mailbox or told both Elaine and Ben that it had arrived and that I didn't want it. Take it, and leave me alone. Instead I am creating the fabled web of intrigue, and somehow that's what I want, I need. In my next stroke of madness, I go to the old dress-up box at the end of the house, rummage through, and find a holster and the large toy pistol that goes with it. I strap it beneath my shirt, under my arm. The motivation for doing this is unclear.

Mick comes out of the house, smiling and bouncing as if life simply couldn't be better. Maybe I should think more kindly of him. Perhaps he really is here to look out for me. Others would think I'm in need of it. He is in jeans and joggers, and a shirt without a collar.

He obviously doesn't think we're going to Ascot. And we're not. There will be men there in ties, and some even in coats, alongside dudes in shorts and thongs.

My father was a punter, in a very coat-and-tie way. In fact, he did everything in a sports-coat-and-wool-tie manner. My family has always had horses: stock horses, polo ponies, and even a couple of draught horses. It was an accepted matter of status that the Martin family always had several top-quality racehorses. The 'old' families always did. My grandfather had paddocks of them, and employed a man whose only job was looking after them.

For Dad, the best thing you could possibly do was to go to the races at one of the big-name city tracks and watch your own horses run. In my memory, Mum never went with him. She told me she used to go when they were young, but after a while she got bored by it. My father never did. He liked to play polo, but he loved everything about the races: the horseflesh, the bloodlines, the people, the punting, the drinks. It was the time when he was the most relaxed and happy. At the races he was always that man on our verandah: the man he wanted to be.

I never liked him. Not for any particular reason. I just didn't. He wasn't a hard man, not for his time anyway, but he wasn't a man to share what he felt. He believed in enduring. Expressing emotion except through laughter was for the weak and the feminine. If you fell or failed or fucked up, you laughed it off. I cannot remember a time when he put his arms around

23

me, but he must have when I was little. I don't suppose any country men hugged their sons in those days. I wouldn't have known what to do if he had.

A few times, Dad took me with him. I would go to the races, and then, at the end of the day, he would drop me at my aunt Alice's so he could go out all night, and pick me up the next afternoon. I enjoyed it as a kid. It was an adventure, and my father was always so excited. It felt like anything was possible. On the drive down to the city, when it was just him and me, I would ask for things that I would never dare to ask for in any other place: could he, Mum, and I go for a beach holiday, or would he buy me a bike, or could we go to a cricket Test one day? He always said yes to my requests, breezily, without thought, but he never delivered on them. I realised that what I thought was the two of us having special fun together, father and son, was nothing of the sort. I could have been anyone he was giving a lift to the city to. I was with him for adult reasons that were beyond my understanding. So after a while I rejected his offers to go. He almost looked relieved.

As I got older, I began to sense there was something a bit off about his visits to the races: indulgent, I guess. I don't know why I felt that. Teenager's intuition, maybe. I didn't know that drought and low stock-prices were making things tough for us, and that his wife, sister, and brother thought he was wasting money on horses and a lifestyle he couldn't afford but believed he was entitled to. It is some quirk of karma that the first time I have spare money to flutter, I am going to the races.

We drive to town, and Mick talks about himself — things he's heard on the radio, and stories that mates have told him. I am not really listening. My brain is churning with Elaine, Ben, the money, and who else might own it, and what the hell am I doing? I tell myself that if the money was theirs they would have said they were missing a box of money. Stands to reason. Somehow, it's comforting to have an idiot alongside me. I say, 'Mick. I've got some stuff to tell you.'

'Yeah?' I can almost hear the wind whistling through his ears.

'I sold a few things — a bit of machinery, a few cows — for cash, like real folding stuff. There's a fair bit of it, and I don't really want the tax department to know about it.'

'Yeah, cool.'

'I'll be putting a fair bit of money on today. Just so you know.' It's a weak premise, but I reckon he'll go for it.

'Want me to put some on for you?'

'That would be great. We'll have to spread it around the bookies and the TAB.'

'You must have sold a fucken lot of cows.'

'I did.'

'What if we win?'

'We share the profits from the local races. I keep the rest.'

'Orright.' I have just provided Mick with the perfect day out.

My phone rings, and I ignore it. Mick looks at me and my phone, and looks away. 'You'll never have any friends if you don't let them talk to you.'

The caller leaves a voice message. I put the phone to my ear as if I am appeasing my brother-in-law. The voice is Elaine's, honeyed as well as distinctly vulnerable. 'Hi, Dave, I just wanted to ring and apologise for yesterday. I was a bit overwrought, and I'm afraid I might have been a bit full-on. My great-aunt was very special to me. So I was wondering if you want to come down for a drink tonight. Just to smooth it over? About six? Let me know. Bye.'

I click off the message, unsure what I have just heard.

'A woman, eh? Got a few fans, have you?' Mick knows what he heard.

'It's a long story.'

'I bet it isn't that long.' He is guffawing now at his joke or at himself, or possibly the way his shoelaces appear to be frayed baling twine.

I refuse to think about the invitation or its implications. I have enough to deal with.

'So, are you going?' Apparently Mick has hearing like a housemistress.

'Mind your own business.'

'Listen, mate, for the next two days you are my business. I know how tough things have been, and I'm sorry my sister couldn't stay, but nothing will be helped by you becoming a hermit.'

'I'm not a hermit.' I change gears for the sake of it. 'I'm going to the races.'

'You'll have to yarn to someone other than me and the bookies.'

I decide that's enough talking. We park near the entrance to the track, and walk. At the gate, I pay Tick Elder, and some other bloke, possibly a Newsome from out on the Barrack Road, the entry fee. Tick asks me how I'm doing, and I tell him, 'Okay.' Mick and I continue. There is a reasonable crowd, which surprises me. It's a long time since I've been, but country race meetings can be pretty quiet. The crowd can only be a good thing. More people means I'll stand out less.

The first race is still half an hour away. We grab a guide each, and examine the form. My strategy is to bet on favourites — the shorter the odds, the better. A small loss each bet would suit me fine. I can hear alongside me that Mick has decided he is an expert.

'Willy's Filly has done well at the distance before, but I do like the look of Great Days.'

'Here's some money — try not to lose it all.'

I stuff $100 notes into his hand.

'Fucken hell!'

'Don't wave them about.' I sidle over to the bookies handling the city races. In between pretending to do something else, I bet on every favourite they chalk up, at every venue. My pocket is bulging with betting cards, and it is only the first race. I go and join Mick at the rails. He is very excited.

'How much did you put on?' I ask.

'A grand. You?' He isn't looking at me; he is leaning over the rail, trying to see what is happening at the barrier.

'Two grand,' I lie.

'Well, here goes.'

It is a small field: six horses. They stay bunched together for most of the race, but towards the end, one chestnut breaks from the pack. Mick is jumping in the air, banging his program against his hip. 'Go, you good thing!' His horse, apparently the chestnut, wins. He leaps about, saying yahoo. When he has stopped, he says to me, 'What percentage are we working on?'

'What do you mean?'

'You said we'd share the winnings. So who gets what?'

'The profit is yours,' I say, and he starts to leap around again, and then ricochets off to collect his winnings.

I feel a hand squeezing me lightly on the upper arm. A woman, my age, short, dark-haired, robust, with large features, says, 'Fancy seeing you at the races.'

It is Helen, the wife of Marko, who's one of my best mates. She has tried very hard to be a good friend. As he has. But I know they don't know what to do or what to say to me. I can't stand hearing their conversations about their kids and their kids' friends. It's like they don't talk about anything else.

'My brother-in-law is visiting. He loves a punt.'

'Well, he's very clever if he can get you out. You never come to anything we invite you to.' She puts an arm around me and gives me a little hug — playful, but pointed.

I don't bother with an excuse. I tell her I promised to put money on in the next, and she takes the hint. 'Come for a drink later on, will you? Please? We're just on the grass in the carpark. There's food, friends.'

'Thanks, I will.' Not a chance. She walks away, and I head back to the bookies.

None of the horses I bet on gets a place. I try again.

Mick bets, and wins. I bet, and lose. I am beginning to feel that betting is not much better than sticking the box back in the mailbox. My small pile of notes is diminishing. I go back to the ute to grab a stash more.

Mick, on the other hand, might need a small bag to carry his winnings. The problem is that the amounts he's winning aren't enough to carry my losses, and they're never going to launder $250,000, even if I were foolish enough to give him that chance. The whole thing is a dumb idea, except it is making Mick happy. If he's got cash, he'll probably go home earlier. So that's a good result.

I think about Elaine's invitation, and whether it's a date or a way to finagle the money out of me. I'm finding it almost impossible to make sense of anything.

On the other side of the betting ring, two swarthy young dudes appear to be watching me: a tall wide one and small wide one. They look, look away, and look back. One holds my gaze, and slaps a form guide hard into an open palm. It's time to get out. I tell Mick this is the last, and put all the money I have on the next race. I feel the swarthy men watching me the whole time. But this time I choose the longest odds I can find. My horse, it turns out, at 20–1, is called Kinky. It seems somehow appropriate. I give each of the four bookies $2,000.

I look across at the swarthy guys, who are still checking me out. And then, without premeditation, I lift my chin at them, and give a lazy eye-roll. I'm thinking I should be saying, 'What?' or 'What's up?' or 'You looking at me?', but I say nothing. The larger of the two lifts his chin at me, dead-eyed, in response. I walk over to them. Nothing in my head makes any sense except a recurring refrain of 'How bad can it be?' I can assure you this is not me. I am not soft, but I am not someone to pick a fight or seek out trouble. I know what tough is, and it isn't me. Suddenly I'm a badarse. I am almost welcoming the pain of a good belting.

I say to them, 'Is there a problem?'

The tall one says, 'Hey,' waves a thumb in the direction of his chest, and offers, 'Sergei.' I know I'm meant to believe he is the coolest guy on the ground. But I think he might have been watching too many gangster videos.

The smaller one says, 'You've got a lot of cash, brother. Everyone round here says you're broke. What are you up to?'

I say, 'I roughed someone up for it. Have you got an issue with that?'

They make little amused sounds to each other, and then the big one says, 'You?'

'Yeah. Me.'

Here's the thing. I'm not doing any thinking at this point, I'm just doing. I don't know where it comes from. I take my right hand and cross my body, and pat underneath my left arm at that gun holster. Somehow it has just the right amount of bulk. Suddenly they lose some of their cool, and have to stop themselves taking a reflexive step back. I get the rush of someone who has just had his ridiculous shtick believed. These guys aren't hard men; they're dopes from the city who thought they could play tough with a bunch of yokels in the bush. I have their mark, and it feels like cocaine is supposed to.

'You want to play?' I give the impression of moving in on their territory.

Now they back away.

'No, man, we're cool.'

'We'll see you around.'

I am about to celebrate, except I feel Mick panting at my elbow. Back to Augie Doggie and Doggie Daddy.

'What are you up to? Trying to get yourself killed?'

'Your race is about to start.'

'I know. I just thought I'd check you weren't getting your head bashed in.'

'Thank you.'

I let Mick cheer his horse at the rail while I watch the TV sets. Kinky, with a jockey in purple polka-dot colours, is a stumbler and a bumbler. He could easily be my mount. He's not cut out for racing. That is, until the 1,500-metre mark, when one of the other horses or jockeys must have sledged him, and he decides that this running thing can't be that hard. He takes the pack on the outside. Mick appears at my side, disappointed at his narrow loss in the last. He's

31

had a good day, though — or so he says — and watches the TV with me. Kinky has the look of an animal that has been pumped with rocket fuel as he sprints round the mob and draws level with the leader. There is an excited noise from the small crowd. Kinky, oblivious to the romance, pushes out in front, and wins by maybe two lengths. I'm guessing the fix was in, but it doesn't matter. I have the betting tickets, and the big winnings are mine. The bookies frown at me when I come to collect and they have to send runners off to pick up more cash. One of them asks me if he can get the money to me next week. Seems I'm not the only one who had money on Kinky. I tell him it's fine, but that I know where he lives. It's a joke, but he looks at me with a confused look, knowing anyone who throws cash around like I do might well know how to call in a debt. Miraculously, he finds the money he owes me.

Mick and I walk briskly to the ute, avoiding the area where Helen and Marko are drinking with friends — my friends. I am carrying supermarket bags of cash, and I can feel Mick looking at me, wanting to ask me, but not knowing how or what. To allay him, I say, 'It went well, so you can keep your winnings and the money I gave you.'

'What the fuck just happened?'

'For the first time in a decade, I was a winner. Don't ask me about it.'

'Right you are.' He pulls cash out of his pocket and counts it, hissing, and bobbing his head with pleasure.

Then Ben Ruder comes striding across towards us, and in the mood I'm in I'm almost glad to see him. He is dressed up for the races, complete with a thick wool tie from a different lifetime and a clean town hat. He stops in front of us, ignoring Mick, and looks me up and down, taking in the bags of money. 'Where did a loser like you get money like that?' He is hoping for derision, but I can see in his black reptile eyes that he really wants to know.

'I won it. Which makes me a winner.'

Mick is staying close, looking like he might bite Ben.

'You can't win like that with ten bucks, can you?'

I give him a stupid 'Maybe' look, and notice his feet are very big for a small man.

He points a gnarled finger at me, and says, 'You're doing something dodgy, aren't you? And someone's paying you for it. Big time.'

'That's right. I've got a brothel on the coast. It's the best way to survive on the land these days. And then I just suck the life out of everything around me.'

He is so angry, the spittle is beginning to froth in the corner of his mouth.

'You won't be laughing when the cops are at your door.' He pushes past, and strides off.

Mick takes on a surprisingly good David Attenborough voice, and says, 'Everyone is so friendly in the country, aren't they? The sense of community, the whole looking-out-for-your-neighbour thing, it's just bloody marvellous.'

I actually laugh.

I drive us home, checking the rear-view mirror for anyone who might be following. There is no one, and in my current state of delirium I am almost disappointed. I feel like I could smack anyone.

'I'm going for a drink at Elaine's tonight. Will you be all right on your own?'

'Great. I'll be fine. Got any food in your fridge?'

'Frozen meals in the freezer.'

'Sounds good to me.'

I shower again, and think about money. I now have enough money in the house to completely refurbish Mick's life. I don't feel it's a good idea to tempt him with that. He slumps in front of the TV, so I take the garbage bags from the linen cupboard and the supermarket bags with my most recent winnings, and put them in the ute.

I say, 'I'll see you later,' and he waves me off.

I'm not sure why I'm going to Elaine's. Intrigue. I suppose. Why is she asking me, and what is her involvement with the box? I haven't accepted an invitation from anyone to anything for months. The arrival of one box has pushed me out into the world. And sitting with Mick, watching TV and not drinking beer, does not sound like a good alternative.

3

I was an only child, but I don't remember ever being lonely. Not lonely like I am now. Except I'm not lonely, because I don't really like to see anyone. But when I was a kid there were always things I wanted to do, and usually someone who would come over and do those things with me. In the holidays, there were people around, and work to do. But when I was with my friends, we didn't work, even if we said we did — we just rode horses and bikes, swam in the dam, caught craybobs in the creek, and had wars at the hiding tree. Later on, I had my own bush-basher car, and we used to fang around in that. My parents expected me to entertain myself, with or without friends. They never thought it was their job to find ways to keep me amused. They both taught me things, and I would never have dared to tell them I was bored or that I wanted a new toy of some sort. If I couldn't amuse myself amongst nature on the farm, or the animals, or the machinery, then I was beneath contempt. It was never a contempt I needed to worry about. It's odd to think that I am the only one on my farm now. But I really don't think about it. Actually, now I feel the place is populated by ghosts, so I'm not really alone.

Elaine's house appears to have every light on. I wonder if she has decided to have a gathering. I sit in the ute tossing up possibilities. The house is very large, as if she and Tito renovated it expecting to have many children or endless visitors. The times I took Tito out to meet people, we met up at his mailbox, so I never got to see the house — or Elaine, for that matter. It's only one storey, but the roof and the ceilings, I can see, are high. Even in the dark, I can pick up the lushness of the lawn and the scope of the garden. It isn't in bad taste, but maybe a bit too keen to let you know how much money is lying about. I don't see any other guests' cars, but I don't want to have to go home to whatever Mick might be doing, so I get out of my vehicle and find my way through a wrought-iron gate in the centre of a hedge, across that lawn, and up the steps to the verandah and the glass front door.

No one is about. No one comes to greet me. I clear my throat as loudly as I can, and then give a half-hearted 'Hello' not in any way reminiscent of Elaine's version at my place. Nothing. I wait for a minute, and then turn to go. I don't really want to be here anyway. I can sit in the car and listen to music if the thought of Mick is too much. And then I hear a faint, single sound. It could be an animal in the paddocks: a cow coughing; a hoot from an owl. I spin around, hoping that facing the paddocks will help me pick it up a bit better. I hear it again, but not from the dark — it is coming from inside. I move quickly, reefing the door open and stepping into a house that is a puzzle to me. The room is as big as a machinery shed: there are couches in a semicircle down one end, and a kitchen bench down the other. There is some sort of indoor fish tank with ... I don't know ... sharks or something in it probably.

'Elaine?'

A sob in response. Maybe from the next room. I run through a massive archway into an even larger room with more couches and chairs, separate in their own nooks, but dominated by a huge fireplace. Sitting on one of the couches is Elaine. Her clothes looked ripped, and she is hunched over with her face in her hands. Every now and then, she lets out a sob that shakes even my soiled heart.

'Elaine?'

She looks up. Tears have smudged her make-up, and wet her cheeks. There is blood mingling with the moisture seeping down her face.

'Are you okay?' I ask, because I am an idiot.

'Yes,' she says, and hunches a little more.

'What happened?'

'The crockery. Someone broke in. Robbed me, hit me, pushed me down, and took the box.'

'Oh shit,' I mumble, because I can't think of anything else to say. I sit next to her, and look closely. I know that cuts to the head bleed profusely, and this one is not doing that. Perhaps that's a bad sign.

'Have you rung an ambulance? The police?'

'I don't need an ambulance. I'm just shaken up. The cut isn't that bad.' She stops, and swallows. 'He just came straight in, out of the garden, through the doors. I was unpacking the box, and he walked right at me, and hit me. I didn't know what was happening. He picked up

37

the box, I tried to grab him, and he shoved me away, and I fell. He walked straight back out, and he was gone. The whole thing only took couple of minutes. He was so strong. I'd only just got the box from the post office. It'd been sent on the wrong mail run. How would he know that I had it?'

While she babbles, the blood begins to stream down her face, bright red.

'You're bleeding.' I have mastered the obvious. I look for something to put on the cut, see nothing, so direct her hand to the wound.

'Push down.'

She does. I jump to my feet and run back to the kitchen. I grab a roll of paper towel, and return quick as. There is blood seeping through her fingers on top of her head. I rip off sheets of paper towel, move her hand, and push down on the cut. I put her hand on the cut, lean her back on the couch, pull out my phone, and dial 000. After I've explained I need an ambulance, that there has been an assault and robbery, and supply an address, I go back to the kitchen, find a bowl, and half-fill it with warm water, and then return to Elaine. She is pale. The paper under her hand is blood-soaked. I remove the bloodied towels, and try to sponge the area. Her hair is caked, but the cut is a white gash between the follicles — only white for as long as I can swab it. I put fresh towels down, and ask her can she hold them. She says, 'Yes,' but weakly, and I wonder how long it will take for the ambulance to arrive. Sometimes, out here, it can take more than an hour and a half.

38

'Are you hurt anywhere else?'

'Not badly. Bruised, I guess. Sorry you had to see this. Supposed to be here for a drink.'

'Did you see his face?' I only ask to keep her distracted and awake.

'Balaclava over his head.'

'Was he wearing anything notable?'

'Black jeans, and jumper.'

I am going to ask if she saw a car, but I think better of it. I don't want her to keep reliving the moment. Instead, a thought becomes words without my permission: 'Must have been pretty special crockery.'

'No. Special to me. Worth a few thousand, maybe ten.'

'That's something.' I consider $10,000 would be worth robbing someone for, but unless you're a crockery nerd, this particular theft doesn't sound like the simplest transaction. I don't believe she is lying to me. I believe she came to my place looking for crockery. I have a dread rising in my gut that the burglar wasn't looking for crockery, and that I may have some responsibility for Elaine getting hurt.

On the road, out the front, there are flashing coloured lights, and I head through the door into the garden. I don't want them to miss us. The ambulance stops at the fence when they see me, and they get out carrying bags and a fold-out stretcher. I direct them, and have the warm rush of knowing competence has arrived. And then more flashing coloured lights break up the night as a police car motors in. A uniformed policewoman and policeman get out. I think she

39

might be the one I saw at my mailbox, but I can't be certain. They start asking me questions, confirming they're in the right place, and who I am, and whether I'm the owner, and what is my version of events. The ambos bring Elaine out on a stretcher.

'Just being safe. No need to worry,' one of the ambos says as she goes past, picking up on my concern. I nod my thanks.

After a while, the police let me go, asking me to make myself available for further questioning. At least they haven't checked my ute.

I drive home feeling I am a magnet for personal pain. As I brood, an older white car I don't recognise goes past in the opposite direction, at pace.

Minutes later, I steer into my garage, and get out. Mick comes out of the house dragging his bag, cursing me, cursing everything.

'Problem?'

'I've just been fucken robbed.'

'Robbed?' I'm not worrying about Mick. I'm worrying about me.

'Yeah, fucken robbed. I'm watching the TV, having a quiet beer, and a car pulls up outside, and someone comes in the door. I figure it's you. So I don't pay any attention. Then this tall dude, badly wired, like he's on something nasty, walks straight into the living room, grabs me, and demands to know where the money is.'

I'm watching Mick to check that he's telling the truth, and thinking that the robber, if he's real, must have come straight from Elaine's to here.

'I go to my bag with him waving a knife at me, get today's winnings, give them to him, and he says, 'That's it?''

'When I nod, he smacks me full in the face, and I go down on one knee. Then, while he's looking about in a sort of rage, I charge him. He's big, but I manage to knock him down. It half-winds him, but he struggles up, and starts waving the knife around at me, saying, 'Where's the rest of the money?' I tell him I don't know. He's taken everything I've got, but if he's going to be threatening me with a knife, he'd better know I've got mates about to come round, and they'll sort him out. Then he just bolts with my dough.'

'You scared him off? Well done.'

'He still got my money.' Mick wipes sweat from his face that hasn't been produced by heat. 'He wasn't real hard-core or anything. Looked like he might have been a local bloke, on the gear. Must have seen us winning at the races, and decided we'd be an easy mark. Didn't think that sort of thing happened in the country. It's different around here, isn't it?'

I walk over to the toolbox, pull out a large wad of money, and hand it to Mick.

'Here. Sorry.'

This significantly brightens his day.

'Thanks.' He looks at the money, and his face changes to a question mark. 'You kept the money in your ute? You knew he might come?'

'No.'

'Then you didn't trust me?'

'I trust you, Mick.'

41

'Either option, you could have told me.'

'I know. I'm sorry.'

He stuffs my money into his bag.

'You're in some trouble, aren't you?'

'Of course not.'

'You'll never get Sarah back if you get involved with crooks.'

'I know that.' I say it like the idea is ridiculous. *Me? Involved with crooks?* But I know he's right. Even though the involvement isn't my fault, I'm starting to get into territory that will give Sarah presumptions that will destroy what remains of our relationship.

'Anyway, I'm gone. This is too far-out for me. Thanks for the cash. I'll come back in a month or so and check on you, if you're still alive.'

The last bit is a joke, I'm sure, but he gives no hint of it — just dawdles to his car, fires it up, gives me an uncommitted wave, and disappears.

I'm relieved, and somehow empty. It wasn't so bad having him around, especially now that I know he's brave enough to knock down a man with a knife. A man who is probably returning right this minute with reinforcements.

I go straight to my gun cabinet, grab the keys, unlock it, and extract my .22, my .222, the 12-gauge shotgun, and ammunition for all three. I take them back to the kitchen and put them where I can easily get to them. Drastic, but the evening has been way too unsettling. When they come for me, I'll be ready. It's only 8.30. Too early for bed. I make myself a peanut-butter sandwich with nearly fresh bread for dinner.

Then I get the box out again. The hammer

drill parts come out, and I count and pack $250,000 in piles back into the box, and then tape it up and take it to the mailbox. I leave it underneath the mailbox so the mailman doesn't have to become involved. It feels like one way of drawing a line beneath everything. They can come and get their loot, and leave me alone. Then I can return to my version of normal. This doesn't sound all that attractive, because now more than ever it is obvious that my life is rubbish. A few violent criminals couldn't make it any worse. But they could make it worse for others, so that is enough motivation to give them back what is theirs. Besides, I now have over $160,000 of my own that will pay a few bills, and even a bit of wooing.

Back at the house, I get out of the ute, and feel my lungs expanding because a downward force has been removed. The night is still and warm, and the stars are a kind of existential joke: perpetually awesome, beautiful, just outside every night, but never looked at, never appreciated. The air has the lightness that suggests the brutal leftover heat of summer is gone and the pleasure of autumn is here. For those who know pleasure.

I watch TV, and sleep on the couch, and wake, and look at crap on my computer, and doze, and am glad to see the morning.

When it is time, I ring the hospital, and the nurse, Jennifer Peach, who nursed my mother and my father at the end, asks seriously if I'm a relative. I say, 'No,' and she apologises, but declines to let me talk to Elaine. It is before visiting hours, and the hospital has strict policies. Then I hear a voice in the background say, 'She checked herself out. With her husband.'

I begin to say, 'That's not possible,' but I stop myself. Lately, anything is possible. I ask, 'Did she look happy to go with him?'

Then Jennifer puts her hand over the mouthpiece, and asks the voice behind her, 'Was she happy to go?' The voice returns, 'Not unhappy. A little anxious, but that was probably because of the night she'd had. We didn't want her to go. She and her husband insisted.'

Jennifer asks me, 'Why?'

I do not give in to the melodramatic choice, and say, *because her husband is dead*. I just respond with, 'No reason. Thank you,' and hang up.

4

The phone rings again. Until the last few days, phone calls and visitors had become a nuisance of the past. Suddenly, I can't get a minute's peace. But I can't let this one go, because it might be Sarah, or even Elaine explaining herself. But when I pick up, it's a man's voice.

'Dave?'

'Yeah.' I immediately curse myself for the naive confirmation.

'You're not going to believe this, but my name is Dave Martin.'

The possibility of an explanation begins to circle.

'Really? That's amazing.' But it's not that amazing, considering that a white-bread name like mine is hardly unusual away from the multicultural cities. 'What can I do for you?'

He laughs an unworried laugh that makes me think he is likeable. 'Well . . . I was wondering that since we've got the same name, whether you might have been accidentally receiving some of my mail?'

I think, *You too*, but don't say it.

'The name is the same, but I'm sure the address is different, and that's what really counts, doesn't it?' Actually, I'm ready to spill all, give him his cash back, and try to forget the whole thing.

He pauses, and I figure I've put him off with

my first parry. Wrong.

'The thing is,' he says, 'my address is 'Fythe Trees'.'

'The road address?'

'696 Wilson Lane.'

This cannot be true. He's just made it up to trick me. I hastily bring up a phone-directory site, and check. Dave Martin seems to be waiting patiently, having anticipated my actions. But he is telling the truth. How come I've never heard of him or his address? Surely someone would have mentioned it or ribbed me about it sometime in the past few decades? Not a word.

'So, what sort of mail do you think I might be getting?'

'Parcels, mostly, of things I've bought online.' This is not spooky.

'And what would be in those parcels?'

'It's not really your business.'

'Drugs? Smuggled wildlife? Bricks of money?'

He is quiet. I can hear currawongs calling somewhere near him. *It must be autumn*, I think.

'It's counterfeit dollars, if you must know.'

'What for?'

'I'm . . . ' He corrects himself. 'My wife . . . is staging a community production of a play called *Money*, and I had a friend print me out large volumes of paper money. I needed them to be as authentic as possible.'

This is an extremely long bow.

'For a community play?' I'm engaging with him far too much. Complete strangers don't do this. The fact doesn't stop me. 'You can buy a colour photocopier, cartridge included, for less than a hundred bucks. Surely that would have been good enough for a community play?'

'So you did receive it?'

'Receive what?'

'The box of money.'

And here I am at the point where the rubber hits the road. Suddenly it all makes sense. Dave Martin is my ticket to safety. *Take it*, I say to myself. *Take it*.

'Sorry, I didn't catch that.'

But guess what? I don't. Despite all the pain I have caused Mick, and Elaine, I'm not quite ready to stop playing. It's something I hadn't comprehended. I had been lying to myself about taking the box back to the mailbox. I want to see this to the end. I want to solve the mystery. I want the money — all of it. And somehow, I'm desperate for the distraction. That box is the first thing to get me out of my head, and off the place, since Sarah left the farm, and almost since things went bad. I want this.

'I'm really sorry, Dave, but I haven't received money of any sort.'

'That's funny, because the mailman said he'd been delivering boxes just like the ones I'm missing.'

I need to talk to my mailman.

'I have received a couple of boxes, but they contained cheap machines . . . a drill, a pump. No money.'

'Well, that's weird, because last week I got a submersible pump that I didn't order. Are you sure you haven't missed a box somewhere?'

'I'm sure. Sorry I couldn't help. Bye.'

I put the phone down. Is he the guy that robbed Mick and assaulted Elaine? Is he Elaine's boyfriend? Or am I just losing my grip? What are the odds of there being a bloke with the same name and nearly the same address in the same district? It's a trick of some sort. As per usual, I feel like I'm the only one who doesn't know what the trick is.

I leave the phone off the hook. All it does is bring misery.

I decide to wash my clothes — a significant moment of achievement for me. I know, as I put them in the machine and add the last of the detergent, that I will forget I've done this, and the clothes will stay in the machine for days before I manage to get them to the clothesline. I take the rake to a thick drift of leaves that rests near the laundry. I keep at it for a while, and then give up after raking only one pile. I think about what I should do with the money. Pay bills and woo Sarah, like I told myself? I don't think so. It would take a lot more than money to get Sarah back. Perhaps I should go on a world trip. Just a backpack and a phone, and see the world. That's what lost people do, isn't it? When you return, you realise how lucky you really are. Bugger that. I know I would just sit in a cheap bar nearest the airport where my plane landed, and drink myself to death. You don't know how lucky you are. I do, actually. I'm really unlucky. As unlucky as I could ever be.

5

It is Sunday, and I am driving around checking stock water: troughs and tanks. The dogs, Ted and Special, are with me, running alongside, their unique ability to show pleasure in the moment on full display. They are kelpies, black and tan, sleek and full of purpose, and if there was any love left in me it would be for them. They chase and smell and play, keeping an eye on me in case there is work to be done. There isn't. Nothing in this world confuses them except perhaps me.

The place has done well with the rain. The grass is green, and even the summer grasses are holding their colour. At this time of year, compared to the height of summer, the stock drink a lot less water, so there isn't as much pressure on the water systems. It is not as likely they'll die of thirst if they happen to empty a water tank through a broken hose or a stuck trough-float. That makes it sound like I give a shit. I don't. Some of the ewes have fly strike, and should be treated. They're not going to be, but as the weather cools they should be all right. The fallowed wheat paddocks are no longer fallow, because now they are bright and thick with different types of weeds of all heights and shapes. It means they are now grazing paddocks. It would take a power of burned diesel, and a lot of sprayed chemical, to get them back to the sort of order needed for crop growing.

My great-grandfather had teams of men in this country: fencing, clearing scrub, shearing sheep, running water points. It must have been a village in itself. They probably shot the local Aborigines, too, but not surprisingly there's no record of that. Many of the people indigenous to the area worked on our place when there was no other way to survive. When I think how much this farm is a part of me, and mine after several generations, I don't like to imagine what it must have been like for them to be forced off it when they had been here forever. The best way to deal with something like this is to not think about it. We are masters of that. We're careful never to write detailed histories. Even my great-grandfather's notebooks hardly mention those original people.

My father had several men working full-time for him, with their families living on the farm. The wives often helped Mum with the house and garden, and someone had to milk the cow, kill sheep for meat, and look after the chooks. There were plenty of others that came in when there were big jobs to be done. Large machinery and then smart machinery replaced those workers, but I could still justify a couple of station hands if I was running the place the way it should be. Maybe I'll get back to that sometime. I still get old Lenny and his son Trevor to help me out now and then. I know they won't talk about what they see. Lenny worked for my father when he was a young man, and his father worked for my grandfather. In those days you inherited a farm, and its stock and working families.

Sunday is the day I think about James. Actually, I think about James every minute of every day, but Sunday is the day I allow myself time with those thoughts. Not today. I'm making sure I think about money, burglars, how Elaine and Mick must both feel, and what Elaine might be doing. Of course she has a boyfriend, and it wouldn't be strange to refer to him as her husband in that sort of circumstance. And she probably wasn't that badly hurt, so it makes sense to go home.

I spin the ute around like I'm in a TV drama, and bounce my way up the rutted edge of the paddock and out the top gate at speed, for no good reason. I'm going to see Elaine because that's what a good neighbour would do. She's either doing well at home with her 'husband' or she's in trouble, and some of that trouble is probably my greedy fault. I could call her, but I don't think a phone call would remove my fears. This is probably not unusual behaviour for normal people, but for me it is out of recent character. I have not reacted to anything or anyone with any energy or speed or purpose for months — except for the trip to the races. Perhaps things are changing. In my rear-view mirror, I see Ted and Special, stopped at the yards, watching me leave. They don't shake their heads in dismay at me. I'm sure they don't.

It only takes me a few minutes to get to Elaine's place. I still don't know what my rush is, but maybe it's the force of intuition. Something is not right about the Elaine thing. Not that intuition has played a large role in my life. If I've felt it, I've usually ignored it. Not now. I spend so much time in my head that intuition seems the only sense offering signposts.

I park at Elaine's sheds out of sight of her house, pretending I've come to ask advice or a favour from the blokes who work for her. I take my time getting out of my vehicle. I reckon I look like the farmer of fables — nothing rushes me, nothing fazes me. 'Ah, g'day.' 'Ah, g'day.' I shut the door of the ute, then look around. No one is about. I see paddocks, distant cattle, and a sorghum crop due for harvest. Then I turn, and look at the house as if it has just occurred to me that there might be a house around here someplace. I cover the distance to the house quickly, let the garden gate clang behind me, and cover the spongy lawn, observing that it is probably in need of a mow if you were going to be fastidious about these things.

At the glass verandah doors, I knock, call out, and feel a slight shiver at what happened the last time I was here. Let's not have that again. But this time there is no response. I pull on the door lightly, and it opens. I didn't think to try to lock it last night, so maybe that means no one has been home. She's stayed over at her husband's place. Which is fine. None of my business. It's not like she's a friend or anything. In fact, I barely know her.

Responsibility discharged, I turn to go home. And then I point out to myself that this is a kind of shirking. Unless the guy who robbed Mick is a crockery aficionado, Elaine's injury is my fault. I step back, and face the door. If I go in, and someone — say, the police — happen to arrive, it will not look good. But even I remember that sometimes you just have to act, and forget consequences. Can't say I care for it, though. It's a very long while since there was anything I felt strongly enough to act on. I guess this is a good thing.

I call again as I step inside the door, and when I walk through the kitchen area I see that there are no plates or cups that have been used, and none of the appliances are warm from use. This is snooping. Unpleasant. I've already accepted that she's gone to her boyfriend's place. And then I hear an engine, and I look back and see a car — Elaine's — stopping out the front. Bloody hell, what was I thinking coming here? There are two people: Elaine and some bloke. Do I walk out, and say, *Hi. Hope you don't mind. I was just checking that the place was safe?* Not a chance. I decide to hide. The alternative is way too creepy. I might as well be sniffing my way through her undies drawer. I squeeze in behind a massive timber-and-glass bookcase in the fire-place room where I found her the night before. I hear Elaine enter the house, jangling keys that she wouldn't have needed.

'Hello?' She asks this without apprehension. I feel an idiot. I left the door open. I should just reveal myself. Elaine will be thankful for last night, and will accept that concern has made me an intruder.

I don't believe it either.

So I wait, swallowing my breathing and trying to think of a plan. But then I hear something I can't place. A breath, a light grunt that I can't imagine Elaine making. The boyfriend? There has been no sound of footsteps on the loud floor. Perhaps he's in socks. And then a faint low rumble, and it might be someone saying, 'Ask again.'

'Is there anyone here?' After what she's just been through, if she thought there was someone in her house, you would expect her to be panicked.

'See?' she says. 'No one. Dave just left the door open after I was taken away.' There is no reply.

It's time to get out. I'm not sure about where the back door might be, but there has to be one. I leave my post, and sprint for the doorway into the next room. They do not appear, and so I guess that she is delaying. The room I'm in is large, filled with ceramic pieces, but not as large as the others. It has more TVs and couches, but one end has exercise machines silhouetted by the light through the floor-to-ceiling glass so you can look outside as you work out. There is a corridor in front of me, but I guess that leads to bedrooms and bathrooms, and not to a quick way out. I run to the gym end, and see a sliding door that opens onto a paved area, push through it, and find myself breathing fresh air in an unseen courtyard. I sidle along the edge of the house in amongst plants and shrubs until I get to the furthest corner. I reckon if I scrabble along the ground out of the garden, and make for the planting rig that sits waiting halfway between the house and the sheds, I should be fine.

From the planting rig I crawl across the ground like an ungainly goanna until I reach the ute, open the door from the ground, slither in, and start it up. I pull forward, and make my way through the gap between two sheds, hoping no one will hear me. I take it slowly — only the guilty would be rushing. But when I look back at the house there is a blond man in the garden watching, waving his arms and becoming agitated. I don't look again, and hold my pace until I hit Wilson Road, and then gun it, knowing he is probably giving chase. He'll be looking for me, and I have to be ready. I'm flying down the road, and then I feel a tyre give. My tyres, which are bald or missing chunks of tread, should have been replaced weeks ago, but because of lack of money and a very low care factor, I haven't bothered. Fine time to pay the price. I veer to the side of the road. In the distance behind me I see dust kicking up, and a vehicle travelling towards me at speed. It can only be him. I figure the tyre is probably buggered anyway, and pull out onto the road and jam my foot on the accelerator again. I might wreck the rim, which would be expensive and inconvenient, but I'm not staying around for this guy.

At my mailbox, I put it into a drift and take the turn, but the soft tyre makes me slide outwards in my arc, and I almost hit a tree planted by my mother in the driveway. I'm a few hundred metres down my drive when the other vehicle catches up. I keep feeding it to my ute, hoping I can get to a gun before he gets to me. But the vehicle behind me doesn't take my turn.

It keeps going at the speed of someone involved in a chase. Except they're not. I recognise Mandy from next door as she goes past like a rocket — the speed she normally drives at — late for something, as per usual.

I'm breathing again as I make my way to the garage. This is playing havoc with my health.

In the house, I find the rifle and bullets, and take a seat in my rocking chair and wait. If the guy from Elaine's comes, I will shoot him if I get the chance. Through the leg or the shoulder. I know the police say that is overestimating your marksmanship on a small target in the heat of the battle. I shut my eyes, and think about it.

When I wake, it is morning and nothing has changed, and I haven't moved. No one waits for me outside. If someone had wanted to kill me, I would be long dead. But now I have no idea what to do. My assailant must know where I live. Perhaps the box at the mailbox has done its job.

I do my best to get myself together, washing, shaving, and eating. If he is coming for me, I want to have a full stomach. But nobody arrives. My phones do not ring. Even the call centres leave me alone. I should talk to Elaine. I walk around turning things on and off, consider mowing James's lawn again (it doesn't need it), and I even water a couple of dying thorny roses. I take Ted and Special, who have waited patiently all night, to their kennels and feed them. Then I return and play patience with real cards, never completing a game. I eat uncooked noodles from the pack.

Then the phone in the house does ring. I

ignore it for two rings, and decide that not knowing is worse than the short period of peace I
might get. I suck in a few breaths, and plunge in.

The voice says, 'Dave? Are you all right?' No
formalities — just a cut to the chase. That's how
we talk these days.

'Hello, Sarah.' The name spoken is enough to
rattle me. No need for the searching lilt of her
voice.

'Mick's worried about you.'

'It's so good to hear you.'

She is quiet. I have said exactly the wrong
thing. It's my specialty.

'He thinks you might be mixed up in
something. Is that true?'

'No. I sold some things to pay some bills.'

'Sold what? You can't do that without telling
me.'

'Just a handful of cows. They were threatening
to send the sheriff out over the unpaid rates.'

I can lie without shame to my still-wife, even
though the fact that she'll accept the lie shows
how low we've sunk. The sheriff probably would
have come for the rates. But Sarah is not
motivated by money, or afraid of its absence.
When Dad died, we found out he still owed
money to his brother, Henry, for his part of the
farm — Henry's inheritance. It was money that
we had to find. We paid Henry out, but not before
a few robust conversations about our need for a
reasonable time to pay. Henry was Dad's younger
brother, and a lifetime after leaving the farm he
was bitter about how long it took for him to be
paid out. Sarah and I toughed it out together.

She was always gracious about hardship. We were a team then.

'But you went to the races?'

'Just to get off the farm. See some people.'

'You don't like the races. You never go to any of your friend's places. Mick says you've got bundles of cash in the house.'

'I had a big win on the horses.'

She doesn't believe me, but she's had enough of the conversation. 'Don't do anything stupid, will you?'

'Course not. How are you going?'

'I'm good. I might have a job. Fran has been terrific.' The line is quiet, and I let it be. Fran is one of her oldest friends — someone who never wanted Sarah to move to the country and marry me. 'I'm feeling like I can do stuff. Cope with stuff. You know, get on with things. I was hoping you might be feeling the same way.'

'Definitely. I'm starting to get some work done on the farm — spraying weeds, fixing some of the machinery, and cleaning things up a bit.'

'Did you get the oats in?'

'Not yet, but I'm about to.'

Sarah knows the oats should have been sown by now. She knows 'not yet' means 'never', but she can't let herself care anymore.

'Are you still off the grog?'

'Yep.'

'Okay. Look after yourself.'

Mick has kept one confidence.

'Try to see some of your mates, won't you?'

'Sure thing.'

When she left it really hurt me, and probably

cut the last of my moorings. I've been floating around like a leaking balloon ever since. But there was a small part of me that was glad to see her go. I knew she wouldn't be able to move forward if she stayed with me, and while she was around she was a constant reminder of how I'd failed. After a while she stopped mentioning it, but I knew she always thought it.

'Dave, I've got a new friend. Lucy. Just a friend. But who knows? I wanted to tell you.' She pauses as if to recover. I'm trying to think why I'm not shocked by this possibility. 'I'll come and visit James in a few weeks. Make sure the house is clean. Bye.'

'Bye.' I would do anything to keep her talking, to keep hearing her, but I have long since destroyed our connection. She doesn't have the will or the energy to put up with me anymore. And now she has a 'friend', as I knew she would. I knew it was coming. I didn't know it would be a she. I wonder if it is a response to the blokey world of the farm that has so comprehensively let her down. I put the phone down and hammer my fist hard into my chest. It is important to think about something else.

I drive to the mailbox, the flat tyre thump-thumping beneath me. I must remember to change it. The box that I repacked and taped up is still there, underneath the mailbox. This is bad news. In the mailbox there are two new boxes. I curse in the most exotic forms that come to mouth. I wonder if I shouldn't leave the boxes there, but then it would become the mailman's problem. I can't think what I should be doing, so

I take the new boxes out of the mailbox, put them in the ute, leave the old box where it is, and drive home. I am thinking of Sarah and the way she is getting her life back on track while I am obviously still derailed. How is she managing that? How does she find enough meaning to get up and go to work? I didn't even ask what she was going to be working as, or where. I don't have the imagination to conceive of it. I don't know who I am or what is worth doing.

Sarah is a nice person, and I don't mean bland or a do-gooder. She is mostly good-natured and generous. She laughs a lot, thinks the best of people, and is slow to judge. She was all of these things when I married her. After the loss, not so much. I know she fought the bitterness, but she couldn't shake it until she left here for good. At least, that's what I thought I observed. Escaping the farm, and me, saved her. It let her leave some things behind that she thought she couldn't; things she believed couldn't be separated from the loss, like rage at how other people could live such happy, undamaged lives. People such as our friends. Turns out, moving away from friends and community helped her dump the bitterness. That's what I think anyway. Of course, I don't know much about Sarah's inner life these days, so I could be talking through my hat. Sarah might be still as screwed up as I am. But I remember the first time she called me after she'd left. There was a tone in her voice I hadn't heard for so long I didn't recognise it until later. I'm pretty sure that sound was hope.

In the past months I have spent a lot of time

on my own. Sometimes I have gone weeks without talking to anyone in anything other than a perfunctory manner — bought groceries, ordered fuel, that sort of thing. I don't answer the phone, and I avoid going out. I really don't do much of anything. I mean to, but it never really happens.

Often I don't notice how much time I have spent without human contact. So much so that the sound of my own voice can startle me. I will be driving along and a thought will put itself into words, and I will wonder who is talking, and then realise it is me. At other times in my life I would have hated to be alone, and would have found excuses to go and talk to people: at the pub; in town; call friends; or just flag someone down on the road. But when being with other people just makes the pain worse, it is easier to set a lone course. And when you want to be alone, after a while you either get used to yourself or go crazy.

All my life I have been anchored here. I have known where I fitted. Wherever I went, people who didn't know me could always place me: because of where I lived, because I was someone's son, grandson, friend, then husband, and then father. Now it is all gone, and I am untethered, unplaceable. If I met myself in the supermarket, I wouldn't know who I was. I never imagined I could be so totally isolated. The farm is the only thing that defines me.

I put the boxes on the kitchen island, and look at them. They are the same size as the last one, but in better condition. I feel a bit afraid of them. Do they contain more money from crooks unknown? I know it's blood money of some sort. The boxes feel like a taunt from my conscience: *You were happy enough to take the last one. What are you going to do with two more? Maybe half a million dollars more?* Why didn't I leave them at the mailbox with the other one?

I grab the knife, and open one of them. There is a plastic bag inside, white, thick-walled and heavy-duty, but no bricks. It gets worse. Everything always gets worse. I slice the top of the bag, and peel it back. The bag is full of something that might be ash — fine, grey-white ash. *What the fuck?* seems an understatement. I dip my finger in, and the ash sticks to it like fine powder. I scrape the ash back to see if anything is buried under the fine material, but there is nothing. It is a bag of ash. Then I notice, in the corner, a half-submerged gold ring with a tag tied to it. The tag says, 'Fatboy Cakestand'. It doesn't make any sense, but it unnerves me because it is written in a childish freehand that suggests Fatboy Cakestand is a nickname. My half-dead imagination brings forth a picture of a bikie gang rival, assassinated; a large, sweaty enemy called 'Fatboy' with the ridiculous surname of Cakestand. Fatboy has been eliminated and cremated. I simply don't have the horsepower to summon what the reasons for this might be. Maybe Fatboy is the revered leader of an outlaw gang whose remains are due to be scattered somewhere.

I spear open the other, lighter box, and uncover another bag that stretches to every corner of the box and is filled with the same material. There is no ring in this one. I'm confused yet again. I close the boxes. I cannot think of anything useful, and I begin to understand that I am an insignificant bystander in a complex underworld game. They've accidentally sent me stuff, and they'll probably kill me for it and not think another thing about it. I'm going to take the boxes back to the mailbox, and leave them there. Sooner or later, the robber bloke will come along. Sooner or later, someone will tell the person sending this stuff that they've got the wrong address.

I take one beer out of the fridge, and down it. What if they don't have the wrong address? Who would be hoping to pick up boxes at my address? I hardly even notice the first beer going down. When I'm finished, I look at the bottle a couple of times to make sure it really is all gone. What if the other Dave Martin really is missing a box of play money and has nothing to do with all of this?

In the past year, nobody has lived here except me: before that, Sarah, James, and me, and before that, me, my father and mother. Mum got early-onset Alzheimer's, but died much more quickly than expected. Dad eventually moved to the nursing home, and gave up. This was significantly painful, but ten years ago, and there's been plenty of pain to swamp it since. So there's no one here who could be hoping to receive parcels. If they're not meant for the other Dave, either it's someone who lives nearby, or they have been deliberately sent to me. Why would you send money to a busted-arse farmer? He's likely to spend it, or tell the police, or do a bit of both. I open another beer. There's no reason why not. Reasons for anything escape me.

I take all the boxes back to the mailbox, struggling to keep the ute on the road because the flat tyre is dragging sideways. A storm is developing in the south, and I know if it comes in, it will ruin the boxes. The rain will soften the cardboard, and with a little pressure the sides will fall apart, leaving the bricks of money. I put them all in the ute, and decide to put them out when this change moves through. I must be preoccupied, because out of nothing a vehicle glides in alongside me. Ian Blent, unmarked and smiley, winds down his window, and sticks a big, gnarled paw on the doorframe.

'Looks like you suddenly got popular, Davo.' One finger lazily indicates the boxes.

I push my beer bottle out of sight. 'Huh? Yeah.' Ian is one of the good guys on the planet. He is Ben Ruder's neighbour on this side, and he still talks civilly to Ben, which probably makes him a saint. He is Mandy's husband. I've always thought I'd like to be better friends with him, but we never saw him about that much. Different friends, different parties. We talk about the season, and the weather, and he curses cattle prices. It is calming. I think again about how we didn't try harder to make a link with him.

'Your tyre's a bit soft.' He doesn't bother to indicate which one.

I say, 'Yeah,' and nod, but don't bother with the ludicrous explanations that come to mind.

Then he says, in a guarded way, 'If you wanted a hand with those sheep, I'd be happy to . . . '

'I'm on top of it, thanks.'

'No worries. But you could just give me a call if an extra pair of hands would help.'

'Thanks.'

He makes a face that does its best to say, *It's nothing*. And then, in an offhanded change of topic, he says, 'Terrible news about Elaine Slade,' and pushes his lips together.

'Why? What happened?'

'She's dead. They found her body this morning, in her house, bashed. Bloody awful.'

'Shit.' Reality has smashed its way into my rainbow bubble. 'She's dead?'

'According to the local paper.' He reaches across to his passenger seat, and picks up a newspaper. It is the local weekly. The *Waterglen Times*. Barely news, and only just a paper. No one knows how it still functions. He flattens the paper out to show me the front page, and shows me the article with its headline: 'Local Woman Found Dead in House'. 'I didn't know her very well. Hardly spoken to her. But something like that is just terrible.'

He examines me, sees my distress, and says, 'Sorry, mate. I didn't realise you knew her that well.'

'I don't. I didn't. It's just that . . . '

'Shit. Sorry. How bloody insensitive of me. What you've been through. I should have thought before I spoke.' He looks wretched.

'No. No. That's not it. She called in here the other day. Before that, it's maybe a year since I'd

65

seen her. And now this.'

'Strange, isn't it? The way that happens. You don't see someone for ages, and then you see them once, and suddenly it feels like they're everywhere. The violence, though. We're normally shielded from that sort of stuff. I don't like to think it's come this way.' I think he realises that talking about death is bad territory, so he says, 'Anyway, I'd better get going before that storm catches me,' and points at the clouds that have become black and noisy.

Any other time I would be glad of the rain to make the grass and the oats grow and stay green before winter and its frosts arrive. Now it only means me, and my boxes, will get wet. Ian leaves, and I watch him drive towards the storm. I try not to think on the life that will never be.

Elaine is dead. It doesn't feel like it can be true. She had only just come into my life, dramatically, and now has swiftly gone. I feel pain for someone else for the first time in eighteen months. But not for long. My rational mind is too quick to tell me she had had a good life, a better life than most people on the planet; she got nearly four decades. I have no factual basis for the assertions, but it's better than saying she was lucky.

I know the police will want to talk to me. There's a pretty good chance I've seen her killer. Blond, tall, fit, not yet forty. Those are my guesses, based on the glimpse of him I had. Is that why he hasn't come looking for me? Was the death of Elaine enough to scare him off? Now my death is a genuine possibility.

I put the boxes in the back next to the fridges. By the time I've cracked open another beer, a police car sweeps into the drive, and the rain comes with them in large drops, hitting hard. The two police that I spoke to last night get out and run to my front door. I put my beer down and walk out to meet them, friendly and open. They apologise, dripping, for bothering me, but say there are a couple of things to do with an incident at the Slade house that they need to ask me about. Thunder and delayed lightning dramatise the moment, as if it needs it. I don't invite them in, and they don't suggest it. Under the cover at my front step, they proceed to ask me where I was and what I was doing the night I found Elaine bashed in her house.

I remember the policewoman's name is something Murray. She has red hair pulled back tightly, and it doesn't make her any more friendly. She does not like me — no prizes for guessing that.

I say, 'She's dead, isn't she? That's what the media said.'

'What media?' the policeman questions me with a sudden intensity.

'The local paper.'

'You saw an article?' He is inspecting me like I am a newly discovered species.

'I saw the headline. Didn't read the piece. It's true, isn't it?' I'm losing confidence, even though I trust Ian, and I actually saw the headline.

'No.' They look at each other.

'No? Is the paper lying?' Now they both look at me as if I am a pathetic sort of small-time trouble-maker.

The policeman says, 'There was some confusion at the hospital. A woman called Ellen Sade, who lived on the other side of town, was found dead in her house. The editor of the newspaper has apologised for the mix-up on the radio, reprinted the issue, taken back the copies they can.'

'Is Elaine Slade okay?'

'Yes. Staying over at her boyfriend's place.'

Murray squints a little, and changes tack: 'You didn't give Mrs Slade that gash on her head the first time, did you?' Despite their sodden circumstance, they have the air of people who have already won the war. They weren't like this the first time I met them.

'Of course not. I found her, helped her.' The rain redoubles, causing the road to run a river, and the water to pool in the paddocks.

'Weren't hiding in her house? Snuck up on her, hit her real hard, and then claimed the hero thing when she came around?'

'Did Elaine say that?' It's preposterous, but really unnerving. I have trouble coming at me from all sides.

Murray ignores the question and says, 'Can we suggest you don't leave town?'

I nod, and they leave. Where did they think I was going to go?

Now I am supposed to make sense of this distorted jigsaw. Elaine was hit on the head by Mick's money-stealer, went to hospital, discharged herself with her boyfriend, and stayed at his place. Nothing illogical about any of that. Did the robber know about my boxed money, or did he just see Mick and me raking it in at the

68

races? Seems pretty likely to me that none of this has had anything to do with the money or the ash in the boxes. I grab a beer and open it, realising that Mick has made a significant hole in my supply. I drink like someone else might come along and take the remaining bottles. For a meal, I eat something straight from the pack, and listen to music on the TV.

6

It's morning, and I am dry-mouthed and queasy-stomached. My eyes are sore and crusty, and the TV is still running the country-music channel that I must have been watching. I am hoping I still have some eggs and that the bacon isn't off. It takes a long while for bacon to go off. A stumbling examination gives me an affirmative on both counts, so after water and painkillers I fry up breakfast, which includes a couple of soggy tomatoes. Out the window, the storms have gone, so I resolve to return the boxes to their place under the mailbox. I haul myself out to the ute to change the tyre. A fifteen-minute job takes me nearly an hour. The rim is not damaged, so my day is improving.

When we were first married, Sarah used to change and repair tyres. She had no intention of doing all our cleaning and cooking, and so she said she couldn't leave all the outside chores like changing tyres up to me. I would always prefer to change a tyre than clean a bathroom, but I was happy with the logic.

My father thought we were insane. He had a kind of grudging appreciation for Sarah, but his opinion was that a wife shouldn't work. If your wife had to work anywhere except the house and the garden, then you had obviously failed as a provider, and in some sense failed as a man. Mum never wanted to work on the farm, but I think she would have if she thought she could contribute. Despite the dominance of my father, she grew stronger and more assertive as the years went by. They fought loudly when they thought I was out of earshot. It was mostly about money, but it often seemed to be about the smallest things — things you would not think were worth having a heated argument about.

After James was born, Sarah had enough to do, so we settled back into traditional roles. And as James grew he had to do those outside tasks, and Sarah never went back to changing tyres. It is not helpful for me to think about this stuff.

But I remember now how quickly she got pregnant. We joked about being able to get pregnant by just 'passing each other in the corridor'. (It is my recollection we did a damn sight more than just pass in the corridor.) Which made it so much harder to accept when she couldn't get pregnant again. We saw doctors, nutritionists, and reproductive specialists, and read about turkey basters and fertility gurus. It wasn't me, and it wasn't her. It took us so long to accept that it wasn't going to happen, but by the time we got to the possibility of IVF we decided we couldn't face it and the associated pain. We agreed we should count our blessing: James.

I walk out into the garden. It is a redneck mess, and I am happy with it. The lawn is long, and the leaves are thick on it. Shrubs, vines, and climbing roses are taking the opportunity to increase their territory and smother other plants. Hitler would be proud of them. But one area is under control. In the front corner of the garden is a rectangular patch of green, even manicured, lawn. At the end of the lawn is a small garden bed with roses that have been regularly pruned and are in deep, red flower. In front of the bed are a plaque and a grave. I walk to the grave, kneel, and say, 'Hey.' As I do every time. Council allowed us to have James here. Compassion, I suppose. It means I am anchored to this place forever, whether I like it or not. I ask him if he knows what's going on with the boxes, and he gives me no answer. And this is why I don't want to be me. I don't want to be the bloke who lost his son. I don't want to be the one who cannot escape this story. I don't want to be the father who will always be without James, and will always have to live with the worst possible thing, no matter what good happens. There is not a day when I don't want to lie down here, shut my eyes, and cease to exist.

But it is not going to be today, because I feel a weight of responsibility that is new to me. I have things I need to set right. It is time to go on a trip. I need to be away from this house and the people that are coming to it.

I phone Ian, and tell him I need to get away for a few days, and ask would he mind feeding my dogs. He offers to do a water run and anything else that might help, but I tell him it's fine. I don't know why, but I don't want him to see the mess the place is in, even if he probably already knows. When I hang up, I consider ringing him straight back to tell him not to worry. I'll just give the dogs a really big feed.

What if the bad guys or this Dave bloke turn up and hurt Ian? But surely they know what I look like, and Ian will only be here for half an hour a day, and I might be gone longer than a couple of days. I dismiss the thought.

I put the boxes in a large bag, and then I pack a small one for myself. Where am I going? That's a question as good as any other. A motel somewhere. A caravan park. And then I hit upon the perfect strategy. I won't go anywhere. I'll camp here, above the house, and see who comes and goes. Ian is the perfect cover. He'll tell anyone who asks that I'm away, and I'll be able to piece together who owns the cash. I pull a large esky out of the pantry, and fill it with whatever food is left and the ice bricks that remain. There is a tent, a one-man tent, I remember, and I search until I find it in the laundry — a little mouldy, but in one piece. Then I load the ute, and take the track behind my house across the oats paddock (with no oats in it) up into the low hill that looks over the farm.

It is midafternoon as I set up my camp. I don't want to be seen from the house or the main road, but I need to be able to see out. I pitch my tent on a flat area back from the edge of a steep decline. The light from my fire should be shielded from the lower country, and the smoke blown away before it becomes eye-catching. I lie on my stomach in the leaves and sticks, and look at my house through binoculars. I wonder how long it will be before they come. The roof looks even worse from up here. The red paint is peeling or faded, and the sagging roofline suggests the battens are warped or rotted. Thank goodness my mother can't see it. Thanks goodness I'm the only one who sees it from this vantage. But if I cared that much, I'd do something about it, wouldn't I? And I'm not going to do anything about it.

To the south of the house, a wedge-tailed eagle hangs in the sky, then circles slowly on an updraft. He is twice as large as anything else in the air. He holds his loop, and I know he has noticed something he wants. I've never seen a wedge-tailed eagle take a live lamb, but I know they're keen for the freshly dead. Two ravens that patrol this part of the property as their territory join him for a moment and then drop to the ground, and begin cawing and strutting. Through the binoculars, I see they have a dead rabbit, probably killed by Mixo or one of the other more recent viruses.

The eagle lands heavily nearby, and the ravens retreat and then advance, and start harassing him — first one, and then the other. The wedgie threatens them with his beak, and then picks up the corpse in his huge talons and begins to flap his great wings. It takes several motions to get him off the ground, and for a moment he looks like he never will. Then he is in the air, and flying is suddenly effortless. The ravens keep up their racket of disappointment back and forth across the patch where the rabbit had been lying. Then they do their worst impression of elegance to get themselves into the air, and follow the eagle. They are still complaining as they swoop the big bird, hoping his irritation will cause him to drop his prize. But the wedge-tail is unworried as he makes his way into the trees, where I know he will have a nest at the highest point. There might just be beauty in what I have seen.

As a little boy, I would come up here and hide from the adults. I could look down on everyone and pretend I was the king of the world. James used to take his friends up here when they were just old enough to camp on their own. Then, when they were older, teenagers, the same group came back to camp, and snuck alcohol in with them. Sarah and I knew, and I used to go and check on them, at night mostly, to satisfy the other parents. I always made plenty of noise as I approached their camp so they would have time to stash what they needed to stash. No alcohol was ever found. I think Sarah and I felt that if they were going to experiment, it was as safe here as anywhere. I have often wished to go back in time, for all sorts of reasons. That is certainly a period I would like to go back to: when kids experimenting with alcohol was our biggest worry. 'We were happy,' I say out loud, and the words roll out like obscenities. 'Happy' is now an odd, unlikely concept that is beyond my imagining. I can't think of a world where I could be 'happy'. And now I'm stealing money and hiding on my own property from criminals.

On a flat spot back from the edge, I scratch back the grass and sticks to make a bare area for the fire. When it is crackling, I pitch the tent, and then get sausages and bread from the esky, put them near the fire to defrost, set out my deckchair, and sit to watch the fire. I have that feeling I always have when I camp, that maybe I'll stay here forever and never return to the house, with all its echoing memories and pain. There is much pleasure in being away from a place where every creak of a wall or a contraction in the roof makes me think it's James coming up the hallway or Sarah getting ready for bed.

There was a time, too, when I used to come up here in the afternoon with a sixpack of beers, and just sit, maybe listen, and drink beer till I fell asleep or my phone buzzed with Sarah wondering if I was all right. Now I think maybe I'll bring a bed up and get a little fridge I can run off the car, and the whole world can just go away. I open a beer, and enjoy the creeping autumn dusk.

As darkness falls, the noise of nature recedes with it. The birds give up, as do the remaining blowflies and insects. Even the drone from distant machinery fades. The world can be a quiet place without human things. I sit and think nothing, blissfully. Soon the only light is from my fire.

And then I see the reflection of lights glowing on the road as they approach my house. I hadn't thought anyone would come at night because I had figured it would be too confusing in the dark if you've never done it before. It's not like a town street with lights, evenly spaced housing and regular contours. All the advantage is mine. But now it's happening and I don't have a plan for it. If I drive down they'll see me before I can find out who they are. It's dark, and the moon is slim and weak, and I have about a kilometre and a half to walk, over rocks and tussocks and furrows. But I need to know who they are, so I grab the .22 rifle from the ute, make sure the fire is safe, and set off at a half-run, half-walk, careful of my footing as I watch the headlights arrive and stop at my house. The intruders are not bothering to sneak up on me, but there are no messages or missed calls on my phone from a friend wondering where I am. When I leave the trees, I pull my hat down so my face doesn't shine in the little light there is from the moon. If they are in my house turning it upside down, I'm not sure what I'll do. Do I have the guts to pull the rifle on them?

Where the oats paddock finishes, I cross to the garden fence, bent double, and sneak along the edge of the house until I hear the trespassers. I can't see them, but I know they are standing at the front door. There are at least two of them.

I hear them pull roughly on the door as if they are expecting to have to break a lock, but I never lock my doors, not even now. They find a light switch, and step into my house like old friends.

My breathing is competing with my heart for loudness as I flatten myself again the wall and try to think. I decide to let them search the house. They'll probably wreck the place, but they'll know the money isn't there, at least for the moment. I make my way to the kitchen window, hoping to get a look at them. But I stop after a few paces, because they have turned more lights on, and I can see them from where I stand — three of them, upending couches and emptying drawers. And suddenly my decision to let them wreck the house is the weak, pitiful choice of a loser and a coward. Rage is beating inside me like a confined demon. I take a couple of rounds out of my pocket, load the rifle, point it in the air, fire it, and then bolt around to the front door and wait. I hear them cursing, running for the door. When they burst outside, I have the rifle trained on them.

'Stay where you are.'

They stop, and put their hands in the air. My front door LED lights them up like they are on stage.

'Put the handguns on the ground.' They bend, and put them down, trying to keep their eyes on me the whole time.

'Kick them towards me.' They obey.

'Take it easy, buddy,' the biggest of them says. 'There's no need for anyone to get hurt.'

He is built like a powerlifter. He is pale-skinned with a bleached-blond buzzcut. He gives me the sense that he is not the sort of guy to be afraid of some hick with a rifle.

'Yes, there is.' I sight the rifle at his barrel chest. 'I'm going to hurt you.'

'Hey. We weren't going to do anything to you — we were just told to look for something.' The man alongside him, who is nearly as big, says this. These are the muscled hard men that I had been waiting for.

The third, the tallest and leanest of the group, takes a step towards me. His hands are up, but he is beginning to smile. He knows I'm a bumpkin who is never going to fire on a human being.

'Look, buddy. We don't want any trouble, and I'm pretty sure you don't want to shoot anyone. So let's just put the rifle down, and we'll leave you alone.'

I lower the barrel of the rifle slowly, then take aim and shoot him in an ample calf. The projectile goes right through, and splinters off the concrete paver behind him as he goes down, screaming into the half-light. The other two jump back, look to him, and then quickly look at me. Did I really just do that? Four of us are asking the question.

'So what do you want?'

'Boxes. Could have been accidentally sent here,' the second-biggest of the three says, notes of panic making the words come out in fragments.

'What's supposed to be in the boxes?'

The big fella is whimpering on the ground, but there is hardly any blood.

'Crockery.'

'Crockery?' I nearly drop the rifle.

'Yeah, plates and mugs and shit.'

'Plates and mugs and shit?'

The speaker looks at his big blond mate as if he might have the right answers, but Buzzcut is no help, so he looks back at me.

'Yeah.'

'Are you sure?'

'Ah, yeah.' He thinks I'm playing some sort of weird power game.

'Righto. Get your mate, get in the car, and don't ever come back.' I wave the rifle barrel towards their car. 'And when you get to the ramp, beep your horn twice so the sentries know you're right to leave.'

He nods, and the two lean down to help their mate up and swing him to the car. I keep the rifle on them the whole time until their car is gone. I hear a car horn twice.

And then I am madly sucking air — the rush of shooting a man is surging through me. I can't believe I did what I did. I have probably made things worse, but being able to fight back was fantastic. Next time they'll come with the big guns. But what about the crockery? Is crockery a code word for something, or are their bosses afraid they'll steal it if they know it's money?

After all my big ideas of never returning to the house, collapsing on my couch in front of the TV with several beers feels like the best option, even if I won't be able to calm down and sit for some while. But the fire is still going at my campsite, so I need to check on it, even if the risk of it getting away is very small. There is still enough adrenaline pumping through me to get me walking across the oats paddock towards the hill, thinking about Elaine and wondering what the hell it is with the crockery. They weren't looking for the money — they were looking for 'plates and shit'. It can only be a code word for something else. Nobody wants crockery that much. The various possibilities presented by Elaine revolve in my brain, hitting the sides as they turn.

My campsite seems further away in the dark, and the hill steeper than I remember. When I reach the site, the fire is burned to coals, and the place is dark, cold, and a bit desperate. I pour water on the fire, pack up the camp, and pull the tent down and put it with the other things in the ute.

When I get to my house, the lights of another car have turned off the main road towards me. I am stuck. The house lights have remained on, and whoever's in the car would have seen my ute lights arrive, so there's no point pretending I'm not here. If it's the big guys returning, they've probably got bazookas with them. All I can do is take a secure point and let them come. I grab the shotgun and some shells, run to where I keep the ladder, and take it where I can climb onto the roof that looks over where the car might park. On the roof, I crawl near the edge, lie flat, and look out into the night. The light meanders its way in, and I take a bead on it. Perhaps I should shoot now — scare them, put them off — but I know the shotgun won't do any damage until they are pretty close. The lights keep coming all the way to the house. I breathe, and take aim. I don't think I can pull off a shot as good as the calf shot, and the shotgun won't make a clean hole: it will blow a hole the size of a watermelon.

The driver gets out of the vehicle, and I loop my finger around the trigger. I could blow a foot off from this distance. But only one person gets out of the car, and in the half-dark I see it's Elaine. Surprisingly, she's dishevelled — part of her shirt is hanging out, and from here her hair looks like she slept on it. She walks towards the house, steps past the two handguns lying on the grass without reacting to them, and knocks on the door. My thoughts are back in a maelstrom. I leave my gun where it is, and edge my way back off the roof. When my foot finds the ladder, I push my mouth into my jumper and yell out, 'Coming,' hoping it doesn't sound like I've been on the roof. When I open the front door, she is smiling calmly, with an expectant look. Expecting what, I wonder.

'Elaine.'

'Dave.'

I have left the .22 behind the door, and I can't think whether I should be reaching for it or not.

'Sorry to bother you at this hour. It's just that it's a bit quiet at my place, and after what happened, I'm really jumpy. I thought, if you wouldn't mind some company . . . '

'Sure. Come in.' *Come in?* Where did that issue from?

As she follows me in, I say, 'I thought you were at your boyfriend's house.' I move swiftly to the door between the kitchen and the TV room, and pull it firmly shut. It was a mess even before Buzzcut and his mates got to it.

When she doesn't say anything, I presume she's wondering why I would know that. 'The police called round.'

'Oh, I was. We had a fight, and I guess . . . we split up.' When I look at her, she is more of a mess than I had first thought, even if it is only in the context of how perfectly turned out she normally is.

'I'm sorry about that. Do you want a drink, or a cup of tea or something?'

'If you've got a white wine?'

Against my better, but faulty, judgement, I get two glasses from the cupboard, put them on the island, then grab a bottle from the fridge, hoping it isn't from the $6 section of the supermarket. I pour for both of us. She takes hers, and drinks a little more greedily than is normal.

'You've had a rough week then,' I say. I don't know how to talk to her about what has happened to me, and whether she is the cause of it or the sufferer. 'They called in here, too.'

'Who?'

'Guys looking for crockery.'

'I can tell.' She quickly asks 'Why?' to cover her rudeness.

'No idea.'

'And you never received any crockery, or china, or pottery pieces in the mail?'

'No. Should I have?'

She does a kind of shrug and eye-roll. 'What did you do with these guys?'

'Talked them out of it. Three of them. Big dudes.'

'And you talked them out of it?'

I nod like it wasn't that big a deal. I am thinking about sex for the first time since Sarah left. Not sex with Elaine, but sex in the abstract, because I am feeling powerful and in control in a weird way. Nothing has been in my control for a long time. Maybe it never has been.

'You must be a very good talker.' At this, I see the tip of her tongue slipping into her wine, and she rubs a hand down a thigh. I know this is getting weirder, because it's possible she's trying to seduce me, and I'm not really seducible. Am I?

'They didn't visit you tonight?'

She shakes her head.

'Has this sort of stuff happened to you before?' I ask.

'I'm not sure I came here for an interrogation,' she says.

'Sorry. I didn't mean to make you feel that way. It's just that I'm trying really hard to make sense of the mad things that have been going on around here.'

'You shouldn't spy on me, you know.'

I'm gagging on bullshit responses. 'No.'

'I knew you were in the house. I could see your ute at the sheds.' She pauses, and I wait for both barrels, but instead she says, 'I appreciate you looking out for me.'

'That's okay.'

'No more snooping, though.'

'No.' I should be grateful that she is not screaming at me, and I am, but not grateful enough to swallow a question. 'That blond guy who was with you — that was your boyfriend?'

'Yes.' She says this in an offhand way, because we are talking about a past she no longer wants to talk about. 'You must get lonely up here. On your own.'

'Not really.'

'I do. Even when Tito was around. It's worse now.' She runs a careless hand through her hair.

Is something stirring in me? Am I up for this? For a moment, there is nothing to say. I decide to persist. 'One last question. The bloke who robbed you — can you tell me what he looked like?'

She blanches. 'He had his head covered.'

'Was he big?'

'Muscly. Like a gym junkie. Not very tall. Really strong.'

'That's what the guys that were here looked like.'

She drinks her wine, pretty well glugging it down. 'Maybe we should be at my place. At least they got what they wanted there. There's no reason to come back. I've got plenty of spare beds. You could stay over.'

It seems to me, in the weird rattle of things going on in my head, that going to Elaine's house is the perfect solution. It gets me out of my own house, and I might find some answers at hers. I am aware she's probably made the invitation knowing I won't take it up, giving her an excuse to get out.

'Actually, would you mind if we did go to yours?'

She studies me over her empty glass.

'Sorry. I didn't mean anything by that. I'm not trying to . . . you know. I'd just like to get out of here.'

She puts the glass down and says, 'Okay. Let's go. You need to pack some things?'

'All packed.'

She raises one perfect eyebrow.

'I was going camping.'

'Right.' She rinses her glass, says, 'See you there,' and leaves.

I wonder what Ian would think if he found out the place I 'went away to' was Elaine's. He'd probably say, good for me. I take the half-bottle of wine with me, and then remember I don't have anything decent to sleep in, so I go to my bedroom and toss through clothes for something respectable. I take the shorts and T-shirt that will do the job, collect the .222 and some ammunition, and head to my ute. I know that I am going because I am too frightened to stay still, and even if I won't admit it, I am intrigued by the possibility. There's a chance the boyfriend will turn up, and that just adds heat to the growing fire.

She is waiting for me when I walk in, perched on a shiny designer kitchen stool, a glass in her hand, and another next to a bottle, already poured. I put my bag down and look around. I don't know which is a more weird scenario: that we are sleeping together, or that we aren't. Common sense would tell me she has just, maybe temporarily, broken up with a boyfriend, and I am split from the wife I love, and am generally damaged goods, so there is no likelihood of us being together. Common sense doesn't know everything, though. I arch my eyebrows, and say without any shame of inanity: 'Made it.'

'I see.'

She is no longer dishevelled. The old Elaine has returned, or almost. I pull up a stool, and she offers the wine. It is smooth and dry and a little spicy, and I am surprised she could have even ingested my version of white wine.

'Things move pretty quickly round here, don't they?' I say.

'How's that?' She is looking at me closely, and it is not unpleasant.

'Well, it was only a couple of days ago that you

called in to see about your box, and I had hardly ever spoken to you.'

'And now?' She says it as a caution to a presumption she thinks she's heard.

'And now I'm staying over, after you've been burgled and assaulted, and I've been threatened.'

'Slumber party.' She giggles just a little bit. It is a lovely sound I haven't heard before. I almost ask her to do it again. Instead the wrong question comes to mind. It is one of those that I have developed a burning desire to know the answer to.

'How did Tito die?'

'I killed him.'

And then, with the kind of timing you'd expect from a TV cliffhanger, a rifle shot zings through the room, radiating the sound of making a neat hole in the glass of the front door. Behind Elaine, a plate on the wall collapses and falls to the floor in pieces. We are on the ground before it is. I point furiously towards the back, telling her to go-go-go, and as she slides away along the floor I reach for my bag and the rifle. I take the rifle and load it, then drag myself to the safest place I can find: under the island. I'm trying to look in five places at once. Would they have gone round the back? Why would they have fired first? On the verandah, at the door, looking through the glass at the kitchen, are two of my muscle friends. The blond buzzcut pushes the door open, and says, 'Elaine?' He pauses in the doorway. 'That's enough games now. You need to give us what we want.'

There is no reply from Elaine. Does she know

them, or do they just know her name?

'We've already given that neighbour of yours a seeing-to. And if you don't cooperate, you're next.'

He looks kind of satisfied with this. A man in control. Then he sees my gun barrel, and his cool disappears.

'Drop your guns,' I say.

'You don't need to get involved in this, man. It's not your fight.' He is almost wincing at the pain of having to say this instead of bolting out the door to his ute and his warm, safe home. 'It's more complex than it seems.'

'Drop your fucking guns. Both of you.' They do. They know I'm the dude who isn't afraid to shoot.

I'm tempted to ask how their injured friend is doing, but that would be kind of obscene. I reach for the phone in my pocket. This time I'm calling the police. I hear a noise behind me, and Elaine slithers in next to me. She grabs at my hand, and holds it. It feels intimate.

'No. Don't call anyone. Just get rid of them.'

I don't question her. I just obey. 'Righto, you two, get out of here. If I see you in this area again, I'll shoot you. No questions asked. That's a promise.'

They turn and quickly leave. I stand and follow them, gun pointed. Elaine is at my side. The car leaves. We hug, and she says, 'Wow. Who are you?'

Her flattering stops me asking why she didn't want me to call the police. And now I don't want to know because memory tells me the police aren't on my side. Our side? I unload the rifle and lean it against the door. Elaine says, 'Would you mind putting it away? It scares me.' I put the rifle in my bag, zip it, and then pull up a stool. For a moment, we just sit taking it in, and maybe wondering, *What's next?*

Elaine says, 'I'm going to call the security company. Get someone in for the night.' She walks to the other end of the room, picks up a phone, and punches in some numbers. After a short conversation, she returns.

And then I have to ask, 'You killed your husband?'

Elaine takes a stool too, finds her wine glass, fills it, and then fills mine. 'Not literally.'

This is a relief. We are both still breathing heavily.

'I just pushed him too hard, way too hard. We had some tough times, which is why we bought the farm and moved out here. I was desperate for him to do something with his pottery — not just the popular stuff he had been making, but something significant. I knew he was capable of it.' She slurps. I guzzle.

'He was killed in a plane crash in Africa?' I place the question carefully, letting her know it's a topic she can avoid if she wants to.

'What? No!'

'Oh sorry . . . I thought . . . ' I'm suffering for having jumped in with an unverified rumour. Serves me right.

'It was a car crash . . . out west. Jesus. Africa?'

'Just what I heard.'

'I thought you two were mates.'

'A bit, I guess.'

This looks like it hurts.

'I'm sorry. I . . . '

'No problem. Anyway. He was fascinated with some of the clay soils out west. Thought they had a magic. Made several trips out there. Used to stay at a tiny place called Willi. I teased him that he liked it more out there than at home. Anyway, I pushed him to find interesting clays, come up with better designs, make more pottery, sleep less, work harder. On the way home, he fell asleep and drove into a road train.'

'I really am sorry.' A better person would have left it there. But I am too far down the road to deadshit. 'What did they mean: 'You need to give us what we want'?'

'Tito had a contract with some bad people. To make some vases and things. He never finished the contract, and they seem to think I've got the remaining pieces somewhere. I'm sure he told you about it, didn't he?'

'No. We didn't really talk about serious stuff.'

'He said you were safe.'

I remember him saying something like that, but I don't understand where she is going with this, so I direct us back to the topic.

'He never finished the contract?' I don't know a single thing about bad guys or the underworld, but those words sound like little bombshells going off in the shiny space between us.

'No, as far as I can tell. Didn't deliver the pieces they wanted, or at least the right pieces.'

I hold my tongue. Elaine has sunk into her thoughts.

90

'God, I visited the accident site so many times afterwards. I'd sit there just looking at the place where it happened. The first few times, I found pieces of his car in the long grass, but I stopped looking after a while. I hung out in Willi as if someone there would pop up and give me an explanation, but no one ever did. It was just a car accident. One of many. It was only me who couldn't get it through her head.'

I am thinking I should be saying something consoling and stop with the questions, but I can't.

'What's your boyfriend, ex, got to do with it?'

'Nothing.' She is tired of my questions.

'What have I got to do with it?'

'I don't know.'

I think about the guy who robbed Mick.

'But I'm glad you were here.'

She puts a hand on my shoulder, and I flinch at her second touch. It is a long time since I was touchable.

'So am I. It's just that now I'm worried you're not safe, and neither am I.'

'You seem like you can handle yourself.' Every thrust seems to have a parry that deflects me from working out what to do.

She gets up, walks to the fridge, opens it, and peruses. 'Want something to eat?'

Until the last two days I haven't been in any scrapes with firearms, but I can't imagine anyone remaining as calm as she has after a potential armed robbery. My left leg is beginning to shake in its place on the stool rung as a reminder that I am not as calm as I pretend, and I put a hand down to still it. 'Sure.'

'How about a stir fry?'

'Terrific.' I stand, and wobble my head around trying to ease the knots in my neck. 'I'm going to have a little look around.' I don't know why I didn't do this before. She nods as she puts out things on the bench. There might never have been a rifle shot in the house. We are neighbours having a late dinner.

Outside, the stars are keen to point out my insignificance. They are the only light not thrown by the house. The harvesters no longer work on the plain. There are no cars passing. I walk around the garden and the lawn, soft under my feet, listening for anything out of place. There is hardly a sound. One circuit of the house takes me back to the door with the bullet hole in it, and the stir fry Elaine is serving. Before I enter, I watch Elaine and imagine she is whistling while she works. I cannot make sense of what I am feeling. Her story is plausible, but her actions feel wrong. Why not call the police? What crockery is worth being shot at for? I turn, and step off the verandah. Too many things are out of kilter, and I reckon I know about 'out of kilter'. I walk towards the ute, and hear the door behind me opening on the verandah.

'Dave?'

'I've got to go.'

'Come back.'

'I will.' I keep walking.

On the way home, I consider camping, but I know I'll end up in my own bed with a rifle to hand. But as I make the turn at my mailbox, a car comes towards me, dims its lights, and pulls in alongside. Ian winds down his window and says, 'You're back.'

'Yeah. My plans didn't work out.'

'Oh, bad luck. Mandy thought she had seen lights on at your house, and she insisted I come and have a look. I guess it was you?'

'Yeah. I should have told you. Sorry about that.'

'Not a problem.'

He looks at me carefully and asks, 'Are you all right?' It is not an offhand question.

'Yeah, I'm good. Thanks for helping out. I'll see you.' I put the ute into gear.

'No, Dave.' He gets out of his car and comes over to me. 'You look like shit. I can't just let you go home on your own.' He grabs hold of my door as if by sheer strength he can stop me driving away.

'I'm fine. Just a bit tired.'

'Bullshit, Dave. Come home with me. Just for the night. We'll look after you — have a big breakfast together in the morning. Nothing's so urgent, is it?'

To accept his offer would be an admission of weakness and a nod to desperation. I am a mess, but if I don't concede it to anyone else, I feel like I can pretend that my mess is a secret, or at least most of it.

'Really, I'm okay.'

He is quiet, not letting go of the door. 'Maybe you could come for a cup of tea and a chat?'

'It's midnight.'

'So what? Mandy would love to see you, and

she worries we don't look after you as well as we could when you're on your own down here.'

The cup of tea is a clever get-out clause. I don't want to be in my house tonight, and he wants to make sure I'm not going to kill myself. 'You sure Mandy isn't asleep?'

'She'll have the kettle boiled by the time we get there.'

'I'll come for a cup of tea.'

'Terrific.' He finally lets go of my ute and gets back into his car. He leans out the window, and says, 'If you chicken out, I'll have to come back down here and sleep in your bedroom with you, and you don't want that.' Then he is gone at the steady pace you would expect.

The Blent house is a simple rectangle on the side of a low hill facing north. The garden looks small but heavily populated in the dark. The Blents are not wealthy, but they are not wanting either. They are people in control of their farm, and their lives. Willing to help those out of control.

In the kitchen, Mandy is waiting, dressed for an outing, and almost too bright, and friendly. She is a small woman with bouncy brown hair and quick, busy movements. I know this is not a place where lethargy gets a look-in. I consent to tea, and as the kettle re-boils she puts out homemade biscuits that it seems possible she has baked in the last half-hour. She apologises for sending Ian off to have a look around my place in the middle of the night, and hopes I don't think he was snooping.

'It is just that I thought I saw light coming

from the area of your house, and I even thought I smelt smoke at one stage. You can't be too careful these days.'

I agree, and she goes on to talk about stories she's heard in the news, of cattle and sheep being stolen, and of people deliberately starting fires. Ian drinks his tea and listens, mostly watching Mandy, and occasionally looking over at me. I have the unique sensation of feeling like I'm in good hands.

I know that if they start to ask me questions about what I have been up to, and where I was supposed to be going away to, I will not be able to come up with anything believable. The memory of my doppelganger comes to my rescue.

'I had the strangest thing happen to me. A guy with my name and my address . . . ' I tell them the story, and then ask if they have ever heard of him or the address.

'There is definitely a Wilson Road on the other side of town. Or it might be a Wilson Avenue or something. There were a lot of Wilsons amongst the early settlers in the area.' Ian says. 'And I'm pretty sure there's a 'Fythe Trees' out there somewhere, too. But I've never heard of a David Martin.'

Mandy shakes her head as if she knows nothing, and then says, 'There is a Sue Martin who lives on a farm on that side of town.'

They volley possibilities at each other, and I stop listening. All I really wanted to do was take the focus away from me. But it occurs to me that I should go and have a look at Dave Martin and his place before he turns up at mine.

They are trying to agree on whether a Samson family live on that road, and I give a little laugh, and break into their to and fro. 'Elaine Slade's not dead. Did you hear that? The newspaper stuffed it up.'

Mandy rolls her eyes with a gesture of *What can you expect?* and says, 'We did hear that. We were about to ring and see what we could do to help out when we found out it was a hoax.'

'That newspaper ought to hire a real journalist or close down, as far as I'm concerned,' Ian says, chastened.

'I visited her. She seemed fine.'

I have said something they don't understand, and they both look at me, unguarded in their interest.

'You visited Elaine?' Mandy asks, sounding like she thinks I've made a joke.

'Yes.'

'That was a nice thing to do.'

I nod. I hadn't thought about there being a 'nice' aspect to it.

'I've never had anything to do with her. She doesn't come to any of the fundraisers or open gardens, or any of the other things we put on. She'll give a donation, but she won't socialise. Not that I know of, anyway. Quite beautiful, though.' Mandy gives the impression that something as exotic as genuine beauty could be a reasonable excuse for antisocial behaviour.

'She seems nice, but I can't quite make her out,' I say.

'Why's that?' Ian asks, as if he might be genuinely interested. Perhaps they are both keen for

96

information on a local they know so little about. In a small farming community like ours, people are surprised and discomfited by someone unknown. Or maybe they just want to keep me talking.

'There's a bit of trouble going on down there, but I'm not sure what it is. Bad people turning up, and now her assault. I haven't had anything to do with that sort of stuff before. Maybe she's some sort of criminal.' I pause, and their eyes go wide at the assertion. 'But probably not.'

Ian says, 'But she wasn't assaulted. That was all a mistake by the paper.'

I nearly tell them about the first assault, my first visit to Elaine's place, but it suddenly feels like too much to reveal. 'Yeah, you're right. I might be misreading her.'

When I've finished answering their questions, I thank them for the tea and biscuits, and tell them how tired I feel and that I need to be home. Mandy tries to insist that I stay the night, and then Ian adds his voice. I say the chat has helped, I really will be fine, and leave the room before they can lock the door or something.

At the ute, Ian tries one more time, but the conviction is lost, and before he finds the energy for threats, I am on my way home to where I don't want to be, wondering who'll come for me next.

I left a kitchen light on so I wouldn't have to stumble in, in the dark, but when I walk in the back door I know immediately that something is different. I couldn't say what. I look around, and think it's not like someone could make a mess of the place. But someone has been here. Is here? I reach into the walk-in pantry for the .22, then I stand still and listen. Nothing. The house is as quiet as the creaking hulk ever gets. I stand still, and calm my breathing. There is only the thump of my heart, and then the distant scream of a vixen. It could be a plea from a woman in trouble. I tell myself it's not. I'm sure it's not. I've heard their horny call a thousand times, and every time I've hated them for their relentless procreation.

I step forward, rolling my feet one at a time, and then stop. Nothing.

'All right. You can come out now.' I say it coolly as I can, the man in control, the man with the gun.

No reply. So I walk through the house, the rifle at my shoulder, taking aim at every doorway and cupboard. No one reveals themselves or makes a break for the pitch-black night.

I lean the rifle against the couch, take my boots off, and lie down. Eventually I sleep, or I think I sleep. The line between being awake and not awake is blurred by dreams that lurch across the line of reality.

7

It is mail day, but I don't get to the mailbox until well after lunch, when I've fed and watered the dogs and given them a run. In the mailbox is a rates notice, a mail-out from my local politician, a bank statement, a phone bill, and two more boxes. I have a good mind to put them all in a pile and burn them. I take them home, and take all of the boxes out of the ute and put them in the laundry. Whatever is in the new boxes, I don't want to know. I will look at them another day when I am feeling more resilient. Now I don't even know why I'm going to the trouble of checking my mail. It always turns out to be a disaster.

I shut the laundry door, check my phone, and realise that, sometime in the past few days, Sarah has sent me a text saying that she and Lucy are coming to visit on the day that turns out to be today. They are going to stay in town, but she would be happy if I was around when they were. I'm thinking that visiting your son's grave with your new girlfriend, alongside your old husband, is kind of insane, although insane ideas have become dime a dozen around here, so I can't really complain. But when I see our car, the white four-wheel drive that has become Sarah's, coming towards the house, I do have the feeling that crazy has come to town. And yet it is the least of my problems. The idea of seeing Sarah, no matter who she is with or why, makes me feel better. I know I will be jealous and probably erratic in my response to both of them, but still I welcome Sarah's arrival.

They get out of the car, stretching and looking around as if they are tourists on a pit stop. I walk across the garden to greet them. Sarah kisses me on the cheek, and I am thankful. She looks tense but healthy, and not as tired as I remember her. She introduces Lucy, who smiles sweetly. There is no mention of the state of the garden, and their faces give no clues of their feelings. Lucy is half pretty, but obviously unconcerned by her looks. Her hair is straight and short, but still lank. Her clothes are worn jeans, a simple shirt, and work boots. I have no intelligence on whether she is slim, chubby, or curvaceous. If this is my replacement, I have no idea how to compete.

Everything that Sarah and I have been to each other is so far in the past I am almost disconnected from it. But I still react to the presence of Sarah the way I always have. In my mind's eye she is the embodiment of what I hope a woman I am with will look like: she is pretty but self-effacing, and moves with a sportswoman's confidence. Her smile is enough to light even my dark days. After all we have been through, and all the things I have done to her, she still gives me a sense of her warmth. If we had never met before, I would be thinking about her tomorrow and the day after. Some people just have what you desire, regardless of practicality or convention. If such a thing as 'the one' exists, then she is mine. The fact that it was beyond my capabilities to hold on to her is just another great big well of pain.

But standing where we are standing, the worst of it is obvious: pain is relative. No matter if 'the one' exists or not, that love never compares with the love for a child. For me, anyway. I'm pretty sure it is the same for Sarah. So, no matter the pain we feel for each other, it is a drop in the bucket compared to what we feel about James.

I walk with them to James's area. Sarah is commending me on my maintenance. I point out the bulbs that will flower soon, and idiotically remark on the fertility of the soil. We are standing by a small, obsessively tended plot surrounded by a massive, derelict, unruly garden. I'm sure Lucy has no idea how to behave, but she says how special the area is, and I appreciate the comment as if she has offered a significant positive insight into our lives and not a limp platitude for the ex. And then I walk away, because I figure Sarah will want some time alone with James. Lucy stands with her for a moment and then strolls over to me, obviously drawing a similar conclusion. And we watch like embarrassed voyeurs as Sarah kneels and begins to cry full-body sobs that I have seen so many times. Just as many times she has told me to stay away from her suffering. I am torn between desperate sympathy and self-protection. That's a rough summing up of the failure between Sarah and me.

Lucy puts a hand on my shoulder. It is the nicest thing a person could do for me, but I still have to stop my body from responding like it is under attack. Lucy seems to know this, too. For once, I remember I am not the only one who suffers. Lucy's understanding wins me, and for all the jealousy and confusion I feel, she is a friend. She could have sat in the car, or treated me like a rival or the enemy, and she hasn't. It is not possible for me to dislike her humanity. And so when Sarah stands again and heads towards us, drying her eyes, I offer them a drink, a meal, a coffee — anything. Sarah's lovely face tells me that, for once, I've done the right thing. They decline the offer; both hug me like sisters, and are gone. It feels like a missed opportunity. We could have talked and laughed and drunk until we had got at least some of the darkness out of ourselves. They say they'll be back, and I suppose they will.

I stroll to the chook yard with no real purpose. We used to let the chooks out in the morning and shut them in at night to protect them from the foxes. I haven't bothered with that for a long time. The chooks get to run free, going where they want, and nesting where they want. Most of the time they seemed to end up in the chook shed after dark, and so far all eight of them have survived. I look in the nests that I haven't checked for over a week, and find nearly fifty eggs, some of them laid on the bare dirt next to the nests, and some of them in the open ground of the yard. I put them in a bucket and take them outside. I pick up one of the clean brown eggs and weigh it in my hand. It feels like the perfect missile. I hurl it at the centre of a huge box tree nearby. The egg splatters beautifully, but slightly off mark. I try again, and improve a little bit. I keep throwing until all the eggs are gone and the tree is painted in yellow and egg shells. I feel some pleasure in that.

In the morning I am driving, on my way to Fythe Trees, and after that to track down the mailman and have a word. It is dawn, and I have only slept a couple of hours, but I am fresh enough, and sitting still is an impossibility. My money is now back in the tool box. I pass Elaine's turn-off, and ignore it. I need time to think about Elaine, and thinking about things that upset me isn't my strong suit.

In town I go to the only remaining bank, and deposit $20,000 in cash — half from the box, and half won on the races. The teller looks surprised and a little pleased. I know her. Yvette Hill. Her husband used to be a stockman on Ben Ruder's place until he was smart enough to get out and get a job managing a farm nearer town. But the presence of Yvette means I am probably starting gossip that I don't need to. If the notes turn out to be marked, I'll say they must have come from the bookies. If not, then I'll be able to go for broke, put my money into several accounts, and spend like a . . . well, like my father did. I'll do that in a much bigger town than this one.

'Yvette,' I say, 'you don't happen to know a Dave Martin, another Dave Martin, who lives out on the eastern side of town?'

'Of course,' she says, and smiles at me like I am a cretin. 'Everyone knows Marto. Lovely guy. A real hoot.'

'Has he lived out there long?'

She shrugs, and blows her lips out. 'Probably ten years, I'd say.'

'Oh. Right. Thanks.'

When I step out of the bank onto the pavement, two police are waiting for me: the same two I have encountered twice in the last couple of days.

'Mr Martin, I wonder if you would mind accompanying us to the station to answer a few questions?' It is Murray. She is no more filled with a love of life than the last time I saw her.

I ask if it can wait. I have appointments. But they are not going to give me any leeway, because they don't like me. So I walk with them, and wonder aloud what they might want to question me about. They don't respond.

In a plain room in the brick police station, they give me a simple chair and start asking me about betting. Do I do it regularly? Do I put a lot of money on? Do I have a system? Am I in contact with people in the industry?

I tell them the truth, except for the bit about receiving oodles of cash in the mail. It is obvious where they're going. They think I might be in on the fix with Kinky. It stands to reason. I've never been seen at the races, and suddenly I turn up and put heaps of money (which everyone knows I don't have) on a horse with very long odds that happens to win. I'd lock me up, too. It's circumstantial, but powerful nevertheless. They let me go, and it makes me confident that they are yet to prove the fix, because otherwise I would still be in there. When things go bad, they really go bad. And I'm still not caring that much.

On my way out, I am joined by Mrs Ruth Johnson, a friend of my mother's back in the day, now an elderly woman who I've always liked because of the cheeky sense of humour she maintains in the face of the trials of old age.

'Young Mr Martin, what would you be doing in the police station? Armed robbery again?'

'Nope. Race fixing, but I might ask you the same question, Mrs J.'

'I was here on official business,' she says, raising her eyebrows and reaching out to grab my arm as we descend the few steps, 'assessing the value of stolen porcelain . . . '

Mrs J is an expert in fine china, often called on (in her twilight years) by the Country Women's Association to host assessment and valuation days as charity fundraisers. She has the air of someone who really has played the big time when it comes to fine china.

'Well, that's interesting.' I cannot remove the sarcasm from my voice, but that's okay because it's part of the game we play.

'It is interesting, actually. Because, you see, a box of it was found on the road, just out of town. A lot of it broken. Probably thrown out the window.'

'Pity.' I don't bother to sound like I care.

'No, it isn't. It was complete rubbish. None of it would have been out of place on a $10 table at a garage sale. Don't know why they bothered to call me all the way in.' She only lives up the road, so I'm guessing it really must be rubbish.

'Anyway, how are you holding up?' She looks

up at me, and mouths a grim grin.

'Pretty well, thanks.'

'Liar.' She turns away from me to make her way up the gentle slope to her house. I would have liked to hug her. For her, and for me. 'Don't give up,' she says over her shoulder, 'You can't. None of us can.'

'Nice to see you, Mrs J.'

She thinks that by telling me about the porcelain she was imparting the most useless information possible. An extension of our private joke. And any other week it would have been, but today it was the opposite. If the crockery was crap, then the burglars have been duped. Did Elaine dupe them? Or was her aunt's crockery simply not worth what she thought it was? These are pieces of a complex puzzle I am too dim to put together.

As always, Mrs J makes me think of my mother.

I remember listening in on their conversations, smart conversations about people and politics broken up by caustic comments that they both obviously found very funny.

But my mother was a lighthearted person. 'Take your hands out of your pockets, Dave,' she always said, because her father had always said it to her and her brothers. People with hands in their pockets weren't ready or willing to work. Mum did not like people who weren't keen for work. I think her close friends, like Mrs J, were the same. If you were awake, you were moving — cooking, cleaning, ironing, gardening, looking after old people and young people, arranging flowers, sweeping, vacuuming, washing, and sometimes riding horses. If you were sitting down, you were sewing or mending something, or knitting. The only time you were still and unproductive was when you were asleep. I don't remember her watching television for more than half an hour at a time. She usually read difficult books. There was always something to be done. And maybe she didn't like sitting with my father while he talked about himself and his day. When I started to take notice of their relationship, in my teens, they never seemed to hug or touch each other. I thought it was because of the way they were brought up. Open affection was frowned on, and all that.

And she almost never laughed at his jokes. Not that I remember. I know from the good times with Sarah that when your wife laughs at your jokes, it's not really about how funny you are. It's about how much they like being with you. And it's genuine, because they express it when they don't really mean to. It might even be the highest form of female praise. My mother never allowed my father that praise, but I didn't understand it at the time — I only remembered its absence years later when I felt the joy of making Sarah laugh.

I still think my parents loved each other, but there was just too much they disagreed about. Mum didn't like the betting and the way my father spent money; and she grew out of being his domestic helper and doing what he commanded. I know she wished for independence — something she never really got. She loved the farm, but didn't like the way it constrained her. The only way she could get a job, or meet lots of interesting people, or study to acquire a new skill was to leave the farm and her husband behind. She couldn't do that, so she had to be content with what the farm provided. And my father couldn't stop being his confident, overbearing self. So she couldn't bring herself to laugh at his jokes.

I sometimes think that was why she was always so busy. Being incessantly active stopped her thinking about what she was missing out on. But in the end he didn't let her down. Even when she didn't know who he was, he visited her, took her out, and did as much as he could to look after her. Not that he knew anything about looking after people. But he certainly tried.

At the Fythe Trees turn-off, I pull into the table drain and stop, pretending to be making a phone call.

The Fythe Trees sign is peeling and nearly too faded to read, but the emergency services number, 696, is clean and shiny. Past it, I see a tan brick house, ugly and unloved. The garden is tiny: a messy, greenish strip that rings the house, reminiscent of so many other farm gardens where farmers are reluctant to give up profitable soil for unprofitable pursuits like quality of life. Nearby is a large open shed, and between the shed and the house there are pieces of machinery everywhere — some of them are supposed to be where they are, and others have been left where they stopped.

An old runabout is puttering between house

and sheds, avoiding machinery as it goes. This bloke has no more idea about bundles of cash than I do. Maybe someone offered him a big sum to be involved, and maybe it's just a coincidence. It prompts me to drive in to introduce myself. When I stop alongside a rusting front-end loader, a small man with sticking-out teeth walks over, wiping his hands on a dirty rag. He is bright and bouncing as he says, 'G'day. How can I help you?'

I put my hand out and say, 'Dave Martin.'

He smiles up his teeth. 'Dave fucking Martin. I've been wanting to meet you for some time.' He pumps my hand with the vigour of a man used to compensating for size with effort.

'How the bloody hell have we never met?' He stares at my face so intently, I feel like he's expecting me to start looking like something he understands.

'I really don't know.'

'So you haven't got any of my mail?'

'No. Never have.'

'That is strange. We get the wrong mail all the time — perfectly addressed letters to someone five properties down the road, dropped off here. It's like half the time they don't bother to sort it. And yet two names and addresses very similar, and only one crossover. Bloody hell, eh?'

I shake my head in good-natured agreement.

'How's the season over your way?' he asks.

'Really good. We've been lucky with the rain.'

'Get your oats in?'

'No.' I'm not giving him more than that.

'I've got a pump for you somewhere.'

He bounds off, springs in his feet, electricity in his arms, and returns with a box.

'There you go. Do you want a cup of tea or something?'

'No, thanks. I'd better get going. Nice to meet you finally.'

We shake hands as I cradle the box. He knows it's a pump, so he must have had a look inside.

'How's the play going?' For some reason, I feel this could be the one question that might catch him out. The play, and the need for printed money, don't fit into these surroundings.

Dave rolls his eyes. 'The wife's play? Real good, thanks. Some of the players even know some of their lines.' He laughs like this is a favourite joke, regularly told.

I leave, thinking that nothing could be less strange or sinister. Dave is as true-blue as you get. It's me who's off-centre.

I pass through town without stopping. Since it is mail day, I'm pretty sure I can catch the mailman on his run, but I haven't seen him anywhere. My timing is right, but he is not about. It must be one of those days that he hasn't bothered to come — hangover or something. I reach my own street, Wilson Road, without seeing him, and give up on the idea. At Elaine's turn-off I remember the way I left her, and think of how the encounter with Dave showed me how paranoid I have become. I take the turn, feeling I have some explaining to do, and suffering the guilt of knowing I left her alone when there were crockery bandits about. I tootle in her driveway, rehearsing lines of apology and explanation, and a suggestion: 'Maybe we could get together again some time?'

Her place is peaceful and green. There are no machines running and no action anywhere. I'm beginning to feel regret at my suspicions and for maybe ruining what might have been a friendship. If I need anything in the world, it is probably friendship. In the distance, I can see cotton pickers harvesting cotton, and the trucks and tractors in attendance. But here the butcher birds are whistling a popular tune, and the light sun suggests good times are possible.

As I near the place where I have parked several times in several days, I see something white through the garden gateway on the lush lawn. It is the bright white of cockatoos feeding in a group. If there are cockatoos in the garden, Elaine probably isn't around, and I am wasting my time. But my time isn't valuable, so I proceed.

At the gate, I clap my hands, but no cockatoos rise from the lawn. I step into the garden, and my eyes try to adjust to a picture of a white shirt, ripped and marked, next to jeans both worn by a body lying on the grass. Bloodied hair is matted at the other end of the body. Elaine is face down, not moving. She has died because of my craziness, because I couldn't do what any normal man would have done.

I stumble to her, kneel, and understand that I am wrong: she is breathing, and may be conscious. Her mouth is swollen, and a hank of hair has been ripped out of the back of her head. One hand is bent at an angle at her side. I kneel, and she moans something like, 'No, no,' and I know she thinks I am one of her attackers returning. I shoosh her, and she turns her head a little, and I see her eyes, unfocused but flashing with hope. 'Dave.'

I call the ambulance and wait, talking as soothingly as I can, saying that the ambulance is coming and that everything will be all right, without having any idea what this means.

When the ambos arrive and take Elaine away, I somehow have the presence of mind to collect my bag from the corner of the room. I put it in my ute, and just then the police arrive: the same police, at the same house, with the same result. The police interview me — their suspicion has graduated to a sort of official boredom. And then Murray says, 'Can we have a look at your bag?'

I give the calmest version of 'uncomprehending' that I can, under the circumstances.

She sighs. 'We saw you put a bag in your ute.'

We walk to the ute, and Murray's offsider roughly rips open my bag. The rifle amongst my clothes looks a hell of a lot like a murder weapon.

Murray's offsider pulls on some plastic gloves, and takes the rifle out of the bag.

'You've got a licence?'

I would be an unusual farmer if I didn't. 'Yes.'

'I think we'll hang onto this gun and your bag for a while.'

I consider asking about my pyjamas, but instead I just shrug and nod.

8

A week of insanity, and it's over. Nobody asks me about the cash I've put in the bank; the police don't bother me about race fixing or Elaine's assaults; no one robs me or tries to bash me; no boxes arrive, with or without money. After I find her, Elaine goes to hospital for several days, and then remains for a few more under observation. The wrist is broken, but her teeth are intact. The doctor says she was hit hard several times in the face and thrown around a fair bit. They have no leads. I tell them about Buzzcut and his mates, but it doesn't help.

I visit her every day. We don't talk much. Her body begins to recover, but her confidence has leaked like the colour from her face. She tells me that the men had come back for the crockery she didn't have, and then bashed her in their anger. She doesn't know why they were so upset, and why anyone would care about plates and cups so much.

Then she goes to stay with her mother.

It's as if a violent storm has hit, done its damage, and then cleared to a blue sky. The boxes stay in the laundry, and I stay away from them. In the mornings, I drive around the farm, not doing anything, just driving. It rains again, and the grass stays green, even though it usually grows less and less as the weather gets colder. The phone rings a lot, but I hardly ever answer it. Occasionally I drink myself into a stupor, and stay that way for days. Then I spend several days feeling sick and remorseful, recovering. In this way, several weeks pass.

9

I drive into the windmill paddock, and there is a ewe, cast on her side, on the edge of a gully. As I approach I see her, a large woolly sack slumped on the ground. She is dying, and in her last moments is being taunted by five foxes who have already eaten the soft parts of her and the lamb she has just struggled to give birth to. I've never seen so many fully grown foxes on one sheep. I am unmoved. I should really be upset. Before, I would have been. I call the dogs back, and they reluctantly obey.

I have always hated foxes, even though I know how stupid it is to hate an animal for the way it behaves. They are the worst of nature: ruthless, opportunistic, adaptable, and, of course, cunning. Autumn is the time when they are the biggest pest, because the vixens have cubs to feed, and I reckon it takes a lot of grasshoppers, crickets, native berries, and roots to keep milk up to a couple of fox cubs. A good feed of meat will fix that. This group of scavengers has thick, bushy red coats with no signs of the mange they often suffer from around here that will as good as kill them. They look like they've come out of a stud farm and will go on to successfully reproduce many more killers of the helpless and the native. I train my rifle on one of them, and take her out with a single shot. The others are gone, quickly disappearing into long grass that was never meant to protect them so well. I shoot the ewe, and drag her and the dead fox, and the remains of the lamb, down into the gully. It is as productive as I have been for months.

James didn't like shooting much. It was the one thing that set him apart from his peers. All his mates loved shooting and spotlighting, and dreamed of getting their own rifle. When they got their first, they dreamed of getting a second and a third. James didn't mind the rifle side of it so much, but he was uncomfortable with killing things. I'm not sure why. It's the sort of sensitivity that farmers don't acquire until they're older. I kind of respected it about him. He never felt the need to do something just because everyone else did, which is pretty far-out for a teenager.

Sometimes I drink beer at breakfast, even though it makes me crazy and useless. I don't do it every day, but when I do it makes everything just a little less raw. Another time, I would be cutting and splitting wood for the fire, but now I can't be bothered. One cold night I pick up bundles of sticks and leaves from the garden, and stuff them in my slow-combustion fire. It burns hot and brightly, making the room kinder and homier for a while. Soon it is ash, and the heat is gone, and I go back to lugging around a doona. I vow I will cut a heap of wood the next day, but I never do.

I think about my father, and how he always had tonnes of firewood cut, usually by one of the men. He was organised, and had a plan for every challenge that turned up. Our haysheds were always full in preparation for the next dry time. The cool room overflowed with meat, drink, and provisions. Machinery was always serviced and maintained; weeds were sprayed and slashed, and fences were in perfect order. If an employee was sick or had to leave us, Dad had someone ready to start the minute there was a vacancy. The workshop was stocked with spare tyres, pipe fittings, small motors, pumps, belts, grease, timber, and so on.

Even then, five years of drought took its toll. We didn't grow any crops, and you couldn't store that much feed for animals. We had to sell too many animals at low prices, and later, when it rained and we needed to buy back in, the prices were through the roof. Good old demand and supply. Suddenly we were no longer wealthy farmers. We were farmers with a debt, producing way below our capacity. We never really recovered, because even when things were good we couldn't capitalise on them, and when things were bad we suffered more. My father always said that the golden rule in farming is: *When things are good you have to make a lot of money to cover you for the many times when things will be bad.* We couldn't follow his rule. But his nature didn't allow for anyone's sympathy, and he would not give anyone the pleasure of knowing that Five Trees wasn't the well-managed place it had always been.

It didn't break him or us, but it certainly made a dent. He still went to the races in the city, and spent money like he had plenty of it. Looking back, I suppose it was pride, even though I couldn't see it then — if he hadn't appeared at the races, everyone would have known we were doing it tough.

But I never cared. My father's need to be some sort of bunyip landed gentry burned the concern out of me. Forget the status symbols and the big notes, I just loved the land and the farm. I was always more comfortable with people who knew the trees and the birds and the grasses, rather than those who wanted to carry on about the size of their tractors and the extent of their holdings.

It always seemed to me to be the most precious piece of dumb luck that I was an owner of this country. When I had my own family and a farm, nobody could do better than me.

There was only ever one thing that could have stopped me feeling like that, and that was the loss of James. The loss of James stopped everything.

One night, after downing a few beers during the day, I decide to make a visit to the pub. I don't know if anyone is going to be there, but my store is getting low, and the alcohol I have already drunk is making me feel that it is essential to replenish my supply. I am confident that if I can't cope I can come straight home. My local is the sort of village pub that can have hundreds of people packing it out, or just the girl behind the bar and the publican wandering around the empty tables.

Tonight there is only a handful of people here: some in the front bar, some at the tables outside, and a few playing pool. I buy what I need for home, summon up the courage to order a beer off the tap, and take a seat at a small table in the bar. I am comforted by the casual noise of other human beings. The beer is good, and I figure my nerve will hold for a couple. And then the door from the pool room opens, and someone yells, 'Davo! Bloody hell, what are you doing here?' and Ralph comes through the doorway, sheets to the wind, rubbing his hands together.

'Just thought I'd come for a beer.'

'Well, that is bloody good news. Haven't seen you for ages. Can I buy you one?'

Ralph is a friend from way back — primary school and all the years after. He was a truck driver and now owns a fleet of trucks, but he remains a constant against endless change. I tell him I don't need another beer, and he flops down heavily at my table.

'Geez, it's good to see you, mate.'

Keith, the publican, brings two beers over and says, 'These are on me. Good to see you out, Davo.'

I thank him, and he gives one nod in a way that makes me wonder why I don't come here more often. Ralph asks what has been going on, and I try to think of something he might like to hear, but I can't.

'The usual,' I say, and he accepts it, and proceeds to tell me about his business and how hard it is getting good people, and you wouldn't believe it, but this is his first night off in months. And that's the way it goes: he talks, and we drink. The flow of alcohol is steady, and we gradually succumb. Ralph finally stops talking, and we gaze at the TV so we look like we're doing something. An ad comes on for a lottery, a massive US lottery that is available internationally.

'Fifty million bucks. Fuck me. Imagine winning that,' Ralph says.

'What would you do with it?'

'I'd sell the trucks and travel the world. Buy a place on the coast, maybe get a new missus — ha, kidding — and still have enough dough to live like a king. What about you?'

I look down into my beer, blank. I can't even dream up a fanciful answer. I already have bags of money I'm not using. I guess he's feeling sorry for asking me. I'm wrong.

'You wouldn't do anything with it, would you, mate? You'd stick it in a shed or a cave somewhere, and leave it there. You poor bastard.'

He sits back and slouches in his chair, leaning against the windowsill. 'If I won the lottery and wanted to put it somewhere safe, I'd give it all to you. Safe as houses.'

I don't know what he's getting at, and I figure neither does he.

He leans forward on the small table, and puts his face close to mine.

'You can't keep on like this, mate. It's not good enough. You've got to let people help you. Your friends. You've got to keep fighting, or you'll disappear up your own bumhole.'

I take that as a sign that it's time to leave. When people on the drink start giving you advice, you know it's best to get out. I stand, a little wobbly, and thank everyone for the beers and the evening. Ralph says, 'Don't go, mate. We've only just got started. Stay the night at my place, and we can have a few more, talk this out.' I am out of there before he can mount a proper argument.

The drive home is interesting. I am talking to myself, weaving around on the road, thinking at the last minute that there might be kangaroos ready to jump out of the grass, or cars behind me trying to get past. Somehow the roos and the rest of the world stay away from me. I make it home, and pass out on the couch amongst the empty beer cans, dirty cups, and chip packets.

It is morning. One eyelid flicks open independently, and my revealed eye unwillingly pans the room and its detritus of laziness and self-indulgence. Some of the furniture is still upended from the visit of Buzzcut and his mates. Everything hurts, and my stomach is queasy. I contemplate a beer. The hair of the dog has become my best friend, despite my previous boasts of being on the wagon. I stand, but instead of heading to the fridge, I remain still and look around the room again. It is a disgrace. I am a disgrace.

I begin picking up, cleaning up, wiping down, and righting the furniture. I find the vacuum cleaner, and even though I feel wretched, I vacuum everything in sight: the floor, the furniture, the TV, the paintings, Sarah's ornaments, and the bookcase. I even give my own face a run-over.

Ralph's words about giving me money are crashing around in my sensitive head. I am a man considered so useless that you could give me a truckload of cash, and I wouldn't have the wit or wisdom to do anything with it. James would not have expected me to be a disaster. He might have wanted me to be sad, but not this hopeless. A gormless, gutless pisshead. And now self-pitying.

But I feel a sudden flush of relief, because someone did give me money, and I went to the races with it. I did something with it. They are all wrong about me. I am a doer. See me vacuum the house?

But where is the money now? Pretty much where Ralph predicted it would be. And whose money is it? Elaine's? Ben's? Buzzcut's? Mine?

And I remember something Tito said to me after one of our nights at the pub — the words Elaine reminded me of. We were in the car coming home, and the beer was making us talk more frankly than we normally would, which is kind of the point of beer. He looked at me and said, 'You're a safe guy, aren't you?' I thought 'safe guy' was some sort of city expression for 'good bloke', so I ignored it and talked about something else. Now I'm wondering if there was a different meaning.

When the floors and the furniture are cleaned, and the vacuum cleaner is more than full, I feel a sense of achievement. The sink and the dishes are still a couple of hours' worth of work waiting for me, but one step at a time is enough. Outside, the autumn sun is making itself popular, and I think that perhaps I should try harder. I take a beer from the fridge, open it, and glug a few mouthfuls down. It tastes and feels terrific.

The phone is ringing. I'm guessing it's Marko, because he hasn't rung for a while, and he has tried to make it a habit. I know he will keep calling until I answer. Marko rang me every second day after James's accident, and visited me on the in-between days, whether I wanted him there or not. He kept it up for a long time, but I guess I broke him. He thought I would get over it after a while, or begin to recover at least. He was probably hurt by the fact that I haven't, and that I don't want to hang with him or come to parties or the pub, or even just chat. What is a friend supposed to do?

I pick up the phone, and he is telling me there's a fire brigade meeting on this afternoon, and I should go. The suggestion is so off-track with what I have just experienced and the stuff going through my head that I nearly hang up. I say, 'I'll think about it,' and he says if I don't come he'll come over to stay with me again. I put the phone down, thinking I do not want to go to a fire brigade meeting. Fire brigade meetings are really just an excuse for a yarn and a few beers, even though some official stuff does get done. The meetings are a bit of a joke, because the people who go have generations of experience dealing with bushfires and grassfires. If there's anything farmers do well in a group, it is fight fires. But at some stage the government decided they needed to be involved in rural fire-fighting. Farmers couldn't be trusted to put fires out on their own. There needed to be regulations, rules, and training. So now there are inductions, procedures, courses, bright uniforms, bureaucratic levels of importance, and red fire engines. The fire brigade meetings I've been to (under Fire Captain Marko) have been opportunities for everyone to show how little attention they have been paying to government rules, and the delight they have in that fact.

But if I go, at least a meeting will stop me sitting here, thinking about everything. And it will get Marko off my back. This is no small thing. He is used to me saying, 'No.' I take a beer out of the fridge, examine it, and then put it back. Perhaps a meeting would be a good thing.

When I arrive at the fire shed there are six utes there already, which suggests a good roll-up. I have not been to a public meeting of any sort since the accident. Come to think of it, I haven't been anywhere except on my recent excursions to the races, Elaine's, Dave Martin's, and the pub. I can see Marko, Ian, Jake Cole, Freddie Doolan, Cliff Peters, Bob Handy, and a couple of others. I know the parents, children, wives, brothers, and sisters of every one of them. Freddie has just become a grandfather, so I know four generations of his family. These are my people, but I am not of them. They greet me warmly. They talk about the weather, and sport, and crops, so no one has to go near a topic that might accidentally bring up a comment about James, or sons, or young men, or death. Despite this, Cliff grabs my shoulder, gives it a bit of a shake, and says how good it is to see me. He is a large, solidly built man with a breaking smile and round, shiny cheeks. I reckon soon a doctor or a wife will put him on a diet, and he will become serious and suddenly older like the reduced often are. For now, he sees life as a great joke, one that he can easily laugh his way through. I would be jealous of this if I could imagine myself in someone else's shoes.

Marko starts the meeting. There are apologies, minutes from the last meeting, and correspondence from the state fire brigade hierarchy. We stand in a circle and listen. There is no risk of Ben coming, because he would never bother with an organisation that it is not compulsory to attend and that offers no immediate personal gain. Everybody is serious-faced and respectful, until Jake asks if anyone has learned to work the gadgets on the truck yet. Everyone laughs, except me and Fire Captain Marko. Marko gets up into the cab of the small truck, starts it up, and proceeds to give a lecture on all the features of the truck. By the time he has small and large sprays going, the lights on, and the heat shield down, he can't see what he's doing, and everyone is getting wet and killing themselves laughing. I smile, and get into it the best I can.

When the performance is over, Marko thanks everyone, sets a date for the next get-together, asks if anyone needs to do a training course, and then closes the meeting and hands out the beers. I decline, pat my stomach, and say I'm trying to stay off the beers at the moment. Marko suggests this must be a brand-new idea, and I say it is, and then make to leave. Marko tries to get me to stay, but I am walking before he can get to me. I know the rest of them are shaking their heads, but I just can't get into this sort of stuff anymore. I don't even feel part of it. They live in a different world from me, and I can't find my way back to it. But as I climb into my ute, Cliff runs across the road to get to me. I start the vehicle, so he knows I'm serious. He stands at the door, spreads his hands in resignation, and says, 'I know you've got to go. I just wanted to say, if you ever needed to . . .'

I nod and say thanks, but he's not done yet.

'I know I can't imagine what you've been through, but they say, these days, it helps to talk — you've got to talk. They might be right.'

I thank him again, say goodbye, and leave him by the road, some of the laughter gone from his life.

* * *

Once home, I wander down to the door of James's room — a door that I usually stay away from. I know Sarah has made sure the room is exactly as James left it: his clothes in a small pile on the floor, crowded by footballs and tennis balls, and a couple of computer-controlled toys, in pieces to be repurposed, under his desk. I don't need to look in to know that the desk has a laptop, a few upright books, and some paper with notes and doodles on it. There is a large, white, closed wardrobe that holds the rest of his clothes, shoes, and sports stuff. The walls are a pale blue, marked where James removed or replaced a poster, taking pieces of paint with it.

126

The posters that remain are of motorbikes in the air guided by riders made anonymous by helmets and colourful, branded leathers.

I push the door open, and I remember it is not these things that keep me away. It is the smell: an awesome smell, a faint breath of my son, who went to ride his motorbike and never came back to this room. He was sixteen years old, and never survived the jump over the contour bank that landed him on his head — a head unprotected by a helmet, not enforced by his witless father. Sarah will never forgive me, and I can never forgive myself. This is an awful place, so beautiful that I can't bear to be here.

But now his room reminds me that I used to argue that he had to be allowed to live, to experience risk, and the thrill of it all. He loved me for that. That's got to be worth something. I tried hard to allow him to push his boundaries. I wanted him to know that a bit of pain or a broken limb weren't the end of the world. But as my mother would have said, 'It's all fine until it goes wrong.' And it went so wrong.

I recollect now, without crying, his excitement when we brought that bike home. He had had a bike too small and weak for him for too long. It embarrassed him, but Sarah was convinced he would hurt himself on anything bigger. She allowed the new, bigger bike, but bemoaned its existence at every opportunity, and insisted on that helmet at all times. So it was only when she was away, in town or visiting friends, unable to police her rules, that he was permitted the freedom of riding without a helmet. I told him not to be stupid about it, and that if he was trying out new stunts he had to come back and put the helmet on. Every time he agreed, and every time he laughed it off.

That day, when Sarah got home from town, James hadn't returned from his ride, so we both went to look for him. She had seen the helmet hanging in the garage, and was frantic. I was talking her down, telling both of us that he was fine, just a little late. How many times afterwards did she scream my words of reassurance back at me: 'He's fine. He's just a little late,' condensing the lethal stupidity and carelessness of my character into two short sentences.

We found him in the paddock, in the fading light, next to his upended bike, his head speared into the dirt, his eyes open. It was the worst thing you could ever dream up. You could pull my arm off with a tractor, and I would get over it. I will never get over this. We were everywhere on him, trying to resuscitate him, frantically pumping CPR, but he was already cold. Cold in your son's skin: that is hell right there. I would kill myself rather than feel that again. Eighteen months, and the thought can have me back in those full-body sobs.

You never forget the eyes or the bike or the moment, no matter how much you wish to, and then you hate yourself for dishonouring your child's death by the wishing.

But now, after all this time, and all this pain, I see him again, embarrassed by me, by the fact that I have given up. He was a spirited child, if nothing else. I hear him tossing a ball in the air, catching it, and asking 'Why?' 'Why are you asleep on the couch, Dad? Why is the place a mess? Why don't you do anything? Why is Mum gone?' In my head I make the first steps towards resolving to do better.

Then I open another beer. I know I'm not capable of getting back to farm work. I can't see the point. Farm work needs vision and goals for the future: meaningless abstracts, as far as I am concerned. So what if the fences fall down, or the oats and the wheat don't get planted? I'll just run fewer animals. I'll run no animals. If the troughs and the tanks leak, there's still water in the creek — for now anyway. Time has stood still for me for eighteen months. I have existed in a blurry dream world, wishing to go back and unable to go forward. The only thing that has made the clock move ahead is the boxes, and that is seriously weird.

I push the door to the laundry to where the boxes are. They sit under their sheet like any other piece of discarded furniture, past their time of usefulness. I quickly check that the money is there, as well as the ash, that I'm not imagining their existence, and then shut the door, pulling it tight. I leave my beer behind, walk out into the garden, and try to think. If the boxes are the only thing that gets me out of the house and away from the beer, then I need to think about boxes.

I walk to James's area, make a small promise about doing better, and keep going. I stroll out of the garden and down the road towards the shed. The day is clear, blue, and mild. A bearded dragon sits on a fencepost in the sun, statue-still.

The cooler weather should have slowed him to a near-sleep state, somewhere unseen, but he's out grabbing a last chance at warmth. I feel like I should admire him for his pluck and resilience — things James would be impressed by. But I'm not recovering that quickly.

It is mail day, and I realise I am walking towards the mailbox. It is, after all, where the boxes come from.

My mother would sometimes walk to the mailbox to get the mail for exercise and to 'keep in shape'. When she was sick she did it every mail day. Sarah and I knew something was wrong before Dad did. She would ask for my help with simple things like writing an email to one of her charity groups. The explanation was usually that she 'wasn't very good with computers', and they 'never did what they were told'. It was a believable excuse. She wasn't very good with computers, and she certainly wasn't patient with them. But I realised after a while that she was having trouble putting words together, and she had never had trouble with that. She was always confident in her words, and then she wasn't. She was only in her fifties, and I was in my twenties, and I couldn't work out what was going on. I remember her laughing at herself when she got something wrong or forgot an incident that had only recently happened. Then she would often blame a 'virus thing' she'd had that was 'clogging up her brain', and I suppose I fell for these justifications, even though I knew I had seen moments of stress and fear on her face that were quickly concealed.

I pick up a rusty bolt I notice in the gravel on the side of the road and stick it in my pocket, and then start to talk to her, telling her everything that has happened, that I have felt, that I have done. And I apologise for not having paid enough attention to her. My father and I. Neither of us paid enough attention. My mother would not have wanted attention, and it probably wouldn't have made a difference, but we still should have done it.

I follow the road as it snakes through the trees and straightens in sight of the ramp and the mailbox. I see the mailman's vehicle nearing, and I break into a run. If I'm not quick, I'll miss him.

The vehicle veers in close to the mailbox. He leans out the window and puts the mail in the box, then pulls forward. I think I'm too late, and I sprint a little harder. But he is not leaving; he is getting out to retrieve a newspaper from the back of his ute. He pushes it into my mailbox, and looks up to see me panting to a stop. His expression is suspicious, as if my exertion can only mean trouble.

I breathe hard, and say, 'Hey, Grant, is it? Dave.' He is young, maybe twenty-five — tall, pale, and slim with a light-brown goatee kind of arrangement on his chin. He is in tracksuit bottoms and a T-shirt that promotes a sports team.

'Yeah. You got a letter or something you want me to take?' He doesn't wait for my response. 'You're getting a lot of mail these days.' His forearms are the dirty green of cheap tattoos.

'That's what I wanted to talk to you about.'

131

'Well, talk, brother. I'm busy. People are pretty demanding on this run. Always whingeing if I'm late or if I miss one day in a blue moon.'

'I would prefer if you didn't tell everyone what I was getting in my mail.'

'I haven't. I don't.'

'Yes you have. You told Elaine Slade, and Ben Ruder, and other people that I'm getting boxes in my mail.'

'Oh, that. That was a while ago. Everyone was asking. I just told them you were getting boxes. No big secret. They could have found out for themselves.'

'Well, I'd ask you not to.'

'Sure.' His face tells me this is another ridiculous imposition from another demanding client. He gets back into his ute. He is a busy man. 'So, if I'm not allowed to share unimportant information, you won't want to know your girlfriend is home?'

'My girlfriend?'

'You think no one knows? You think you can keep secrets out here? Like your cheap-shit gadgets in boxes from China?'

He drives off, mouthing a disbelieving 'Fuck' or maybe 'Fuckwit'.

On face value, you'd have to say he doesn't know about the money. It is good news that Elaine is home. I had wondered if she'd ever return. I stride out towards the house, keen to talk to her, wondering how I might protect her.

On the phone, she is cautious, but I think pleased to hear from me. She tells me she's hired a full-time bodyguard and that he makes her feel safe. Without premeditation, I outsmart myself by asking her to come for dinner. There must be something in the freezer I can use, I think. Perhaps she'd be happy with an omelette. Perhaps not. She agrees to come, and asks if there's anything she can bring. Casual as you like, I say, 'Not a thing.' My mouth seems to do what it wants. I already know I was kidding myself thinking there might be something worthwhile in my freezer. Dinner will mean a trip to town for wine, main-course ingredients, and some cheeses and nibbly stuff.

My first job is to tackle the sink, and the dishes that never made it to the dishwasher and now line the bench. I fill the dishwasher, then wash up the remaining stacks. I change the water in the sink twice, leaving my hands pink and wrinkled. Then comes the trip to town.

As I drive, I ask myself, *Am I trying to impress Elaine, or asking her to absolve me?* Midway through that phone conversation, after I'd stunned myself with the invitation, I knew I was going to be trying (insanely) for something like understated sophistication: no trouble taken, but exquisite results. 'I do this sort of thing all the time.'

This is remarkable, considering I have just cleaned my house for the first time in some weeks, and given that my recent cooking decisions have involved choosing between the microwave and the oven for heating frozen meals — sausage rolls and party pies par excellence. I did cook a bit, back in the good old days, and I'm guessing the internet can walk me through it if I can't remember how.

Waterglen has a couple of pretty good supermarkets. When I can be bothered to shop at all, I buy my groceries at eight in the morning, as soon as they open, because it is a good time to avoid seeing people. I know the drill. I won't meet up with parents of school-age children, because they're too busy organising for school; locals looking to buy a couple of things and have a chat won't arrive until midmorning; people hunting for last-minute meal solutions at the end of the day still have many hours' grace; and farmers in town for parts or fertiliser that have been sent to the supermarket with a list won't wander around, lost in the aisles, until well after lunch.

Today, I do not have that security. I am not safe. As I walk in, I pull my hat down, put my collar up, and keep a sideways eye out. A girl on the checkout (Alyssa?) smiles at me, and I give her the quick grin of a man with no time to spare. I move quickly. At the meat section I consider pork and the aphrodisiac of crackling, but know it would turn out soggy, and then ponder the alternative of crispy roast chicken, maybe with lemon, if that's a thing, but I decide that a couple of good-quality steaks will give me the benefit of *I really haven't gone to much trouble*. I can do potatoes served in their jackets, and a salad. Maybe some veggies in the oven. I can cook the steaks while we talk, and the rest can already be in train.

So far, I have seen no one I know. The supermarket is relatively empty, so I push myself along. I buy a brie because I can't remember what some of the other cheeses taste like, and throw in some crackers, and a quince paste. Then I whizz round to the section with air fresheners, grab one that doesn't look too sickly, and head for the checkout.

The checkout is dangerous, because you are exposed. Anyone can see you, and once you're caught in the line there is no way of making a run for it. I am nervous at the checkout, and I make sure I don't select the one manned by the girl I am supposed to know, even though it might have been quicker to do so. I am through quickly, painlessly, and push my trolley at pace towards the grog shop. But standing at the sliding doors, waiting for me, is a young man. One I cannot avoid: Tom Little. He was a year older than James, but still in his group. He has visited us, stayed, camped, partied, played board games, and stretched out on couches eating snacks and watching movies. A mate.

'Hi, Dave. Mr Martin.' Tom is tall and slim, with broad, angular shoulders and pale, still-adolescent skin that I'm sure annoys him.

'Tommy. How are you?' He is one of the kids who took James's death very hard. There was even a stage when his parents were worried about him; he was so down, they thought he might be at risk. I remember he wanted to come out to our place all the time after we lost James. He didn't want to be near the grave; he just wanted to be around what had existed before. Like all of us. We tried to be supportive, but we had too much of our own stuff to be of much help. Another person I failed.

'I'm okay, thanks. How are you?'

I remember how much I like Tom. He is a quality kid: modest; good-hearted; interested in the world. I don't need any more reasons to like him. But there is another significant one: he was a friend of James's and the fact that he's the best of what young men can be, not the worst, reflects well on my son and my memory of my son. My reasons for liking him are nothing to be proud of.

'Pretty good, all in all. Did you get yourself a job?'

'Yep. At the paper. *Waterglen Times*.' I remember that Tom wanted to be a reporter, even though the job had become quaint and kind of old-fashioned. His parents don't have much money, so I guess he's decided to hold off on university until he can get some cash together himself.

'Well, good on you.' He looks slightly embarrassed, which might be from my encouragement, or the fact that he is working at a newspaper which is only just that. 'Been there long?'

'Few months.'

'Excellent — a working man.' I'm trying to choose between hugging and walking away without saying another word. Neither option would be fair to him. 'How's it going?'

'I think I'm getting the hang of it. Made one mistake, though.'

One big mistake by the local newspaper comes to mind, though it is no orphan. 'Elaine Slade?' I say it wincing, not meaning to make him relive it, but unable to go in any other direction.

'Yes. I got the names mixed up, and I was the only one in the office. Guess I would have been fired anywhere else.' He looks embarrassed, but I can tell he's almost past worrying about it. He must have had to explain himself many times.

'Shit happens, eh?'

He gives me a half-chuckle, and agrees. I ask him if his parents are all right, and then leave him with a weak joke about going to the grog shop, the most important grocery shop. I look back, and see him turn and walk out into the car park alone and unsure, and I feel a good old stab of self-hatred. I direct my trolley towards the security of alcohol.

There are some stands to hide behind in the liquor section, but I also know it is easy to be cornered there, with only one checkout, one way out. Ambush territory. I'm selecting a shiraz, and I hear a voice I know. It is a man's voice, and not one I want to hear: Ben Ruder. He is asking the young, dopey guy behind the counter why they've put the price up on a particular whisky. The young guy doesn't have any answers, and Ben demands he go and get a manager to explain. The young man disappears, and Ben strolls away from the counter, obviously waiting for a result. I move further down the display of reds to the merlots, which I consider unsuitable, and keep my back to Ben, showing I'm far too engrossed in my potential purchase to engage in any other sort of interaction. It doesn't stop him. He takes a few loud steps in my direction and says, 'Martin, I'd stay away from that Slade woman if I were you. Lot of bad rumours going around about her.' He sniggers. 'She'd be too much for a wuss like you to handle.'

It's dirty and nasty, and I ignore him. The young attendant returns with his explanation. I stay perusing the reds until I hear Ben complaining again about the price, and maintaining he'll take his business elsewhere. I pick two shirazes, grab a sav blanc in case Elaine's not a red drinker, and add a case of beer to my trolley. And then I move to the section with expensive reds, choose one at the top end of the price range, turn, yell 'Ben!' and then toss the pricey bottle at him. He swivels to see the missile arcing through the air at him. His instinct won't allow him to drop something that might be very valuable. His face reddens and his eyes widen, and his unthinking response is to juggle the bottle from side to side, eventually grasping it by the neck and stopping it crashing to the floor. He expels a breath, looks at me fiercely, puts the bottle on the counter, and leaves.

The young guy lets out a stifled laugh. I purse my lips, shake my head, and say, 'Dickhead.'

He swallows a grin as he keys in my purchases. 'Does it every week. Miserable bastard. Complains about price. No matter what he buys, he complains about the cost. I could call my supervisor in, over the mic, but he won't come. So I just pretend to go and see him.'

I push my trolley to the ute, and almost ask aloud: 'Are there really rumours about Elaine? What sort?' A large woman in a maroon tracksuit alongside a maroon sedan watches me mumble my way past. Tonight I am going to give Elaine a few drinks and a nice meal, and ask her everything.

At the approach to the roundabout on the way out of town, I stop behind a sixteen-wheeler flatbed truck with a bogie drive. The truck driver is being overly cautious, but you can't complain about that. Then I feel something nudge me from behind. I'm not even sure if I really feel it, but when I turn around, I see Ben in his old ute, grinning, sticking a finger up at me. He uses all the steel in his old machine to push into me, and I begin to skid towards the back of the truck. I jam the footbrake on, and then the handbrake, and I almost stop. I don't give Ben the pleasure of seeing me scream at him. I can smell rubber and asphalt. Then my ute lurches forward until the tyres catch and hold for a moment before letting go. I slide, and the back of the truck rises before me like a cliff face. I'd jam the ute into reverse, but shifting through neutral might make things worse. I don't have any alternative except to jump out, but that feels like it would be a sort of cowardice. My ute moves again and draws level with the tray of the truck. If Ben pushes hard enough I will slide in under the tray, and the front of my vehicle will crumple, and maybe I will, too. Ben is still pushing, and I can hear how hard his machine is working. And then, as if there was never anything to worry about, the truck takes off and leaves me, the slow guy in the fast lane, behind. Ben retreats and then swings out past me, blowing his horn as he goes.

10

As I turn at my mailbox, I see the lid partly open, suggesting that someone has left me something. I stop, open it, and see two more boxes, the same as the last two. I slam the lid shut, and sit back in the ute with my hands on my head. More boxes. More fucking boxes. Does this mean more dead people? More money? Did Grant put them in on his way back, or has someone else dropped them off? I agree with myself that I will not think about this. I put them in the back, and drive home. I leave the boxes in the laundry, and then set about organising myself for Elaine's arrival.

When she takes a seat at my kitchen island, she looks fully repaired. But in response to a question about how she feels, she claims the wrist is still sore, and displays a support that irritates her. To me, she is back to her beautiful self, almost haughty. She sips at her wine (white), and asks me how I've been.

'Messy,' I tell her, and begin to apologise for walking out and not being around to protect her.

She dismisses my apology, and claims to know how hard the last year must have been. I lean down, and open the oven to check the vegetables in the oven. They smell like they are going to be fabulous.

'Thanks for finding me.' It is a lonely thing to say. She makes it sound like there is no one else in her life who would have found her.

'I thought you were dead.'

'So did I.' Then she corrects herself: 'I thought I was going to be . . . '

I set the salad things out as a deflection. 'Shit, I forgot to ask, is steak okay? I can whip up something else . . . '

'No, steak will be great.'

I take them out of the fridge and put them on the bench. They are moist and pink, but not too pale. I am rocking it.

My confidence gets out of control, and I decide to share: 'Someone sent me some money. A lot of money. I don't know who.' I don't look at her until I've said the last words. Her face is serene and, if anything, a little pleased for me. I had hoped I would get a sign of something else: guilt, acknowledgement, even panic. But there is none of it. Not that I think she is responsible or involved. It's just that I can't help feeling she's had something like this happen either to her or to someone she knows, and I have no idea why.

'Cash?'

'Yes. Folding stuff.'

'You're a lucky boy then, aren't you?' I get 'playful' instead of 'panic'. There's my intuitive skill on full display.

'I'm not sure what to do with it. I don't know whether to spend it or send it back to the post office.'

'I would normally say 'Spend it', but I've had too many close calls with tough guys to think that anymore.' The only thing that is odd here is the calmness of her response. She is not alarmed, surprised, or intrigued. It's just a thing that has happened to me. I take the steaks to the barbie, which is just outside the kitchen door. They sizzle nicely when I put them on and return to my waiting guest.

'The 'tough guys' are the ones who were blackmailing Tito?'

She nods sadly. I take the veggies out, and let them sit on the oven top while I go out and turn the steaks. Elaine doesn't offer to help, and I don't need it.

'He didn't live up to his end of the bargain.'

'No.' She is sounding a little drunk already. Maybe she had a couple before she came, because she's taken up drinking after everything that's happened to her. 'Well, actually, he told me he'd finished the six pieces they had demanded. I never saw them, but that's what he told me before he died. And then I get these attacks and threats. I don't know what he did with the pieces, and I don't know how I'm supposed to find them.'

'You could tell the police.'

'So could you.'

'What?'

'About the money.'

'The money?' I forget for a moment that I have told her about the money. 'Oh, yeah. So what are you going to do?'

'I don't know. Keep asking around, and hope something turns up. I'm looking everywhere on the farm, in case he hid them there somewhere. Ben's helping me out.'

'Ben Ruder?'

142

'Uh-huh.'

'Really?'

She smiles at my annoyance. 'You don't like him?'

'Not really, and I wouldn't say I was the only one.'

'He's okay. He's Tito's uncle.' She is still talking, saying, 'He found the farm for us. Helped us out.' But all I am hearing is 'Tito's uncle'.

This is really bad, and I'm not even sure why. I know I'm looking like a jealous adolescent, so I ask, 'Tito's pottery must have been really valuable?' I put the rest of the salad together, and add a few sliced grapes and a little balsamic dressing.

'Yeah. Flavour of the month, year, or whatever. There is still a lot of prestige in saying you have a piece by Tito Slade.' She reaches a hand out towards me, and touches my forearm. I stay rigid to stop the jump. I'm sure it is only a friendly touch, a way of saying thanks for dinner and the other stuff. I head for the steaks, showing I'm too preoccupied with my responsibilities to respond to the contact.

Then we eat quietly, and she commends me on my skills. I seem to be filling her glass a lot with the red she has switched to, but I am keeping my own glass topped up, too. She tells me about growing up in the city, privileged and insulated from the kind of hardship that seems integral to the country. I tell her about my childhood, which I remember as fun on horses and bikes, and in dams and creeks. The fun-on-bikes reference makes my spine arch protectively. I tell her about helping my father, and camping with my friends. I don't remember it as hardship.

With no lead-in, she says, 'Did you ever find yourself in something you didn't like, but you were so far in you couldn't find a way out of it?'

It's an odd question, and I stop and try to give her a thoughtful answer, but there isn't one. Except maybe the grief at the death of my son. That's something deep enough to suffocate you, and I'm not sure I've found the way out yet. But I don't tell her that. I just say, 'No, not really. You?'

'Me neither.'

I ask what she means, and she tells me something vague about a friend in trouble. It sounds sort of false, so I don't ask too many questions.

I make coffee in the plunger that hasn't had a run for over a year, using coffee I can't remember buying. It tastes okay. Elaine doesn't complain. When I get up to remove the cups, she grabs my wrist, pulls me down to her, and puts her mouth on mine. It is pleasant and even arousing, but I'm still not sure I want it. She is undoing my shirt and kissing me, then opening her top and putting her arms around me. Her beauty is scary-powerful, but instead of giving in to the action, I kind of split in two. I take a seat outside myself somewhere in the air, and watch a guy (who is me), and a girl (Elaine) getting it on. They seem pretty well matched, although the girl is much more enthusiastic. You might say mad for it. There is kissing. There are clothes being removed, attended by various forms of grappling and stroking. They don't look like they're going to make it to the bedroom or the bed. And then I witness the man whisper, 'Sarah,' and it is like a hidden director has yelled, 'Cut.' The feverish need disappears, and both part and fall like collapsed tents, and I am back on the couch.

'I'm sorry,' I say, although I don't know if I am. I didn't mean to say it, but I couldn't help it.

'It's okay,' she says, 'I know these things take time.' But she is getting up, putting her clothes back on briskly, as if I had walked in on her getting dressed. 'Thanks so much for dinner.'

The emotion is forced, but I can't think of anything to say to make it better. 'Thanks for coming up. It was really nice.' And then, as if I'd been involved in a different engagement, I say, 'Perhaps we could do it again ... ' *Do what again? Disappoint each other?*

'Sure.'

And she is gone, still putting together her confidence.

I get another beer and slump on the couch, unable to think what I was hoping for. My heart is still beating from her touch, from her body, but my brain is in neutral. Elaine's car leaves, and I turn off the lights in my house, and sit in the dark. I let one small sob squeeze its way out, and then I shut it down, all of it. It was there for me, and I didn't go through with it, so I mustn't have wanted it. End of story.

I think of Sarah, and the stupidity of mentioning her name. She would be embarrassed for me. She would ask me not to mention her, and certainly not think of her, especially when I am with someone else. After James died, Sarah and I hardly even touched each other except for desperate supportive hugs that could have been between any two strangers. And yet, even now, when I think of sex, I think of Sarah. When I think of the female body, I think of Sarah. All this is made even more pathetic by Sarah's new orientation. It's pretty obvious, no matter what I feel about Elaine, that Sarah's dominance in my imagination has to stop. I've got to admit that my suspicions about Elaine have not entirely disappeared, and they are an ingredient in this muddled mix. My head is a pudding. Beer is the only answer I have found for that.

★   ★   ★

In the morning, I wake with the remnants of embarrassment and an idea of asking the post office where the boxes might have come from. I can't find a postage mark on any of them, but I'm not certain that postmarks still exist anyway. I call Cooper at the post office in Waterglen, but he can't recall anything about the boxes. He remembers some that came from China a few weeks back, but has no knowledge of more recent deliveries. I ring the post office in Stony Creek, which is a shop as well as the sorting house for my mail run. Marg, who is some sort of distant cousin, is amused by my question. She says if I'm getting boxes that aren't from cheap-machinery wholesalers in Asia, then she doesn't know a thing about it. And then she laughingly suggests I must be up to something else. Maybe drug smuggling? I laugh along with her, and ask if she saw the boxes arrive on a batch of dates I supply her with, but I have the words 'drug smuggling' tumbling over in my head.

I had not thought about smuggling, partly because I had been blinded by the money. Perhaps Tito was smuggling something, and that's what Buzzcut and his mates are demanding. Maybe they were putting illegal things instead of his pottery in boxes, and sending them somewhere. Or maybe he was putting illegal stuff in the pottery itself. I don't know what this has to do with the boxes of ash. When Marg assures me she knows nothing about the recent boxes, I am left with the possibility that they are coming to me from within the closed loop of the mail run. And then she says something strange: 'Your neighbour, Mrs Slade, she asked the same questions as you a few weeks ago. What is it with you guys and boxes?' I laugh, and pretend there is no significance to her comment, and tell her I'll talk to her later.

In my kitchen, I open my laptop, hope that I've paid my internet account, and do some research on pottery smuggling. It seems that the really expensive pottery is ancient stuff, mostly from China, and it doesn't seem the sort of thing that Buzzcut and his mates could handle. I run through references to antique vases and the big names in modern pottery, but none of it seems to fit with a country operation. And then I hit upon a 2009 article about a cocaine smuggler who made crockery out of, or including, cocaine. I am a bloody genius. A few quick searches, and

I have cracked the crockery case before the police even get close to working it out. Elaine's husband must have been incorporating cocaine in the crockery and then selling it to drug dealers, who broke it down and sold the drug for big bucks. I have accidentally received a box of ill-gotten gains. Where this puts Elaine, I don't know.

I phone Constable Murray, doing my best to keep the triumph out of my voice.

'How can I help you, Mr Martin?' She is expending as little energy on talking as possible.

'I believe I have some information that might be helpful in solving the assault and battery on Elaine Slade.'

'Really?'

'Yes.' I let the line hang dead for a moment. She thinks I'm being a pest or trying to take the focus off myself, but the dramatic pause is in my favour.

'I have reason to believe that a cocaine-smuggling business was being run out of the Slades' farm.' Boom.

'Is that so?' She almost yawns.

'They were turning the cocaine into pottery, and then selling it — exporting it maybe. The box of crockery you guys found on the side of the road was Elaine Slade's. The guys who took it from her were disappointed it was just normal old crockery.'

'I'll inform the detectives handling the case.'

This is not the response I had expected. I am tempted to inform her how ignorant and incompetent she must be, and that she has just

148

passed on the tip-off of a lifetime. 'You sound sceptical?'

'Mr Martin, it is very difficult to get cocaine into Australia. It still gets in, though. There is huge demand. My question would be, if a drug smuggler has managed to get cocaine here at an enormous profit, why would he turn it into something else? I can see why you'd do it to get the cocaine into the country, but doing it when it is already here seems a bit unlikely.'

The logic of her statement is enough to slap me down. I don't have a response, but she has more: 'And, anyway, the detectives had the crockery tested for everything you can think of.'

I end the phone call quickly and politely.

I wander around the garden trying to make my brain go in a useful direction. It refuses to. Instead it notices without emotion that the garden is in transition. The deciduous trees are losing their leaves after their colourful showing on the autumn stage. It is the time for the native trees to take back the limelight. The lemon-scented gums and the pink-flowering ironbarks are in rude, leafy health that I'm sure is intended to embarrass their foreign counterparts. King parrots still race between the trees as currawongs call out their beautiful threat to every other bird in the garden. I hear and see it all, but it doesn't register as anything more than the clatter of a life that I'm only just involved in. It could be traffic noise from a suburban street.

For some reason my mailman is sharing information about my mail. I don't know why he would do that, and I don't trust him. If Mrs

149

Crowther was still my mail lady and Elaine asked her what was in my mail, I'm sure Elaine would have received a curt 'None of your business'. The mailman is involved in what is going on, but I don't know how. The thing is, when he is coming from the post office he has to come past Elaine's place to get to mine. So if he has boxes, she's going to know before me, and if she's giving the boxes to him, she can do it without me knowing.

The only information I have is that the boxes don't seem to have been sent from anywhere — or at least haven't passed through the post office — which may mean they have come from a neighbour close by who hands them directly to the postie. It is mail day, and another outlandish idea takes hold: I'll go and catch the mailman on the road and ask him for any mail he has for me. If he has boxes with him, I'll know the sender has to be someone from closer to town than where I meet up with the mailman. That is, of course, if there are more boxes coming. If he doesn't have any boxes for me, I won't know if he was never going to have them, or if he is yet to pick them up.

I know he leaves Stony Creek at around eleven. If I get going now, I'll catch him not far out of town. If he has boxes today, I'll catch him closer to Stony Creek on the next mail day. I run across the garden to the garage, and feel the pleasure of the urgency and my decisiveness. I drive fast, unjustifiably fast, but I'm on a mission to solve a mystery and make my son proud.

At the funeral, when they took the coffin away, I could hardly stand, even though the too-small box was on its way to our garden. That was when I first really believed in James's death. Until then I had been fighting it with everything I could fight it with. Even when we entered the church for the service, I felt strong and positive because of that iron-clad denial. People must have thought I was strong, the way I smiled warmly and shook hands meaningfully. But the sight of the coffin going into the hearse, with all those weeping friends looking on, was simply too much for even the greatest barriers of delusion. Our only son, James, was dead. And I didn't want to be me.

That makes it sound as if the loss of James is one thing only: a child gone. It is not that. It is so many things. We threw and kicked balls around in the backyard, teasing each other, making up heroic commentaries, whenever I was available. We talked about school and sport and our observations of people, and made stupid jokes that Sarah couldn't stand, or pretended she couldn't stand. I taught him things that my father had taught me, and sometimes he was openly bored with my teaching. I watched him closely — growing, reaching out, connecting with others, and he didn't mind my gaze. I like to think we had given him enough love and confidence that it didn't bother him. And he fucking well liked me. I'm sure he did. We got on. Which was the greatest surprise in my life. That's not what my father's generation hoped for. They wanted respect, hard work, and strength. Open dislike was accepted, as long as integrity or at least toughness prevailed. They could be proud, but friendship was so far down the list of priorities it barely made it onto the page. So the loss is not just one thing. It is so many things that I cannot name them all.

As I get close to Stony Creek, I realise that catching the mailman near the village won't be as helpful as I'd thought. If I really think Elaine or someone to do with her is involved, I should meet the mailman halfway between my place and the village, and work towards home. But if I do this, it means I'm certain no one in the village is sending the boxes — and I'm not sure that's true.

As I drive past crop stubble and fresh green wheat, I try to calculate the best approach to take, but I give up and go with my gut. There is too much odd stuff going on at Elaine's for her not to be the most likely suspect.

When I reach the Burger family's mailbox (a small mailbox made of an oil drum, in contrast to the ones I have talked about), which is about halfway between Stony Creek and my place, I turn and drive my ute into the long grass. It takes about ten minutes for Grant's vehicle to appear, cruising along the road as though he has nowhere he needs to be. I get out and stand at the mailbox so he knows he'll have to hand out two lots of mail, and not just drop the Burgers' and leave. As he gets a bit closer he speeds up, and I guess he feels like he's been caught daydreaming and not focusing on the important job at hand. He keeps the pace up until he's within about twenty metres of the mailbox, when he suddenly slows. I'm relieved, because it looked like he was going to go right past me.

He freewheels the ute in close to the mailbox, winds his window down, lifts the flap on the box, and drops the mail in. I step up close, ready to explain myself, but he accelerates right past me, his middle finger in the air, his tyres as close to my toes as they can be without crushing them. I watch him head off, ridiculing myself for believing that any plan will go as I expect. Should I chase him? Run him off the road, or stop with him at every mailbox between here and home? But I cool down, and I know a better plan is to follow a hunch I've developed.

I drive out onto the road and go back the way Grant came. At the next intersection, I turn left and take the slightly longer way home. Because he has to stop at every mailbox, I can be much quicker than him, but I'm not going to be waiting for him at my mailbox. I'm going to watch him.

The only people I see on the road are old Glen Pye in his Dodge truck moving hay, and a couple of guys on motorbikes on their way through. I approach the Wilson Road turn-off from the opposite direction to Grant. I drive down into an extended hollow in the table drain, and get out. From here, using binoculars that I always keep in my ute, I can see Elaine's mailbox without her seeing me. I wait.

Nobody passes. Nothing happens. I begin to get impatient, and I start to worry that he has decided to give up and go home before he's finished the job. But when he does come down the road, I'm not surprised by his appearance, but by the speed he is doing. He is really motoring. He takes the corner at Wilson Road in a four-wheel drift, and keeps pushing it until he reaches Elaine's mailbox, where he slides to a stop in a spray of dust and gravel.

There is a car already there, waiting. A man in an old hat gets out of the car, walks to the back of Grant's ute, and starts looking through the packages of mail — everyone's mail. Grant does not get out of his machine or even acknowledge what is going on. When the man in the hat is finished, he passes something from his pocket through the window to Grant, then goes back to his car empty-handed, gets in, and drives away, up Wilson Road. When he is gone, Grant gets out of his vehicle, drops mail in Elaine's mailbox, gets back in his ute, and casually makes his way up Wilson Road.

I trip trying to get into the driver's seat too quickly. When I gather myself, I start my vehicle, pull out of the table drain, and flatten it. The ute leaps over the incline on the edge of the road, and I fang it down the gravel, the tyres only just holding. I reach my mailbox, but Grant has come and gone. He must be up the end of the road. I park my ute perpendicular, across the width of the road, blocking anyone who might try to pass. I check the mail: letters, brochures, but no boxes. What can this mean? Have I got it completely wrong again? Grant reappears, coming back from Ben's and Ian's. I stand and wait, expecting he will veer out into the paddock to go round me. He doesn't. He slows, stops just short of the door of my ute, and then puts his head out of his window.

'What the fuck are you doing now, you loony?'

Since he hasn't delivered any boxes, I'm not exactly sure what I'm doing.

'Got any boxes for me?'

'No. Fuck off out of the way. It's probably an offence to get in the road of a postman.'

'Who gave you the boxes that were delivered to me?'

'What? No one. The fucking mail service. Get out of the way, or I'll call the cops. Dickwit.'

I can't think of my next step, so I edge my ute forward enough for him to get around me. He over-revs the motor as he goes past.

I take my mail, and go home. I stand in the garage, as lost as I've ever been, feeling like the one thing that's been keeping me going has evaporated. I almost wish someone would come in and rob and hit me. Anything as a distraction. Even the thought of a beer is no comfort. I slump to the concrete floor. I cannot unravel the boxes mystery — it's like a puzzle that is just too complex, wearing away my desire to solve it.

I want it to end. My living just makes things worse. My death would be the solution — it would be much better for Sarah. She could put a manager on this place, and he might even get some things done. A manager with a family would be good for the local school and the district, and contribute more to the community than me. Everybody would be better off if I just moved on. A simple equation.

In the country, men kill themselves. It's what

we do. No one ever suspects it. Suicidal farmers are far too practical to ever let on that they might be about to do away with themselves. Like me, they see it as the ultimate solution. Their families never do. But I'm not depressed, not clinically, like they are. I'm just crazy, but the solution is the same, and I love the idea of putting a stop to everything forever. Like a line drawn on a page that says, *After this, nothing.*

I do not hear James's voice telling me to get up and dust myself off, because his voice doesn't exist anymore. He does not exist anywhere except in my head. This is the fact that I have been avoiding ever since I saw his blank eyes in his broken body. I have him in my heart. I have his bedroom, and I have his things, but they are just artefacts and remnants, and nothing more. I cannot conjure a lonelier thought, and it brings a bleakness I do not want to live with.

I think about how I should kill myself. Shooting would involve the least amount of organising, but I know it would be easy to stuff up: any loss of conviction for the smallest moment, and the rifle moves, leaving you disfigured and disabled, but alive. You remain in a worse state than you ever were. Pills work, but if someone finds you before the job is done, there is a good chance they will revive you. The best way for me to die would be to have someone do it for me — someone like Buzzcut.

I can leave the money to Sarah in my will, but to do that I have to hang on to it. It will need to be put in a safe place, a place where she can find it. And I know where. This thought at least gets me off the ground. I get the boxes from the house and put them in the ute. I'm not thinking about anything more than boxes, ute, hiding tree. The hiding tree is a massive river gum in the centre of a thick copse of trees in the middle of our farm. The tree is hollowed out at the base, with a large-enough area for an adult to crawl in. My father played here as a child, as I did, and as James did. You have to know where it is to see it, and it is the perfect place to hide from cranky or demanding adults.

I drive, thinking practically about the end of days. My will needs updating. I'll have to find someone who can manage the farm or get it in shape for sale. There needs to be a note for Sarah, and maybe even Elaine.

I park alongside the tree, and begin to carry the boxes in. There are seven of them, and I remember I never checked the contents of the final four. I reluctantly cut the tape, and lift the flaps on all three. No bricks of money. More bags of ash. None have rings, but two have tags. One reads 'SvenGzhel'; the other, 'BryanLomonsov'. I repack them, and take them to their place in the hiding tree. I hate to think what this all means. I have to look up those names to see if their deaths were recorded in the media.

I drive home in the dark, ignoring the beauty of the moon and the Milky Way, not bothering to stick my head out the window to luxuriate in the fresh, clean air. There is the faint sound of a motor in the distance. I walk into my house brain-dead and tired out, but still I pick up a different smell in the kitchen. I don't have time to place it, because, as I open the back door and step through it, I feel a sudden brutal pain, and the day is finished.

11

'My husband was being blackmailed.'

It is Elaine's voice, but all I hear is, 'Something, something was being hobnailed.'

I could be dead. I may have succeeded in killing myself. It is comforting to know that Elaine, or at least Elaine's voice, has come with me. I attempt to open my eyes, but they are already open. I'm pretty sure I'm in a blurry hospital ward; the whites and greys in the simple room look the same, blurry or not. This suggests I'm alive, unless the afterlife is some sort of bargain-basement existence.

The voice says it again, and this time I get it.

'Hi,' I say, as best I can, without moving my lips.

Elaine gets a surprise. She was obviously talking to herself.

'How are you feeling?' she asks, sitting up, or making a movement something like that.

'Crabpp.' My lips are like blubber. 'Did I try to kill myself?' I am not embarrassed about this likelihood. Unlike suicide failures I've read about, I don't seem to be disappointed that I am alive. Despite the pain and the general blur, I am glad to still exist. Who knew?

'No. Someone hit you over the head. I found you. Ian and Mandy helped me.'

Maybe I remember that — being hit — but maybe not. I look around the room. There are other beds and other people. We have a curtain that is pulled part of the way around us. There is a small table sort of thing next to me, and not much else. Hospital. Then I think about the ash and the hiding tree. I remember having returned from the hiding tree, so my attacker probably didn't find the boxes. I fall back asleep.

When I wake again, Elaine is still there, head bowed, her phone taking her attention.

'Hi,' I say again, and she looks up and smiles.

Elaine is examining me closely, so I must look pretty odd. Nothing new there. I feel a bit like I did when we were kissing: out of body. The pain brings me back. I could throw up, but I don't. At least the blurriness is lifting. I can see Elaine's beautiful face lined by concern. Hopefully, the concern is for me. A random question presents itself, and, as is my current habit, I ask it.

'You said Tito had a contract. What was the contract?' This obviously comes out jumbled, because Elaine just says, 'Ah, sorry?'

I say it again, and this time it is her turn to get it on the second round. 'My husband was being blackmailed.'

'I know. You said that.'

'He had a gambling problem. It got out of hand. I paid his debt with my own money, and we moved. I thought we had beaten it, and I think for a while we had. Then I found out Tito had been punting on the side and he'd racked up a debt with the same criminals. They said he could pay it off by making pottery for them.'

My head is suddenly fuzzy again. Underworld crime bosses demanding clay coil pots? I guess she sees my confusion, because she shrugs and says, 'He was just really good at what he did.'

And then there are more people in the room: Marko and Helen, Ian and Mandy, Ralph and his wife, Reedy. All of them seem slightly embarrassed by arriving at the same time in a place where they clearly don't feel comfortable. Are they surprised to see Elaine here? I can't tell. Marko comes in close to the bed, grips my hand tightly, and shakes it. He looks worried and confused. I'm sure he doesn't believe that someone hit me. I point to the back of my head where the pain is centred and I can feel a dressing. He gets the message, and gives me a relieved laugh.

Ian says, 'You look a lot better than when I last saw you.'

I thank him and Mandy, and they shake their heads at me to refuse my thanks.

'We think we scared him off. Don't know what he could have been looking for.' His eyes crinkle a little bit, I guess because he realises he's suggested there's nothing worth stealing in my house.

'I had a big win at the races a while ago.' I nod in Helen's direction, and she gives a little nod of confirmation that at least the attending-the-races bit is true. 'Maybe they saw that.'

'You went to the races? I didn't know you went to the races,' Ralph says. 'You could have taken me.'

I realise that only Ian and Mandy know Elaine. 'Everyone, this is Elaine Slade. Lives down the road from me.' Elaine gets out of her chair, and shakes hands.

'Have you put the money somewhere safe?' Helen is more worried than I've seen her.

I tell her yes, and then Marko says, in a kind of committee-member voice, 'We think you should come and stay with us, just for a while. You don't seem to be looking after yourself, Sarah's worried about you, and now this.' He indicates my bed. 'But if you didn't want to stay with us, you could stay with someone else.'

'There's plenty of room at our place, and it's close by.' Mandy jumps in, maybe to show how worried she is.

'Sarah's been talking to you?'

Helen lets her head make a downward movement.

'She thinks it would be a good idea if you stayed with one of us.' Reedy has pushed forward a little, her frame long and scrawny, as her name suggests. I am suddenly very angry. Sarah doesn't talk to me, but she talks to these people so they can all decide what is good for me. I don't want to live in anyone else's house, or share their table. Their team goodwill is going to take me away from James.

'Actually, I think I'd like you all to leave.'

They are stunned and upset. 'Dave,' Ian says, and Marko follows with, 'Mate.'

'It was just a knock on the head. I'm perfectly capable of looking after myself. I'd appreciate it if you all went.'

They look at each other, wring their hands, and do things with their eyebrows.

'Nurse?' I give it a little urgency. 'Nurse?'

162

Jenny Bolling, the nurse who has been looking after me, comes to the ward, and the group accepts defeat, shaking their heads. I tell her I'm tired, and she looks apologetically at my visitors and suggests they be on their way. Elaine puts a hand on my blanket-covered knee. 'When you want to go home, give me a call.' The hand leaves my knee and gives a little wave, and she leaves, too. I realise I really am tired, and am almost asleep by the time the nurse pulls the curtain all the way around my bed.

★ ★ ★

The hospital lets me stay until the morning. Nobody is allowed to stay in hospital very long anymore. I call Marko and ask him if he can run me home. I don't feel any embarrassment at asking him for a favour when I booted them all out of the hospital last night. He immediately offers to come straight in, even though I can hear he is on some sort of heavy machinery and I suspect is probably in the middle of something important. Then I ring Elaine, and tell her Marko has offered to take me home. I don't know why I do this, except that some sort of instinct tells me I don't need to be any closer to Elaine. She is noncommittal, and says she'll see me soon. I have to acknowledge that it is possible Elaine is the one who knocked me out. That's not fair, I know, but it is a possibility.

I am waiting for Marko on the kerb in front of casualty. His king cab ute swings in too fast for an emergency area. He almost leaps out of his

163

machine, and takes a few large steps to stand next to me as if I were an invalid in need of help. I'm not keen on moving my head rapidly, but otherwise I feel pretty good. Marko shakes my hand, looking like he has enough vitality for both of us. He is a big man with huge hands, a large head, and thick, brown, disorderly hair. He is nervously saying things like, 'How ya going, mate?' and 'You're looking better.'

When we get into his ute, he points a thumb towards the back seat. 'The women cooked you a whole lot of meals. You're not going to starve.'

I don't look back. I know what casseroles and lasagnes look like. There are painkillers to pick up from the pharmacy, and then we are out of town, and I feel myself relax. Marko is only just sitting still in his seat. There are things on his mind.

'I know you get cranky at us, but if someone's hassling you, you've only got to call. I'll have a mob of good men round there in a flash.'

'Thanks. I'll be okay.'

'Geez, you're a hard man to help. Bloody hell, there are people everywhere wanting to do something for you, and you just keep throwing things back in our faces.'

I look out the window, and sulk. The idea of people doing things for me, fussing around, getting in my space, telling me what to do, is a version of hell. So I ignore his frustration. He is driving so fast that the country is ripping past too quickly to study. The McPherson's massive house, built only a hundred metres from the road, whizzes past, as do the Bruces' skinny cows and the Hailstons' poorly picked cotton crop. Marko goes on about me a bit more, and I think how he and the rest of them will never understand until it happens to them, and then they won't want all the help being offered. I'm not being fair. I know that. They're just searching for ways to do the best for me, and they can't find one. It is not my problem.

Marko is the one sulking now. He is not talking, gripping the steering wheel too hard and pushing his top row of teeth into his bottom lip. Eventually he gets over himself, and says, 'Elaine?'

'A neighbour. Pretty much.'

'A hot neighbour.'

'Sarah's got a girlfriend.'

'We were wondering if she told you.'

I am the last to know everything. Up ahead, a black car has stopped on the side of the road. Either the driver is making a phone call or he is lost. The car is not fully off the road, which tells us it is someone from the city; someone who thinks there won't be any other cars on a back road like this, and if there are they will just be driven by stupid rednecks.

Marko slows to check there's no trouble. A man in a dark-blue suit is sitting in the driver's seat, and looks like he's been bashing his phone against the dashboard. His face is deep red beneath short, black hair. He winds his window down, and looks like he's going to tell us to piss off.

Marko gives him a bored 'Everything okay?'

'Fucking GPS, fucking hopeless fucking thing.'

'Where are you trying to get to?'

'I'm supposed to see a guy called Tito Slade who lives at Five Trees. It's out this way somewhere, but the fucking GPS keeps telling me it's on the other side of Waterglen. Fucking stupid thing.'

I look at Marko, and shake my head.

'Never heard of him, mate. Sorry.'

'Yeah, well, fuck you too, you stupid hicks.' He winds his window up.

We leave him, and Marko asks, 'You want to tell me what's going on?'

'I don't know why someone would give my address for Tito.'

'He looked nasty.'

'Uh-huh.'

'You seem to be attracting 'nasty' all of a sudden.'

'Tito got himself into trouble with some bad people. I think I'm getting a bit of his overflow.'

We take Wilson Road, and then turn off at my mailbox. Marko helps me carry the food in, and, as I stack it into the fridge and freezer, he returns to his ute and gets an overnight bag. He dumps it on the kitchen floor. 'I was thinking about staying the night, but when we saw that angry bloke on the road, it made up my mind for me. I'm here, whether you like it or not. I hope your girlfriend doesn't turn up.'

I don't argue.

The phone rings, and he looks a question at me. It seems a good idea to ignore the phone, but I answer it anyway. It is Sarah.

'Are you okay?'

'I'm fine.'

'You're not fine. You've just been in the hospital because someone attacked you.'

'Yeah, but I'm out, and I'm all good. Just a knock on the head.' I tilt my head in accusation at Marko, and he doesn't pretend he wasn't involved.

'You're going to get yourself killed, you bloody idiot, being mixed up in whatever you're mixed up in.'

'It's all under control.'

'You know as well as I do that nothing is under control.'

'Well . . . '

'Do me a favour, Dave, and get yourself away from these people that are hurting you. Stay with Marko. Be a farmer. Look after yourself.'

'Will do.' I put the phone down. I don't need to think about Sarah being annoyed with me. She has been annoyed with me ever since she stopped hating me.

Marko takes a plastic container, which looks like it holds a casserole, out of the fridge.

'I've got to run round and check a couple of things before we eat.'

He puts the container back. 'I'll come with you.'

'No need. I'll be right.'

'You probably should be just sitting down, taking it easy, after that knock on the head.'

'I will after I've checked a couple of water troughs for the stock.'

'I'm coming.'

'Seriously, I don't need you to. I'll be fine.'

He squints at me, and I know he's thinking

there's something I don't want him to see — probably the mess the place is in. I know he doesn't want to shame me, so he says, 'Well, be quick.'

I drive towards the hiding tree, my head still thumping. Marko's assumption is right. There is something I don't want him to see, but it's nothing to do with the farm. I need to check that the boxes are still there and haven't been taken while I was in hospital by whoever knocked me out.

I drive as fast as the track will allow me, and pull in close to the hiding tree. The boxes are still there, dry, and they haven't been chewed by curious animals. I thought it was a safe place for them, but now I can't convince myself of that. I feel like I need to be able to keep an eye on them at all times. I put them in the ute, and then speed back to the house. Before I go inside I take the box of money and put it in the meat room under a wheat bag behind a timber chopping block.

'That was quick.' Marko says when I enter the kitchen. He looks pleased to see that I am still alive.

He heats up a casserole for lunch, and I'm stunned to see him working at the stove. We eat without talking, and I am glad of it. The sound of a car, a powerful, expensive car, makes me look out the window and see the black sedan arrive. There is a forceful, impatient knock at the door. I take the shotgun out and give it Marko, who looks alarmed. He breaks it to confirm it is empty. I answer the door to a pacing man. He sees me, and the recognition is instant.

'You!' His anger has obviously not dissipated. 'You're fucking Tito Slade!'

'No.'

'Then who are you?'

'Since you're on my property, I think I get to ask that question first.'

He pushes his mouth shut, and fumes. Then: 'Frank. Tito Slade has something that belongs to me. I've come to collect it.'

'Tito Slade never lived here. He's dead.'

Silence. Frank's head bobbles just once, and he contains it. This is bad news, and it softens him.

'I'm looking for my brother's remains.'

'Why do you think they'd be here?' In the history of the world, there have never been so many people so poorly directed.

'He fucking sent me a weird note. It had my name on it, but the street address was wrong. I don't know how I even got it. It had this address, his name, and the words 'bones/ remains'.'

Frank stops to take in the air he is suddenly in need of. 'I presumed Tito lived here. Now you claim he doesn't live anywhere.'

'How would he have come by your brother's remains?'

Angryman shuts his mouth, and stares at me. His face is puce again. 'The Vasiliev family had my brother killed, then they took his body. They were going to do something with it, but I think Tito saved it, sent me the note.'

'Tito lived . . . ' It's better not to tell. 'What was your brother's name?'

'Greg.'

'Don't know any Gregs, sorry.'

'Also known as Fatboy.'

'Fatboy Cakestand?'

'What? No! Fatboy Costello.'

As he says it, Marko walks over, the shotgun slung over his arm as though he were a pheasant hunter. 'Were you here the other day?'

'Me? No. Hard enough to find it today.'

Marko looks at him, suspicious. 'Well, I hope you weren't. And you won't want to be coming back, either.'

The angry man looks at Marko and the shotgun without concern. Maybe everybody totes a shotgun in his world.

'So where did Tito Slade live? Can you tell me that?'

'I don't know. I just heard he died. He's certainly never lived here.'

Angryman's frustration returns red and hot. 'What am I supposed to fucking do now?'

Marko moves the shotgun to his other arm. 'How about you stop harassing people, and bloody well piss off home?'

The angry man turns away, then turns back, as if he has something to add. After a couple of rapid steps in our direction, he leaps at Marko, his palms outstretched, reaching for Marko's throat. They both go down, and the gun clatters across the floor. They roll, grabbing at each other, and I retrieve the shotgun, take a cartridge from my pocket, load the gun, click the barrel shut, and fire it into the back of the couch. The confined space makes the shot sound like a bazooka. The couch slips forward and blows stuffing out of its new hat-sized hole.

'Let him go.'

Angryman has already let Marko go. He and Marko sit up and look at me like I might be the crazy one. I break the gun, and put it down. They refocus on each other.

'What the fuck is wrong with you?' Marko spits this at the man who has put red welts on his neck. They are both breathing heavily.

'My brother was murdered. His body hasn't been found. How the fuck would you feel?' Frank is calming down, but slowly.

I tell him that I think he's confused. There are no murderers here. He stands, brushes himself down, straightens his coat and tie, and says, 'So you normally have a shotgun at the ready when people visit?'

We don't have an answer, so I ask, 'Who is the Vasiliev family?'

'Crooks in the city. Real nasty. Professional killers. They take people out, and the body is never found.'

'Never heard of them.' Marko, who is also standing again, makes this sound like it is a significant statement, which it isn't. He still looks keen to throw Frank out the door.

'You've never heard of Sergei Vasiliev?'

'No.'

'You don't have TV, internet?'

'Fuck off.'

'And what do you do?' I ask. The shotgun shot has given me a particular authority.

'I'm a car salesman. Clean. Had some trouble

171

when I was young, but nothing since. My brother is a different story.' His anger is gone, and he looks like a different person, maybe even a reasonable person.

'You want a beer?'

'What?' He and Marko say this simultaneously.

'There's something going on here, and I don't know what it is. I think we need to talk.'

'Oh, fuck off, Dave.' Marko cannot believe me.

'I'm serious.' I go to the fridge, extract three beers, hand one each to the other two, and open one myself. They look at the beer in their hands in wonder. 'Come on, drink up. Take a seat.' I push a stool at the now not-so-angry man. His name is Frank Costello, and his brother has been missing for some months. He did a bad deal with the Vasilievs, and they put a contract out on him.

'So he may not even be dead,' Marko points out, still not happy with my idea of friendship.

'He's dead, all right. They sent me a message. Said there'd be a gift from the Vasilievs. But nothing ever came, except one day I got a note from some Tito guy.'

I've finished my drink, but the other two have hardly had a mouthful of theirs. I get out three more, and hand them around. They look at me like I have a problem.

'So why would you believe Tito and come all the way out here looking for him?'

'I didn't know what else to do. Everybody tells me my brother is dead, but there's no body, and the police have got nothing. Everyone is asking questions. Someone sends you a note saying they've got pieces of your brother — you follow it up, don't you?' He lets us see the desperate man he is.

'I guess so.' Marko finishes his first beer, and seems to be relaxing. 'The Vasilievs send out gifts after they murder someone?'

Frank shrugs. 'Apparently.' He is just Frank now — a car salesman who probably gets ribbed for using too much cologne. Not a bad guy, though. 'It's actually pretty hard to get someone killed discreetly. It's easy to do a drive-by or a shooting on a front porch, you know, in front of your family. But to remove someone, body and all, with no witnesses, is a real art. Most hitmen don't get the significance of killing someone. It's just fish in a barrel to them.'

'You know this how?' Marko is almost sneering.

'Like I said, I had some trouble when I was younger.'

'What sort of gifts? Chocolates? Flowers?' Marko is not disguising his disbelief.

'I don't know.'

'Did you get lunch? You want something to eat?' I ask.

Frank waves a hand and says he's fine, but his face says he'd love to eat.

'We've got some curry. It's not bad. Go on.'

He doesn't respond, so I get out a bowl, fill it and put it in the microwave. When it is hot I shove a fork into it, and pass it to him. He eats like it is a long time since he has.

Frank finishes, and passes the bowl back to

173

me. 'That was delicious. Thank you. Sorry — I'm not used to not having a takeaway place on hand. I was too early to have breakfast in town, and I've been driving around for hours with no food, and no shops in sight.' We have crossed some sort of social threshold whereby he is now talking to me like we met in a pub or a service station.

'You going to give him a tank of fuel now?' Marko is derisive, but now it's an act.

'Had you heard of Tito Slade before?'

'No. Don't know a thing about him.'

'Ever seen a reference to my address anywhere before?'

'No.'

I tell them the things Elaine told me, and everything that has happened at Elaine's and at my place, except for the deliveries of the boxes.

Marko is open-mouthed. 'Why didn't you tell me about this, Dave?'

I say something meaningless, and then Frank says, 'So maybe it was the Vasiliev family that was blackmailing Tito.'

It seems like a reasonable link.

'What would the Vasiliev family want from a bloke who does pottery and lives in the country?' Marko has given up on the act. The intrigue has got the better of him.

'I guess they'd want him to make pottery.'

'Which means they'd want him to put something illegal in the pottery: it has to be drugs.' And now Marko is talking as if he is a fictional detective, several steps ahead of us, the case already solved.

I tell him I had the same thought. 'But the police kind of laughed at me.'

'But . . . ' Frank is thinking out loud. 'I saw an article on the net where this guy made crockery out of . . . '

'I know. I saw something about that, too. I think the police probably did as well.' I explain to Marko, and he looks like he's not sure whether to laugh or be horrified. The fictional detective is back in the book. His face changes, and he asks, 'So, the note suggested to you that Tito might know where your brother was buried?'

Frank nods. 'Stupid, I suppose, but I didn't have anything else.'

I make a decision. 'Marko. Frank. I've got to get something from my ute. Can you both stay here, and not attack each other or do anything stupid?'

Frank and Marko nod begrudgingly. I walk out to the ute, choose the box I want, and return.

I put the Fatboy box on the island in front of Frank and say, 'I got this in the mail. It doesn't have Greg Costello's name anywhere on it, so it might be nothing to do with him.' I put my hand on top of the box. I know Marko is probably gobsmacked behind me, since this is another thing I neglected to mention. 'The name on it is 'Fatboy Cakestand', and I warn you it might be human remains.'

Frank gets up and comes over to the box. There are already tears welling in his eyes.

'Like I say, it was his nickname: 'Fatboy'. I don't know about the other bit.'

Frank opens the box. His face suggests that for one moment he thinks I'm playing a game with him. He touches the ash uncertainly. I realise he has no way of telling if he is looking at what is left of his brother, or the remains of a pet or a log. I pick out the ring and hand it to him. One sob hiccups its way out, and then he begins to howl. Marko and I don't know where to look or what to do. Frank pushes the ring against his cheek, and in between sobs says, 'It's him. It's him.'

After some time, he controls himself, wipes his eyes, and says, 'Thank you. Thank you so much.' He puts the ring into his pocket, carefully closes the box, and slumps on the stool. He takes a white handkerchief out of his pocket, blows his nose, and then puts the handkerchief back.

'I knew he was dead. I was only hoping to find some remains, but I guess you never really believe.' He sniffs. 'The family will be relieved. At least we have something.'

Dry-eyed, he looks around the room as if searching for context or explanation. 'So how the fuck do you two fit into all of this?'

'The trouble just turned up on my doorstep. Marko's being a mate.'

And then the three of us talk for a while about nothing: sport and stupid people. It's our way of building a defence against what we suddenly know. I am telling myself that Tito sent the boxes. But he must have had someone handle this for them to arrive this long after his death. Why me? Why money?

Marko breaks the mutual support, and says, 'If

the Vasiliev family are the ones sending tough guys to hassle Dave, what can we do about them?'

Frank gives a half-hearted laugh. 'Nothing. They're way too powerful, and I don't think you two are killers.'

'We could report them to the police.'

'Good luck with that.'

We are silent, so far out of our league that we have nothing to say.

Frank finishes his beer, and says he'd better go. 'Are there ever any cops around here? Like, to breathalyse me?'

I tell him, 'Only when they have reason.'

We shake hands like old friends, and he takes his box and leaves. It is dark outside. The three of us have been together for hours. My head is beginning to hurt again, and I am ready for sleep. I tell Marko there are clean sheets in the cupboard if he wants them, but I'm not up to doing it for him. I'd like to talk to him about what he thinks of the things we learned today, but I'm too tired.

I leave him settled down in front of the TV.

★   ★   ★

When I get out of bed in the morning, Marko is up, showered and chirpy, a body of barely contained energy. He is not used to sitting around.

'You didn't think getting human ash in the mail was worth telling me about?'

'I didn't want to worry you.'

'You are a very frustrating person, Dave Martin.'

'I know.'

'And I don't believe that someone has just accidentally sent you stuff like that.'

'No.'

'That makes this a dangerous place, so you'd better come and live with me until it blows over.'

'What am I going to do at your place?'

'You're that busy here?' He is cooking eggs like it's a ground-breaking science experiment that no one has attempted before.

'I've got plenty to do here, and I can handle myself.'

'Mate, I don't think there's evidence for either of those things.'

'And you wonder why I don't tell you everything.'

I'm not really listening to him. I'm thinking about Elaine and what she knows about this whole business. Plenty of husbands do things their wives never know about. Or is she more compromised than I know, and more evil? Did she send the money as a thank you, or maybe to keep me quiet?

'Are you going to tell me about Elaine?'

'What do you mean?'

'Anything you like.' He serves scrambled eggs with tomatoes and toast, and we sit together to eat, and drink hot black tea.

'She's not my girlfriend.'

'Right.'

'I don't know what she knows. She just said Tito got in some trouble, and that someone was blackmailing him.'

'So what happens now?'

'No idea.'

'You can't have a relationship with someone when you don't know important things about her. And you can't pretend that the problem, and the bloke who hit you on the head, have just gone away.'

'I could.'

'You'll probably try. I get a feeling there's more to this than you're telling me, and it makes me worry that you're in over your head.'

'I'm not.'

'You're just a farmer. You don't know anything about this sort of underworld thing. So stop carrying on like you do. I think you should come and stay with us.'

'I'm not going to, so give it up.'

He finishes his meal, takes his plate to the sink, turns to me, and I know it's speech time. 'You've been through a hell of a lot. Everyone's worried about you. Now is not the time to turn into some sort of vigilante private detective.'

'I'm not. I won't. I swear.' The thought of staying with people, even the best people, is something I just can't do.

He smacks his lips, and walks across the room and back. 'Righto then, but I expect phone calls, and if you don't call, I'll come over every day and check on you.'

He gets into his ute shaking his head at me, fires it up, backs out, and then obviously has second thoughts. He winds down his window and says, 'No bloke is an island. You know that, don't you?'

'Of course.'

179

'No you don't. But to prove to you that two heads could be better than one, here's a thought: fine-bone china. I did some reading about it this morning. Think about it. See ya.'

I watch him drive away, a little queasy in the stomach from his suggestion, and feeling the smallest sensation that if Marko exists I am not completely unlucky. I don't know if he's onto something, but I guess we're both thinking there has to be a link between Tito's pottery and the ash of assassinated enemies of the Vasiliev family.

The problem of Elaine presents itself again. If Tito sent the ash and the money as a diversion, this suggests that Tito and presumably Elaine were on the side of the good guys: trying to subvert the blackmailers. But even if that is true, she's put me in a considerable amount of danger for no reason. She hasn't even warned me. Is the money a salve for that?

Somehow, Tito must have decided not to do what the Vasilievs were expecting him to do. He was in trouble. Perhaps they were threatening to kill him, and later on did kill him. For some reason, he started sending things to me, but made sure they wouldn't arrive for a year. Was he protecting Elaine, or hiding it from her?

There is a knock on the door. I have been so entranced by my thoughts that I haven't heard a vehicle arrive. It unsettles me. I feel like I've lost touch and anyone could appear at any time without me hearing them. Standing at the doorway in clothes that look too serious for him is Tom Little, with some sort of computer tablet in one hand. He smiles at me when I open the door, and sticks out his other hand to shake mine, way too quickly.

'Hello, Dave — Mr Martin.'

Behind him is the small car he has parked at the entrance.

'Tommy — what a nice surprise.'

'Yeah. It's a long time since I've been out here.' The silence is awkward, but I know he has attempted an acknowledgement of what used to be.

'Come in.'

'Actually, I won't, Mr Martin, if that's all right?' He pauses for me to indicate that it is. 'I'm not here for a social call. It's a work thing.'

I'm enjoying the way he's expressed it as he holds up the tablet as proof.

'So how can I help you?'

'Well, according to the police and the hospital, there's been two incidents — assaults maybe — out here in the past couple of weeks. You and Mrs Slade.' He says the last name carefully. 'I wanted to get your first-hand account of all that. I'm not too keen to interview Mrs Slade.'

I think hard about this. In local news terms, it probably is a story. Bashings are hardly a common event on the farm. But what can I give him? I tell him about my win at the races, and that I believe it was just a one-off by some opportunist. It seems his device is recording me.

'What do you know about the Slade incident?'

'I can't say for sure at the moment. All I know is that I found her in a pretty bad state.'

He asks me about when, how, and why I was there, and I do my best to answer. When we've

181

finished, I say, trying not to be too pretentious: 'But, off the record, there is actually a big story behind it. One that you should stay on if you really want to be a journalist. For the moment it is two assaults, unrelated.'

He scrapes his feet and squeezes his eyes shut. 'A big story?'

I tell him how I was hit from behind, how I have been threatened by people looking for crockery, and then about all the things that have happened to Elaine. When I am finished, he looks at me with a wry, not-quite-amused smile.

'Mr Martin? Crockery? I mean, I know I made a fool of myself over Mrs Slade, and I'm sure everyone had a good laugh, but I'm not an idiot. If you're making fun of me, I don't think it's very fair.' His fingers fidget on the edge of his tablet.

'I know it sounds ridiculous, but I'm not making fun. I promise. And, like I say, there's a lot more to come.'

'So someone tried to rob you once, and did rob your brother-in-law?'

'Yes.'

'And then, a fair bit later, someone assaulted you in your home, but didn't take anything?'

'Yes.'

'Can you guess at the reason for the second incident?

'I can't say why at the moment.'

'At the moment?'

'At the moment.'

'It's quite a drive to come out here, sneak up on you, hit you on the head, and steal nothing, isn't it?'

'It is.'

'And you can't help me with any reasons for that?'

'Not really.'

'How long were you in hospital?'

'Forty-eight hours or so.'

'Any injury sustained?'

'I lost consciousness. Had a big cut to the back of my head, but the doctor said no concussion as such.'

'Are you okay now?'

'Yes. Thank you for asking.'

'That's about it.' He holds his computer by his side. 'Thanks for everything, Mr Martin. I might call in on you another time, if that's okay?'

'Please do. And stay in touch.'

He smiles inscrutably, turns, and walks to the tiny, battered car.

'Tom, someone sent me a large amount of money.' He stops where he is, and listens. 'And human remains, in boxes. There's a real story here.'

He nods, and then keeps walking, and I'm not sure whether he's agreeing or confirming that he thinks I've lost it.

12

I have successfully not thought about Elaine for some hours, but I know I should be talking to her, telling her everything that's happened, and asking for her take on it. I get in my vehicle and drive to her place. In the front of my mind is the fact that nothing good has happened for me when we've met up. Twice I've found her hurt, once I got myself into trouble, and once I declined a pretty significant offer. What's on the agenda this time? As I approach her mailbox, I see an old ute bumping up the drive towards her house. I stop. Ben was happy to say some pretty nasty things about Elaine in public. But Elaine said he was helping her with something. Why would she rely on him? I could drive in there and ask her, but I know that turning up at her place again unannounced with some sort of foreknowledge will be creepy. She will know I'm spying on her. I turn the ute around and head home, the sunlight disappearing around me.

The best way to get a handle on what Elaine is really up to is to spy on her. Or maybe it's the worst way, but it is a way, and it gives me something to do that I am willing to do. That first day, when she came to my place looking for a box of crockery and later received it in the mail, doesn't fit with my theory. Perhaps Tito had sent it as a decoy, and Elaine was expecting it. But he's been dead for a year. This suggests that someone else sent it. And it turned out to be just rubbish, didn't it? And why did Ben also come looking on that day? Was that just a coincidence? There are plenty of reasons for people to get parcels in the mail or have one go missing.

In the dark, I ride my old pushbike halfway to Elaine's, and pull off the road past the table drain and into the long grass alongside the fence that runs up to a nearby ramp. I still have a couple of kilometres to walk across wheat paddocks and sorghum stubble, but if I don't want to be seen, there's no choice. There is only a half moon, but it is bright, and the night is clear, so I can make out detail in everything around me. My shadow is defined as though it were daylight. I climb the fence and set out with long strides, sticking to the wheel tracks in between the perfect crop rows, and keeping an eye out for random vehicles and errant piggers. The cicadas sing their persistent background song: the sort of quiet noise you can't get closer to or further away from.

I am walking on Jack Turnbull's place, the neighbour I never see. He and his wife, Ruth, are away a lot, and have managed to give people the impression that they would rather not live around here. It's a form of insult, even if unintended. When I am halfway across the wheat paddock, a spotlight lights up white out of nowhere, and sweeps across the earth towards me. I dive forward, and flatten myself, hoping the furrow will shield me. The light pans the paddock, glides over the top of me, and is gone. I begin to breathe again, and the dirt sticks in small clods around my mouth. Now I can hear the diesel throb of a vehicle in low gear. It is distant, so whoever it is must be on the edge of the paddock, avoiding driving all over Jack's faultless plantings. Then the light swings back, and I try to sink into the dirt, wondering if they are the kind of mad city shooters who take pot shots at anything that moves. The beam disappears, and I find myself whispering my hope that they have given up. But I barely finish getting the words out when a boom in the air, followed by a thudding sound ahead of me, momentarily lifts me out of my slough and bangs my heart against the sides of my chest. For someone who wants to die, I am showing a commendable fear of being collateral damage.

I shut my eyes, and lie still for maybe ten minutes. My breathing is still loud, but I can no longer hear the engine. If I walk again in this open paddock before they are gone, there is the risk that their spotlight will find me accidentally, maybe on the back swing. I stay down a little longer, and think, *Be calm*. Eventually, I'm sure I hear the vehicle in the distance, moving away from me. I put my head up as though I'm engaged in trench warfare, and see no vehicle and no lights. I get slowly to my knees, ready for the crack of a rifle and a sudden, searing pain. When neither happens, I stride out again, alert to the palest reflection of man-made light.

I walk for another half an hour until I get to Elaine's machinery sheds near her house. All the lights are off except at the house, and as usual it is lit up as if there is excess electricity in the world that needs to be used up. There are no cars out the front, which might mean no visitors, and indicates that the security guard has been given the night off. I take a spot in close, pushed into the hedge, where I can see Elaine and not be exposed by the lights of any car that turns up.

I see her at the kitchen island, writing or drawing something. Her hair is hanging down, obscuring her face. There is music, instrumental and low-key. Elaine takes a sip from a tumbler without looking up, and then continues to do what she has been doing. My idea of spying suddenly seems very stupid: watching a normal woman at home, at night, doing normal things. Soon I might be perving on her doing the ironing. I lean back into the hedge, and think about the walk back to my bike. And then what? Ring Marko, and ask if I can stay with him? I concede the main reason I came on this foray was to do something — anything except sit in my house, think painful thoughts, and drink myself into oblivion.

I look back at Elaine, and she is in the same position, still doing whatever she was doing. Then a man appears from another part of the house, and she doesn't acknowledge his existence. He is short, older. He walks to her, and puts a hand on her back. She still doesn't look up. I know who he is. It is Ben Ruder, in her kitchen, treating her like an old friend or even a lover. I think I'm choking, and begin hoping that alcohol abuse is causing me to have delusions or sight problems. Elaine gets up and goes to the stove, and I focus on the man. I was right the first time — it is Ben, of all people, and I am jealous. Jealous of this awful little man. I realise I was enjoying just watching her, and if Ben hadn't materialised I probably would have gone on being a peeping Tom as she went about her normal life: washing the dishes, doing the accounts, finishing a meal. Even more startling is the fact that, through all this, I haven't had a thought of Sarah. This fact means she might even condone my voyeurism.

With her back to the stove, Elaine shakes her head at Ben over something that seems trivial. He steps closer to her, and could be talking, but I can't tell because I can only see his back. Then he hits her with an open hand, full to the face. I fall sideways into the hedge, break a branch going down, and then have to hang on to it to stop myself running in to defend her. I try to tell myself this is not my business and that nothing will be helped by a surprise visit. I do not know what is going on here. He was Tito's uncle. He helped them find the farm and to relocate when they were desperate. Is he helping her with something now? To fight the Vasilievs? Or is he controlling her? Either way, they have to be involved in the boxes. They want what is in those boxes, even if they don't know what's in them. Perhaps Elaine has her own plan, or has committed her own crimes. Nevertheless, my heart is insistent in my chest, and I know if I am capable of doing good for someone else, this is the time and place — whether Elaine wants me to or not.

With one hand she is holding her cheek where

Ben hit her, and with the other she clings to the stove. Ben remains close to her, and looks like he will do it again with only the smallest provocation. Now she tosses her hair back and stands tall. I have the stupid thought of my rifle and of what I could do with it. Could I really shoot Ben? But I don't have my rifle, and I do need to do something. Ben's open hand moves out from his side, and I get to my feet and then duck down again. I cannot sit here and do nothing.

An idea of an action sprouts in my head, comical and misplaced, but it's all I've got. Instead of running in to save Elaine, I begin to moo like a cow that has lost its calf. It's a reasonable impersonation, without the bovine volume. Ben jerks his head back. Perhaps he thinks there's a cow in the garden, or maybe he is unsettled by the strangeness of the sound. I am sweating trying to think of another distraction. I would throw pebbles at the other windows if there were any in reach, but there aren't. So I opt for a butcherbird whistle: one long note, then a series of ups and downs just discernible from a magpie's call. Ben nearly runs to the door, his feigned hobble an afterthought. He pokes his head out, and looks one way and then the other, concerned, but not sure what to be concerned about. As he shuts the door again, I give him a made-up trill from a non-existent bird that carries clear, lonesome, and ridiculous in the night air. I can see immediately how much it annoys him. For me, the thrill is unmatchable. But after a moment he manages to ignore the sound. No one is going to be sitting in Elaine's garden making fake bird noises. But I haven't finished. When he takes two steps back towards Elaine, I bark like a dog. Sometimes, certainly not all the time, my bark can fool my dogs. Ben hears it, and I'm sure he's only half-fooled. He steps out, and walks up and down the verandah, yelling obscenities into the night. It takes him some time, but eventually he cools, and decides he's frightened off whatever it was that was making the noises, goes back inside, and pulls the door firmly shut behind him.

When he turns to face Elaine again, she is holding a kitchen knife, jabbing it towards him. It's possible she is saying the name 'Greg Costello', but I can't be sure. Ben puts his hands up as she points with the knife towards the part of the house that he originally appeared from. Then he says something I can't hear, and she drops the knife and her shoulders. Her face is covered by her hair, and he steps in close and puts his arms around her. She does not push him away. This is as insane as everything else that has been happening. Ben hugging Elaine means I am on my own.

He leaves, heading back out the door he arrived through. Elaine watches him the whole way. His car disappears at speed, and I understand that the hand on Elaine's back was a gesture of power more than intimacy. I slump against the hedge, and watch her. She paces, distressed, picks up something and throws it at the wall, and then sits with her head in her hands, and sobs. Why don't I go to her? Is it because it would be too creepy for her to know I was out here spying? Or is it because I don't understand what I have just witnessed?

I crawl on hands and knees until I reach the sheds, and then I run, stumbling and tripping just to burn the adrenaline that is bursting in my body. The spotlight is now in the far distance, several paddocks away, so at least I am safe from that. My steps in the soft soil keep time with the battering of thoughts in my head. Is Elaine being forced to do something she doesn't want to do and is too afraid to tell me about? That would put her in the clear. Sort of. If everything is linked, then Ben is a definite bad guy, more involved than I realised. I walk and then ride, and reach home.

I wander around my house, hoping a way forward will blossom in my head. I see Ben hitting Elaine again, and the fury with which she held that knife. Maybe they are in an abusive relationship that is also a crime partnership. That feels possible for Ben, but not Elaine. Then I watch TV for a while, not seeing it, which is good because I hate TV. It is full of stories of relationships, and failure, and loss, which make me hurt. Eventually, I sleep, not having come up with any answers.

In the morning, I drive around the farm, sticking to my pointless routine. The landscape is still green, abundant, and awesome. The weather is so mild and faultless that even I feel the beauty of it. Is there a perfect temperature for a human being? One that lifts your spirit, no matter how low? That's how it feels, and I am desperate for the goodness of it. I know that Keats and his mates thought of autumn as decline, but round here it can match spring for splendour, and the threat of winter is no more fatal than the threat of summer.

I get out and walk the paddock for a while, and actually pay attention — like I used to. The summer grasses are holding their green, because there still hasn't been a frost, while the winter grasses are shooting up, sticking their optimistic heads in the air. The landscape is rich and diverse, probably because I haven't pushed it in the last few years. All good signs. I should have oats in. I should have steers grazing. I should have wheat in, and up. I should . . . I am clear-headed enough to know that this is bullshit. The paddocks are not prepared — they're thick with weeds, which means that moisture hasn't been retained and that anything planted will struggle. So the seedbed is full of weed seeds waiting for their chance. And weeds take their chance better than anything. My farm is a mess. But for a moment I am not thinking about Elaine and Ben, or James. It's a good feeling.

And then I remember I have to tidy up James's area, and weed the garden bed. So I drive home, and walk past the disorder of my garden to the fastidiously looked-after plot. There really isn't anything for me to do. A weed never gets a chance in this garden bed, and the lawn is clipped, even, and clearly marked out. In two months he would have been eighteen. That one sentence has enough pain in it to last me for a thousand sleeps.

* * *

At lunchtime, I ring Elaine, and ask her if she's all right.

'I'm fine. That's the question I should be asking you. Is your head okay?'

'Back to normal.'

'I should put you on to the company that hires my security guard.'

'Is he around all the time?'

'Twenty-four/seven, except when I give him the night off, which I don't do much, because it makes me feel insecure.'

'Yeah, I bet it would. By the way, I saw Ben's ute driving in to your place.' When the words come out, I realise how odd they sound — how odd I sound.

'I did warn you about spying on me, didn't I?' The tone is jokey.

'I just saw the ute go in. That's not spying. That's just driving past.'

'Okay.'

'He's a nasty bit of work, though.'

'You think?'

'I know.'

'I think he's kinda sweet.'

Here's an answer that bowls me over. Even if I hadn't seen him hit her, I would struggle to believe she could think Ben was 'sweet'. Now I know for sure she's being dishonest with me. There is something significant she's hiding. Even so, I can't stop the word 'Sweet?' slipping out on its own as a question. She laughs that laugh. I can picture it tinkling up out of her throat.

'I'm kidding. He's definitely not sweet. But he's not that bad when you get to know him. He's helped us out a lot.'

My tongue does not have the dexterity to allow me to say, *Is being hit by him part of getting to know him?* I just give a 'Hmm.'

Her rejoinder is something like, 'He is, I promise. You should make an effort with him. He's actually very interesting. Knows lots of things. Is in contact with all sorts of people.'

'I don't think I'll be making any effort with Ben Ruder.'

'He was a good support to Tito through all our troubles.'

I don't say I can't imagine it.

'Used to get the cow bones for Tito's pottery. Tito always appreciated that.'

I tell her I'm just glad she's okay, which seems out of context given that we haven't discussed what I saw, and then I hang up.

13

In the evening, I shower for a long time, because it seems like it's something I should do. I repeat to myself that Ben was supportive of Tito. What the hell does that mean? Then I think about Tito and what might have been driving him.

I cook a barbecue for myself, and make sure there are veggies on the plate. Apparently, that's how you live longer, and that seems a weird thing for me to be thinking about. At the current level of my vegetable consumption, I should be dead tomorrow. James liked peas, but no other vegetable I could think of. This never stopped Sarah thinking up new ways to trick and blackmail him into eating them. Sometimes she succeeded, and sometimes she succeeded because he knew he had to please someone who was trying so hard.

And then I search for the name of the small village that Elaine said Tito liked to visit. I don't know anything else about Tito, except what we talked about and what Elaine has told me. The internet has a few articles and pictures of him winning prizes and awards over the years, but nothing of any help to me. Willi comes up on the map, but not before the algorithm has tried to send me to a dozen similar-sounding places. It is about five hours' drive west of here, and according to various websites it is a thriving metropolis. It has hotels and motels, and schools and industry. But when I refine the search on each of these categories, I discover that Willi has none of them. All I can find is that it has something called a sub post office, but the internet can't really explain what this is. All the references are to licensed post offices and community postal agents. I guess these are modern rebadgings of the old half post office, half small businesses that used to exist around here. I remember one on the other side of Waterglen that sold booze as well.

I call the Willi number provided. I know with these sorts of establishments I have just as much chance of catching the proprietors at night as I do during work hours.

'Hello.' The voice is pleasant, but unconcerned.

'Is that the Willi post office?'

'Sure is. How can I help?' It is not the voice of someone from the west. He has not bothered to take up the distinct way they talk out there. A newcomer, I'm guessing, but maybe new a decade or so ago.

'I just wanted to check that you were still in business.'

'Business? We're still open, and we do the mail, if that's what you're asking.'

'Yeah. That's good to hear. Do you remember a bloke called Tito Slade?'

He does not say anything for a long time. A dog yaps a small-dog bark in the background. No one hushes him. 'Who am I talking to?' The voice is now tense and on-guard.

'Dave Martin from Stony Creek.'

'Dave.' His voice relaxes. 'How are you, Dave?'

'I'm well, thanks. You've heard of me, my name?'

196

'Well, I would have, wouldn't I?'

'Why is that?'

'If you want to find that out, you'd better come and visit.' The line goes dead.

I ring Ian, and Mandy answers the phone. I tell her I need to go on a little trip, and this time I really will go away, and would Ian mind feeding the dogs? She is quick to agree to do anything I ask, and then wonders aloud if I would like Ian to go with me.

'Thanks, Mandy, but I need to do this on my own.'

'Are you sure?'

'I promise I'll look after myself.'

At daylight, I fuel the ute, throw some things in, and head out. I'll be driving west for five hours: a little south-west, and bit north-west, but west over all. I put my sunglasses on, and turn the radio up. I reckon I'm driving towards answers and away from something, and that's a feeling I'm going to hang on to for all of those five hours. I'm not going to think about what I'll do with the answers I may or may not get. And as the country changes from undulating to fairly flat, to really bloody flat, I keep guiding my thoughts away from who would be interested in those answers, why they would be, and what they might do.

I sing along loudly to old songs, and disagree with opinionated radio announcers. It borders on fun, and is definitely a type of peace. My phone is off, and nothing can touch me in my cab. There is just me and the whirring of my tyres on the black top. I check off towns as I go

— none of them the same, and none dissimilar. Some look like they've been boosted by mining or some other new industry, and others look like they should have 'If we don't do something soon' written across their 'Welcome to . . . ' signs. The trees on either side of the road change as I cruise through different districts. Eventually the trees take a back seat, and forms of shrub and low bush dominate.

When James was a small boy he was always asking me the names of things, especially plants and animals. I would explain box trees, Myall trees, red river gums, and kurrajongs, and he would say them back to me, rolling the words around in his mouth and trying them out until he got them right, or close to right. He demanded to know grass types, thistles, and birds until I was running for books to expand my own knowledge. I know so much more of my world because of him. Just one of his legacies, I guess.

Late morning, I pull over in a small river town and buy a hamburger and a drink in a cafe that feels like it refuses to notice it is the twenty-first century. There is a large coffee machine, but I'm not willing to risk it. I take my lunch down to the riverside, sit at a shaded council bench, and look at the slowly flowing water, glad that it actually exists. I've made such good time that some of my urgency has dropped off. After I've eaten I put my feet up and half doze for an hour or so. It is almost like being on holiday: no one knows me and nothing is familiar.

I go for a drive along the river, which winds

198

away from the direction I'm supposed to be heading. By the time I've found my way back to the main track, I realise I've wasted a few hours. Well wasted, though. I'm calm and as positive as I get.

I take a turn off the highway, even though the faded signposts do not mention Willi. The country gets paler and harder, and I know the farmers here must own an awful lot of land to run enough animals to exist. I haven't seen any animals other than kangaroos for over half an hour. There is some feed in the paddocks, but I don't think my cows would eat it. The GPS says Willi is only twenty minutes away, but I know GPS doesn't always have the right information in country like this. I stick to the track, and see a gravel right-hand turn that has its own sign pointing to the village I'm looking for. On the map, Willi is at the junction of three roads, but the sign makes no such suggestion. Willi is the end of the line.

I reach the village around three in the afternoon. There is a main street and a strip of tar again, so you know you're in a settlement. There are six houses to my right, and a hall, and maybe eight houses on my left. I drive down the main drag, and look. The houses are okay, their gardens better kept than mine, and there aren't too many vehicles on blocks in the long grass. At what I think is the end of the street I turn left into a street that takes me past the backs of the houses I've seen, and in front of another row of maybe five more houses. These ones have large yards, and one of them has a prime mover parked out the front. I'm guessing the inhabitants are workers who service the surrounding farming district, but I can't imagine there is much work for them. There will be people on welfare, too, as there always is in small villages. Then again, it isn't the place I'd pick to be on welfare, so perhaps no one else has.

A loop of the village takes me back to a house with a phone box out the front. In my memory, a phone box used to be a sign of civilisation: if you were broken down, or lost, or desperate, it was the one way to call someone. No phone box, no phone call. Now it looks quaint, and old-world in the legion of a parked horse and buggy. Behind the phone box on the front of the house is a faded sign with the 'P' symbol of the post office on it. There is no other evidence that this is the place I'm looking for. I park next to the phone box, get out, and push my way through a small wire gate. The house looks unloved but solid, more solid than mine. A screen door that has been poorly repaired a couple of times swings loosely on its hinges. I open it, and step into the past. In front of me is a smooth timber counter with no one behind it so I can see the rows of empty pigeonholes on the back wall. There are a few parcels on the floor, and some small dusty piles of letters, and post packs that you can buy. A bell sits on the counter on top of a sticky-taped note to ring it if you need service.

To the left, I can see, side-on, an upright communications board with wires coming out of it, and a headset lying next to it. I know what it is, but it is so long since I've seen one that it takes me a moment to comprehend. It is an old party-line phone switchboard. We had one when we were small children. You wound the handle a few times to get the operator, and then you asked him or her to put you through to the number you wanted. It was a party line because only one caller could use it at a time, and anyone could pick up the phone and listen in to any conversation. Everyone had a Morse code identifier assigned to them, and when you heard your Morse code you knew the call was for you. Everyone else knew you were getting a phone call. There were seven or eight families to each line. We were one of the last areas to be upgraded to an automatic exchange with phones that you could dial a number with, like they did on the television.

This switchboard has not been used in a very long time, and I'm sure the lines no longer exist, but it is still strange to see it. I am floating around in the time when everything was so different, even though it doesn't seem that long ago, when a man's voice says, 'Can I help you?'

He is probably in his mid-thirties, tall, slim, with long, thick hair that is only one combing short of being dreadlocks. He has a loose look about him, and his eyes are odd, not quite able to hold focus. The clothes he's wearing are a light fabric that might even have been tie-dyed at one stage but are now just a faded blue. 'Alternative' comes to mind, or maybe 'artist'. But out here?

I stick out a hand and say, 'My name is Dave Martin. From Stony Creek. We spoke on the phone?'

'Shit. You really did come?' There's something like panic in his mad eyes. 'Shiflon Vasser.' He shakes my hand with a firm but irregular shake. 'Is your car out the front?'

I tell him yes.

'Would you mind taking it round the back? There's a little track right next to the house. If you follow it down until you pull in under a really bushy tree, it will be much harder to see you.' He gives a sort of whinny after he speaks, which I think is involuntary.

I want to ask why he wants me to park around the back, but he's already been a bit secret-agenty with me on the phone, so I figure if I want information I'd better play along.

It is warm and clear outside, and I am glad of the fresh air. I do as he says. The bushy tree, which I hadn't noticed in my lap around town, does a good job of hiding my ute. You might almost think it was pruned for the purpose. Shiflon sticks his head out of a door at the back of his house, and waves me in. Inside, the house is dark but fairly clean. There are couches and beanbags with Indian-looking sheets and rugs thrown over them. Here and there, instruments that look like guitars rest against walls and chairs. It looks like an interior (and maybe even weight-bearing) wall has been removed, because the area is one big room that opens onto a kitchen at one end and a bathroom at the other. The ceiling droops. A single, bare globe on a long lead hangs at the lowest point. He ushers me towards the kitchen, and I ask, 'Is someone watching us?'

He peers at me as if I'm stupid or perhaps joking, and then looks concerned. A whinny escapes from somewhere between his nose and his mouth. I notice his feet are bare, and his toes are very long.

'You are Dave Martin, who lives near Tito Slade's place, aren't you?' He puts his hands on his hips, and looks like he's ready for some sort of fight.

'I am.'

'And why are you here?'

'I think Tito involved me in something, but I'm not sure what. His wife said he loved to spend time in this village.'

Shiflon waggles his shaggy head, and turns away from me, saying, 'Yes, yes, yes,' grabs two stools and passes one to me. 'He did like this place.' He perches on a stool, and so do I. The kitchen is out of the 1950s — checked linoleum, pale-green cupboards with glass windows and green Masonite bench tops. There is a present-day coffee machine in one corner.

'But when I saw him towards the end, he would have liked any place except home.'

'He was scared?'

'I thought you knew him, man.'

'Not very well. I certainly didn't know he was into any of the stuff I now think he was into.'

'Really? He told me you were his closest friend. The only man he could trust. Apart from me.'

'If that's true, it's pretty sad.'

'It's true. That's why he had me send you the boxes. You did get the boxes, right?'

All I hear is *had me send you the boxes.*

203

'Seven of them. You sent the money?'

'It was money?'

'Yeah. In one of them.'

'Makes sense, I suppose.'

'So why did he do it? Why did you?'

Shiflon sighs heavily. 'Let me see. I've known Tito forever: since art school. Best buddies. Kindred spirits, you know? But when we left, his work got really popular, everyone wanted it, and he started charging a fortune for it. Became a bit of an A-lister, or whatever you call it. He changed — got sucked in by the high life, hanging with rich people, doing what rich people do. He was into the booger sugar, and the punt, and it took hold. Turns out he was a gambler. Would bet on anything at any time. Started to get into some trouble. He married one of the rich girls, and things just got worse. So she decided to get him out of town. Fresh start in the country — you know the deal.'

'Elaine told me the same story.'

'Elaine?'

'Tito's wife.'

'Yes. She did? That's good. Anyway, he was straight for a while. Got in contact. I told him about the clays out here, and he started visiting. We kind of got our vibe back on, you know?'

I nod that I know.

'You want a cup of coffee? It's good — the real thing.'

'No, thanks.'

'I think I'll have one. It is excellent for my thought energy. Do you mind?'

'Go ahead.'

He walks across to his machine, and begins the process of grinding a small amount of beans and then pouring them into the machine. For a moment I think he's forgotten that he's explaining something to me. But he returns to his stool with his cup, and continues. 'And then the bad guys, who'd lent him money for his dice-rolling, offered him a line of credit or something, and he got back into it. Didn't tell his wife. He lost all the money, of course, and so they had one over him. You don't like coffee?'

'I do. Just not at the moment.' I'm thinking I should have said yes just to keep the peace.

'So then he had to tell his wife, maybe thinking she would bail him out again. But they didn't want his money, or his wife's money. They wanted him to make some pieces for them. Seemed like a pretty good deal to me. I mean, they could have kneecapped him, or pulled out his toenails, or something.'

I make a noise of agreement.

'Then, one night, he comes in here, desperate and all shaking kind of thing. He told me he'd got himself in a bad position. Bad dudes were forcing him to do shit stuff.' He looks around, giving me the sense that someone else might be listening.

I am nodding, keeping myself in check, because Shiflon is giving me all the answers in one sitting. He's taken a deep drink of his coffee, and smacks his lips. I'm pushing my mad thoughts about human ash in pottery to one side so I don't miss anything Shiflon might share with me.

'He never told me what was going on, but he asked me to mail the boxes to you. He dropped them off here, and then he drove in front of a truck.' The whinny returns.

'The bad guys didn't kill him?'

'Don't think so. The road-train driver was in a bad way after it. He wasn't a killer. Mind you, it's very hard to tell these days.' He gives me something like a knowing look.

'And Tito asked you to send the boxes?'

'I didn't know what to do, so I didn't do anything for a while. Just hid them in the back room, and tried to forget about them.' He sniffs his coffee, and the pleasure he gets from this is clear on his face.

'Is Elaine involved?'

'Nah. He thought she was the greatest, and hated the fact he had put her in this position, you know, because of his gambling and everything. She came and saw me after the accident. Came and saw everyone round here.'

I nod supportively, unwilling to ask a question that might put him off-track.

'I didn't tell her I had the boxes in my own house,' I say.

He finishes his coffee, adds an 'Aah', and puts the cup down on the bench.

'But then one day, out of the blue, they just started to freak me out. Like they had an energy of their own. You ever had that happen?'

I try to suggest I sort of have, but he's not listening.

'I have. Plenty of times. They were talking to me, warning me that bad shit would happen if I didn't do something. I guessed sooner or later the gangster dudes would come looking for me. They haven't yet.' He trains those eyes on me for a moment, expecting something. Does he think I'm with the Vasilievs?

'Then the wife rings me again, like a couple of weeks ago, and starts questioning me about boxes. I hadn't told her anything about them. She just came up with it.'

'What did you tell her?'

'I said I thought I remembered Tito saying something to do with mailing the boxes to someone, but I didn't know who.' He suddenly shakes his head fiercely. 'That's not true. I told her Tito said he was going to mail the boxes to you.'

I feel my heart turn over. Elaine had been waiting for me to receive the boxes. She knew all along. Shiflon looks calm and unburdened. He's told the story he's been wanting to tell for months.

'Actually, in the end, I didn't mail the boxes. I drove them down to you. Took me three trips. Crazy shit. Didn't want the bad guys tracking me down when they worked out where they were mailed from. But I did mail the letter.'

'Letter?'

'Yeah. To a . . . Costello family.' He screws up his face like he doesn't remember.

'You told Frank Costello about his brother?'

'I wouldn't know. It was just a letter Tito gave me. I never looked inside. I swear.' Shiflon suddenly looks panicked. 'Was it important?'

'No. Just like a get well card or something.'

Shiflon does not need to know any more than he already does.

'Cool,' he says.

I'm wondering if this can be real. Would Tito really have given someone like Shiflon all this responsibility? Maybe Shiflon has appropriated the things Tito told him about and now somehow thinks it happened to him. I change tack, figuring that if his knowledge is stolen, then a different angle might show him up.

'Does a guy called Ben Ruder have anything to do with all this?'

At this, he gets up and walks over to a kitchen drawer, making strange growling noises. His back is to me, but I can see him pulling something out of the drawer, something that fits in his hand. He turns and faces me, pointing a small-calibre pistol.

Without saying another word, he scrunches up his face and pulls the trigger. The bullet goes nowhere near me, and wangs into the wall behind. A piece of gyprock breaks away, and slides down the wall. Shiflon says, 'Sorry, man. I've decided I can't trust you.'

I hit the floor, and he opens his eyes and looks around. He sees me, and repeats the exact process: scrunches his face, and fires. This one embeds itself in the lino, lifting one of the squares upwards as it does so. On hands and knees, I scramble across the floor to a couch that I try to use as a shield.

'I've got to protect myself.' He's yelling it now.

He fires again, and this time knocks out the light. Glass and sparks shower the room. That's

208

enough for me. I am out the door, screaming 'Help' and diving through the thick foliage of the tree to the front seat of my car.

The car starts, and I back up the road at a crazy pace, which doesn't put Shiflon off, and neither does the fact that we're out in public. He is firing at me in that optimistic way, bullets spraying all around me, echoing off the buildings, but none of them doing any harm. I'm out on the main street, over-revving the motor and gone, and I can hear him still shooting. I turn onto the dirt, looking back to see if he's following, or if he's got an army of friends out to give chase. There is no sign of him or them. My heart is pumping so hard my hands are hot. The ute fishtails in the loose gravel, and I tell myself to steady up or I'll die in a car crash like Tito did.

Did Shiflon just tell me the truth, or was it another game? He certainly isn't a practised assassin. If he's taking orders from the Vasiliev family, then I have just confirmed that I received the boxes. But more likely he's just taking orders from a fried, paranoid brain. So I drive, nonstop, my pulse at its peak, for nearly three hours, barely blinking until I reach a good-sized town called Bogan, where I think shooting in public would be frowned upon. I stop at a clean, colourful service station, fuel up, use the toilet block, and then go to pay my bill. There is no one in the shop except the young guy behind the counter. He is in high spirits, but I can't help thinking he knows what has just happened to me, and has probably had a call from the Vasiliev family telling him to keep an eye out for me.

'How's it going?' he asks, almost humming his pleasure as he takes my card. He has 'Kent' written on his bright shirt.

'Good, thanks.' I don't want to invite any attention.

On a small TV behind him, a young woman inexpertly reports a shooting incident in the village of Willi. 'See this?' he says, indicating the screen with his head. 'Didn't think there'd be enough people in Willi for a shooting incident. You know that saying about shooting a rifle down the main street, and not hitting anyone? That's Willi for you.' The primitive nature of other western towns is terribly amusing for Kent.

'Yeah, crazy.' I check that the vision has nothing of me, or my ute, or Shiflon. It doesn't. It is simply shots of the main street, the post office, and the stiff-limbed young reporter. At least someone in Willi thought shooting in the street was unacceptable.

'Thanks, mate,' I say, taking my card back, keeping a tight rein on myself. I would like to bolt, out to my ute, get in, lock the doors, and gun it.

He says, 'Have a good one,' in a happy way, and I walk out calmly. I turn my phone back on but it is out of service.

I am driving again, breathing, leaving the quiet streets of Bogan behind. I am calming down, but wondering if the Vasilievs will see the report on Willi. It is on a regional station, and the city stations don't always pick up regional stories. A shooting in Willi where no one got hurt and no one was robbed probably isn't hot enough to make it to the next level.

My phone returns to service with a voice message on it. It is Elaine, claiming to be 'just checking in'. But this time, despite the extra throb I get in my blood when I hear her voice, I am circumspect. I don't know what is going on, but something definitely is, and Shiflon has just confirmed she is part of it.

The phone rings as soon I click off voice messages. It is Marko, and I nearly say that if he's going to ring all the time I'm going to change my number, but he jumps in.

'Where are you?'

'On my way home.'

'From where?'

'Just a little trip to clear my head.'

'Right. There's an article in the media about the Costello family burying Fatboy, or at least having a memorial service for him. It was supposed to be private, a secret, but some journalist got wind of it. The family did a DNA test on the ashes, and someone in the clinic leaked the information.'

'That's no good.' I'm feeling like an intrusion from the media is probably the least of Frank's concerns.

'Mate, don't you see? If I know about it, the Vasilievs will have known about it the minute it happened.'

I'm still not really with what he's on about, and I nearly say, *Got to go.*

'If the Vasilievs know about it, they will probably have found out, by pressuring Frank, where the ashes came from. So, mate, if you've got any more boxes, or even if they just think you've got more boxes, they're going be sending someone after you, and this time it will probably be a professional — someone competent, someone who can actually do the job.'

I push out one long breath, finally understanding Marko's concern. I could tell him he doesn't know the half of it, but I don't see how that would help anything.

'Shit.'

'Yeah, shit is right.'

'It's okay. I'm going to give them back their bones.' The idea has just jumped into my head: a kangaroo in the top paddock. 'Ben Ruder is involved with them, so I can just stick them in his mailbox, and everything will be cool.'

'Ben Ruder is involved?'

'He's Tito's uncle, and . . . I don't know.' And I don't know. My dislike of him has made me leap to conclusions that have no basis, except for the fact that he's a turd.

'This is all just too far-out, isn't it? Next thing you'll be telling me there are bodies buried all over your farm.'

'No. There's not. All I've got to do is return the bones, and everything is cool.'

'So you do have more ashes.'

'I do.'

'Bloody hell. Get rid of them. If Ben's not the one to take them, I'll find out how to contact the Vasiliev family and tell them I found something of theirs.'

'Oh, terrific plan, Marko. Then they'll

probably send your bones to me in some fucking beer stein.'

He almost laughs.

'Well, that's one solution,' he says, and is quiet. I don't fill the space. Then he offers, 'Do you reckon something like this ever just gets 'cool'?'

'Never been involved with something like this before, so I don't have a clue. Just doing my best.'

'Righto.' Marko's probably immune to my shit attitude, but you've still got to give him points. 'I'll talk to you later when I've had a chance to make sense of this stuff. Be careful,' he says.

'What did you mean by your fine-bone china thing?'

'Nothing. Just my imagination getting away from me.'

'Yeah. So what was it?'

'Well, you've got a bloke who makes pottery, a neighbour with boxes of ash, and some gangsters who want pottery made for them. Fine-bone china was literally made using a certain amount of bone from animals. I just thought . . . stupid, really.'

'Yeah. Stupid.'

After I stop talking to Marko, I suddenly realise I am dangerously tired. I'm only two hours from home, and the sun hasn't even set, but I can't drive any further. I pull off the road into a roadside rest area protected by yellow box trees, kill the motor, put my seat back, and fall asleep. I sleep for hours, waking occasionally, but never able to properly open my eyes.

And then, in the small hours, the sound of someone crawling through the grass jerks me fully awake. Buzzcut and the Vasilievs have tracked me down and are going to liquidate me on the side of the road in the middle of nowhere. I slide down low in my seat. The noise stops. I inch up and try to look over the window. The sound starts again, but this time there is snuffling and snorting. I sit up and look out into the gloom.

A feral sow and her suckers have found something interesting in the grass next to my ute and are rooting up the soil. So much for bravery. I open the door and shoo them away, but there is no chance of a return to sleep. When the pigs have disappeared, I take a walk, relieve myself, and make sure my head is clear for the drive.

I hit the road again, taking it slow and telling myself there is no rush, aware that I am just about on peak hour for roadside kangaroos.

14

By the time I reach home, the sun is starting to make itself known, and I realise how glad I am to be back. The line of the horizon, the particular colours and smells, are more of an unacknowledged part of me than I ever realise. It isn't just a piece of real estate that my family has owned for a long time. It's part of me, or maybe me it.

I take a shower, and lie down on a fairly clean bed. I just have to breathe and not think too much. There is so much in my head, and so little of it makes sense. And except that my life is threatened, I'm not sure that I really care. But I can't sit on my verandah and drink beer for the rest of my life. I put on some of my safe music, and drink the rest of the cheap white wine, and then some, but I don't fall asleep. Not for long, anyway. The morning is too bright — my body clock might be screwed up, but it still thinks sleeping while there's daylight is wrong.

I think the morning I've had deserves a beer. I take one from the fridge, and sip it like a connoisseur. Somewhere in the mush of my brain I am putting two and two together.

I sit down at the computer, and I tap in 'Sven Gzhel' and 'Bryan Lomonosov' into the search engine. I expect to be directed to crime story sites where the gruesome deaths of individuals with these names are reported. Instead, I find listings for two types of Russian porcelain. 'Sven' and 'Bryan' are crossed out in the search list. It is just Gzhel and Lomonosov that have created the responses. Both have been around for some centuries, but neither mentions fine-bone china.

I find my phone and run through the contacts, looking for Mrs J's number. I call it, and she answers with a calm, slightly amused tone. It's as if she thinks anyone who would bother to call her must be an idiot.

'I have a weird question for you.'

'Of course you do. You're a weird boy.'

'Can you make fine-bone china using human bones?'

She doesn't need time to think of her answer. 'Yes. I don't know what the quality would be like. Should be okay. Adding bone creates a kind of translucence. There are people who will do it for you.'

'You can pay to have your loved one made into crockery?'

'Yes, you can. Either mixed with the clay to make the object, or incorporated into the glaze.'

'Wow.'

'Yes, wow. Of course, if the potter isn't a very skilled artisan, you're going to run into big problems.'

'Problems?'

'Well, they're likely to be fragile, brittle, easily broken, and of course really, really ugly.'

'Okay. Thanks. Have you heard of Gzhel or Lomonosov porcelain?'

'Russian. Not to my taste, but not bad quality.'

'Could someone make something in a Gzhel or Lomonosov style?'

'With human remains?' Mum used to say Mrs was always the smartest human in the room.

'Yes.'

'I suppose so. Both of them have a distinctive style. Gzhel is traditionally white with blue decorations. Lomonosov is known for a thing called 'cobalt net'. In crudest terms, which might suit you, it is a kind of bluish fishing-net design on a white background.'

'You do know what you're talking about.'

'I do.'

I put the phone and my beer down, rolling the names Cakestand, Gzhel, and Lomonosov over in my mouth. My thinking isn't as clear as it would have been before I started the beers, but it's clear enough.

At the kitchen table, I open a new file on my computer. I start from the beginning, and write down everything I can remember that has happened since the first box arrived. I'm trying to get some clarity in my thinking. If I'm going to believe the theory that the Vasiliev family were blackmailing Tito to incorporate their victims' bones in porcelain pieces, I need to have the details set out. How do you prove a theory like that? I have ashes and some incriminating money. Unless someone finds a vase or some such with human bone material in it, I've pretty well got nothing. Except Marko said the Costello family did a DNA test on their box. That's a link.

But there's a good chance Tito never made any of the pieces that the Vasilievs wanted him to. So, no evidence. It's not as if I'm going to find Buzzcut and force a confession out of him. Shiflon is hardly a reliable witness, and nobody else is implicated. Ben and Elaine are my only keys, and I don't know for sure if they know anything. But I feel like it is worth writing down and then at least sending it to my young reporter friend, if nothing else. Who knows? He might make a career out of it. Because I do have ashes and the Costello family. The forensic police on the TV would be able to work out who the bones belong to, so I guess the real police would be able to do that, too, and they're my next stop.

I make a cup of tea, put on some music, and take a chair out into the late sun. I think about Sarah. Is the fact that she has taken up with Lucy some sort of comment about me? To me? Probably not, but sort of. Her intention might be to stay away from everything that was, and anything like it. And then again, it could be just good old love. You have to take that where you find it. Elaine is having an effect on me, but it's not love. Attraction, sure, which has got to be healthy. And the first re-emergence of something like lust. It suggests I'm recovering a bit. I mean, lust has to be a primal life force, right? I don't imagine you can be lusting and suicidal at the same time. Perhaps I have a future.

My tea is too milky, but the sun is perfect. I toss the tea on the lawn, and shut my eyes to doze. But James's voice rouses me, saying, *Dad, you've got to take a risk. It's boring otherwise.* I know it's not James's voice, so I guess it's me talking to myself, using his voice. But both of us are right. I go to the phone, and ring Elaine.

218

'Elaine?'

'Hi there.'

'Was it fine-bone china Tito was being forced to make?'

'I don't know. It's possible.'

'What if Tito, as part of the blackmailing, was being forced to put other materials into his pottery?'

'Like drugs?'

'Maybe.'

'I really don't know. Seems unlikely. They really liked his pottery.'

'The Vasilievs?'

'Who?'

'They're like an underworld family in the city. I was thinking they might be Tito's blackmailers.'

'Never heard of them. I only ever dealt with an intermediary. I didn't know who Tito's gambling debt was owed to, either time. Have you been on your own a lot since hospital?'

'No. Marko stayed for a night, and, and . . . ' I almost mention Frank's visit.

'Then maybe you know something that I don't.'

Maybe I do.

'I talked to Shiflon. He said he told you Tito was mailing boxes to me.' It sounds ridiculous, and I suppose if Elaine doesn't know anything about it, it is ridiculous. She is quiet for a long time.

'I don't know what's going on here, Dave. I thought we were friends, maybe something more. But you always seem to be trying to catch me out somehow. Why would you go to the trouble of speaking to Shiflon? The guy has serious problems. He lives in Willi because it's the only place where his conspiracy theories about the world can't come true.'

I silently agree with her point, and avoid mentioning that he shot at me. 'I know. It's just that I received money and human ash in the mail. Then a guy called in, looking for the remains of his brother, saying he'd got a note from Tito. He identified the ashes as being his brother. His brother had been executed by the Vasilievs. I'm just trying to work out what is going on. Shiflon seemed to know about it.'

'I'm not sure I get the connection.'

'I'm wondering if it's possible that Tito was being forced to put ash from human bodies into his pottery pieces.'

'Ash from human bodies?'

'People who were murdered by the Vasilievs.'

'Why?'

'To make a kind of trophy, a memento, that says, 'Don't fuck with the Vasilievs.''

She sighs loudly. 'All right then. Let's go through it. You think Tito was making pieces out of the bones of people who were executed?' I can hear that she is doing her best to take me seriously.

'Yes.'

'So he was doing that on this farm. I've had them in this house?' Her breathing is heavy, and I am sorry to have brought the news to her. But then she shows me how poorly I've assessed her take on this. She says, 'Are you taking anything? Drugs?'

220

'No.'

'I know about grief, and I would understand if you had to lean on something like that occasionally.'

The conversation has changed, and I am no longer a friend, or, if I am, a pitiful one.

'I drink, but I don't do any other leaning.'

'Well, you must be spending too much time on your own, because the idea that Tito was doing something like that is just bonkers. He wasn't that kind of person. I mean, you're suggesting someone brought the bodies here, and then we chopped them up, cooked the bones, and then made things out of them. Do you seriously believe any of this yourself?'

'Frank Costello came and got the ashes of his brother.' I get this in before she can hang up.

'And that is just too bizarre. How do you know he was on the level? Did you ever think that someone might be playing games with you, Dave? Is there anything in your life that is real? Is there one thing you can guarantee me is true?' She is sneering, and I'm almost feeling she's right to sneer. It is outlandish.

'You were bashed and robbed.'

'Tito made very valuable works of art. People like to steal valuable things. It's logical. Not everything turns out to be a criminal conspiracy.'

'You said Ben provided Tito with bones for his pottery.'

'Cow bones, roo bones. They're lying around in the paddock on his place. It was a simple favour. No murder, no mutilation, nothing weird. Get a hold of yourself, Dave. You're the

221

one who thinks you received a box of money for no reason. Do you think that happens to normal people in normal lives? I suggest you visit a doctor. ASAP.'

Then she does hang up.

What does Ben have to do with this? I want to ask, but I am stunned by her response, and feeling insecure about my convictions. She could be right. I don't have the greatest grip on reality. It is a stretch to believe that she and Tito were doing things with human bones.

I put the phone down, and think of how desperate Frank was to get back what was left of his brother. That did not seem fake to me, but it so easily could have been.

But what if she's in on the game? What if she killed Tito, knows all about the bones, and has for some reason involved me in it?

Despite still smarting from the feeling of a slap-down, I ring her back.

'What is it?'

'I think the Vasiliev family is about to make a visit.'

'Then send them my best, will you?' She hangs up. Elaine is not easily scared.

And then, straight away, the phone rings, and I pick it up because I assume it's Elaine with one more rebuke. But it's not. It's Tom Little, saying, 'Hi, Mr Martin. How are you?' The way he asks it makes me think he believes it's a worthwhile question, not just a meaningless greeting.

'I'm fine, thanks, Tom. How are you?'

'Well. Going well.'

And then he is silent, and I'm not sure what is

going on. I figure I should be making conversation, but I don't want to mention his job again in case there are more hiccups. And then he breaks it with, 'I was wondering if I could come and stay for a night?'

'For work? For an interview?'

'No. No. Just to stay. I . . . '

It doesn't seem like such a weird request, given how much he wanted to be here after James died, but he is making heavy going of it. I suppose now that it is just me, the prospect of a sleepover is much more daunting. Who is going to cook the meals? Who will handle the small talk?

'I'd like to have another night out there, and just remember how it all was, if that's okay?'

'Sure. I'd like that.'

'And to tell the truth, the last time I spoke to you, you worried me a bit, the way you were talking.'

'You thought you'd keep an eye on me?'

'When I told Marko how you were talking, he asked if I still liked the idea of staying over. I said I did.'

'Bloody Marko. Listen, Tom, you are welcome to come, but come for your own stuff — don't come thinking you'll be my nurse or babysitter.'

'I wasn't thinking that. The thing is, after our conversation I did a bit of research into your . . . situation . . . I thought you might want to hear it.'

'My situation?' I don't know whether he means my trouble with boxes and Buzzcut, or that he thinks I might be bonkers. 'I would certainly like to hear what you've found, whatever it is. When do you want to come?'

'Um, tonight?'

'Tonight?'

'I just found out I don't have to work Saturday — tomorrow. So it would fit in fine, if it works for you?'

'Yeah. Whenever suits.' No point standing on ceremony now.

'All right. I'll see you tonight.'

'Great. See you then. Bye.'

I put the phone down, and consider ringing Marko to tell him to back off. Instead, I focus on whether there is a bed in one of the spare rooms with sheets on it — clean sheets. I think Mick put his stuff in the main guest bedroom, but he didn't get a chance to sleep there. Then Marko slept in there. I check the room next to it, across from James's room, and find that Sarah has left it with crisp sheets and a doona in a bright cover. At least Tom won't think I'm a complete disaster. But if he does, it won't change anything.

I try to tidy up a bit, and tackle the washing that has accumulated again on the sink. Then I go to the back freezer, and find some mince. I decide to make a spag bol that will cover meals for a few nights, including tonight.

Spaghetti bolognaise was the only meal besides steak and salad that I ever saw my father cook. When he moved to town, and visited Mum every day, he lived in a small unit near the hospital. He got meals on wheels occasionally, and he would often eat meat pies or order takeaway Chinese from the only place in town that offered it. It was a miserable existence, but he didn't want to live with us, and he wanted to be near Mum. I took that to be a sentimental thing to do with old age. She was one of the few things, the few people, left of his old life. He hadn't ever really taken Mum's feelings into consideration. When he got round to it, for whatever reason, she was too far gone to know it.

By the time Tom's car pulls into the driveway I have managed to waste the hours, and I'm not really sure how. He walks in, smiley and upbeat, in a clumsy cover for his nerves, but I like him for it. He has a small bag with him, which he drops in the corner. I offer him a beer, and am glad when he accepts. It is always good to have a partner in crime. We struggle through conversation about his work and his family.

I say I've made dinner, and he tells me there's no need. I'm pretty sure he's pretending he doesn't need dinner because he completely forgot about that practicality. The way he's eating my stale chips would suggest that I am right. So I serve spaghetti, meat, and sauce, and ask him about his research. Mid-mouthful, he gets up, goes to his bag, extracts his computer tablet, and returns. He turns it on, and is immediately more relaxed.

Without looking at the screen, he says, 'My dad worked with a guy who knows a local detective really well. This guy knows I'm trying to be a journalist, and he heard about the trouble I had . . . ' Tom pauses as if giving me a chance to remember. 'So he asks this detective if there is anything he can pass on to me about a local case.

A story. Maybe a scoop sort of thing. This detective says he can't really tell him anything about his current cases — it wouldn't be right. Then he remembers a case concerning a family called the Vasilievs, and there's a link to this area.' Tom waves a fork at the room, takes a large mouthful, and chews quickly.

My ears are leaping off their fittings. I want to tell him that I know about the Vasilievs, but I don't want to detract from his moment.

'The detective says there is this crime family in the city calling themselves the Vasilievs, headed by a guy called Sergei Vasiliev. Not big time, but not small either. Every now and then, the rumour mill attributes a murder to them. The police don't have anything on them, but they seem to be a presence.'

Now Tom looks at the screen. 'The police believe they are professional hitmen. If you want someone *whacked*, you go to the Vasilievs.'

He looks up at me. 'Word has it that they have a link to this area, but it's kind of vague. People with connections to the family have been seen up this way. They kind of stand out, because the country is the last place these sorts of people like to go to. Anyway, the police do a bit of research into the Vasiliev family. They ask their sources, follow up rumours, conduct an internet search, or whatever they do. It turns out that the Vasilievs don't exist. There is no Vasiliev crime family. No credit details, no tax numbers, no bank records, no passport record, and so on. The only Vasilievs they can find are a couple of oldies living quietly in the west, and some grannies in nursing homes.

'The Vasilievs don't exist?' All my theories have just been quashed under Tom's polite heel. He holds a hand up to steady me.

'They're fake, but they exist, if that makes sense. Sergei Vasiliev isn't a real person. The guy who turns up every now and then pretending to be Sergei is someone else. He's like a pretend tough guy. The way the detective explains it, he's a bit of an idiot. The police back off from the case, because nothing makes any sense and there is no real evidence.'

I'm going to need to go over this again. 'So someone has made up the Vasiliev family as a front for their, what? Business? Organisation?'

'I guess so, but the police don't know what to do with this sort of information. There are no bodies and no genuine accusations. The Vasilievs are a false name for something that doesn't exist. Their guess is that if you're going to be in the business of having people whacked, it's better for your brand to be a crime family called Vasiliev that lives in the shadows, rather than crazy brothers who live in a caravan at the back of their parents' house in the suburbs.'

When I look confused, he shrugs and says, 'Just an example.'

'Can't they go undercover? Find out who is what?'

'Maybe, but, according to the detective, they can't really justify spending money and time on something so vague.'

'So you think they might be involved in the assaults on Elaine Slade and me?' I don't know if that's what he's thinking, but I'm not ready to

227

tell him my far-out theories.

He pushes the computer away, and leans back. 'I don't have a clue. It just seemed weird that you and Mrs Slade got attacked and neither of you seem to know why. I wondered if it was a coincidence that people with a connection to a crime family, or a fake crime family, happened to be in the area.'

'Good thinking.' And it is. It gives me sudden confidence, and I tell him about the visit from Frank Costello.

'Wow. So you think Mr Slade had something to do with the Vasiliev family?'

'I do.' I get up and take the plates to the sink, as if I care about these sorts of things. I need a moment's breather before I tell him any more. I rinse the plates, and stack them to dry. I get a cloth, wet it, and wipe down the island. 'I believe that Tito was being forced to put human remains, ash, in his pottery. People do that sort of thing. I thought it was the Vasiliev family, who he owed gambling debts to, who were forcing him to do this. He decided to trick them and not do what they were forcing him to do, but he died before he could carry out his plan to return the ashes to the families.'

Tom's mouth is open, and his eyes bright.

'That is far-out. Have you got any evidence?'

'Not really. Sort of. I've got boxes of ashes. And a box of money that was sent to me. Like I told you.'

Tom looks down. 'I thought you were off your rocker when you said that.'

'Yeah. It doesn't mean I'm not.' This brings a

small laugh. He asks about how and why I think this might have been happening, and I tell him everything I know. He sifts through my logic like a professional until he is satisfied that I'm not just fantasising.

'What are you going to do now?' he asks.

'I think it's time to go to the police.'

'Can you keep me in the loop? It could be a big story for me.'

'Absolutely. You want ice cream or something?'

'That'd be nice.'

'Chocolate sauce?'

'You have chocolate sauce?'

'Now that I think about it, no.'

'Plain ice cream is fine.'

'Lucky you weren't hungry.'

I grab the ice cream from the freezer, and put out two bowls.

'I thought you'd move from here,' Tom says.

I look up at him, because I'm not sure whether he's talking about James or my knock on the head.

'After James. There's just so much of him in this place. Not just the grave.' He's embarrassed. It has come out wrongly. 'Everywhere. I mean, in this house, the farm, and everything around it. I feel like he's on his way in from the paddock or somewhere, and we'll see him in a minute.'

'Yep, I know. I feel it all the time. I thought about moving. But when you let go of that, it feels like you're letting go of him. So I can't leave, and not just because of the grave.' I go back to the ice cream.

'Is Mrs Martin okay?'

'I think so. She's happy in the city. Some of that's because of exactly what you say — away from the memories and the reminders of the way life could have been. Maybe being away from me helps, too.'

Then we are quiet. We eat, and examine our bowls. The conversation has been too much. I get up and turn the TV on, and Tom takes our bowls to the sink. As I flick through the channels, he says, 'How are they cremating the bodies? Is there a crooked crematorium somewhere?'

'I guess so.'

'That would be pretty hard to do, wouldn't it? Get a body in, and remains out, of a public business like that?'

'How else could they do it? Maybe one of their crooked mates owns a crematorium. But you'd think the police would work that out pretty quickly. I mean, if Tony Soprano owns a crematorium, you're going to be keeping a close eye on it, aren't you?'

Tom goes back to the tablet, and taps it several times. 'To do a proper job, bodies have to be cooked at 870 to 980 degrees Celsius. You can't reach that heat in a normal bonfire or barbecue. You need a furnace or . . . '

'A kiln.' The light-bulb moment is mine.

'You know people with a kiln? Oh, the Slades. Right.'

Once again, I go over my deductions out loud, because otherwise they'll become another theory piled on top of another theory. 'That means Tito, and possibly Elaine, are behind this. The Vasilievs or whoever they represent were forcing them to cremate the bodies and then put the ashes into his artworks.'

Tom nods thoughtfully. 'It's kind of circumstantial. I mean, we don't know if there are other kilns about, or if they used a kiln a hundred kilometres from here.'

'No. But I'm thinking, if you're dealing with dead bodies, and you've got enough power over one guy to make him put human ash into pottery, and he has kilns, then it would be really convenient to force him to do the cremation.'

'Yeah. No one else needs to be involved.'

I feel the sadness of what I am saying. Elaine is mixed up in this, and she has deliberately played me along. Tom must see my distress, because he says, 'You can't blame them, can you? They were being forced. And it's not like they did the killing or anything.'

'And it seems like Tito did his best to get out of it.' Once again, I am prepared to grasp at any straw when it comes to Elaine. 'So how does Ben Ruder fit into this?'

'Why would he fit?'

'I saw him fighting with Elaine, and the crazy guy told me . . . the crazy guy went crazy when I mentioned Ben's name.'

'He lives near you, doesn't he?'

'Further up my road. He was an uncle and a friend of Tito's. I can't help thinking he was the link to the Vasilievs.'

We go round and round various theories, but without anything solid we don't make any progress. It is enough to send us to bed. It is good to have him in the house, and I go to sleep looking forward to seeing him at breakfast.

He sleeps late — something I'd forgotten young men like to do. By the time he appears, slow and sleepy-eyed, I have been pacing the floor for a while. The breakfast things have been in and out of the fridge several times.

I offer him eggs, but he declines, and pours himself a bowl of cereal.

Then he says, 'It's possible Elaine knows about the boxes, knows you are supposed to have them, but doesn't know how sinister the contents are. The same might be true for Ben. Maybe only the Vasilievs and Tito knew what was supposed to go into the pottery pieces.'

'Yes.'

'So don't feel so bad.'

'I'll try not to. But I don't see how Tito could do all that on his own: receive the bodies, somehow get them in the kiln, and cook them without Elaine or anyone else knowing.'

'True.'

'It's really hard to see how any of them get in the clear.'

'I guess so.'

He leaves after he has eaten, thanking me and saying how much he enjoyed it. I say, 'Come again,' and hope that he means what he's said.

15

And it is time to go to the police. I should have done this when I first got the money and the cremains. I'm not a detective or a vigilante. I'm not even a properly functioning human being. I ring the police station beforehand as a kind of self-defence, after my last experience with them. My idea is to let them know I'm about to give them something important that I need help with, so they don't make me feel like a goose when I walk in there.

It is Constable Murray who takes the call. I am sober-voiced and serious. But before I can begin on the spiel I have been practising, she says, 'We know about the box, Mr Martin.'

'You do?'

'Yes.' The same tired tone. I really am a headache for her. 'I delivered it.'

'You delivered it?'

'Yes, Mr Martin. Hand-delivered it. By the time we'd dropped it off, taken a run up your road, and turned around, you were waiting at your mailbox.'

'I don't understand.'

She sighs loudly. I am a ten-year-old who has been told many times. 'My mother nursed your father in his final days in the nursing home.'

'Okay.'

'And he told her he had a big box of money, his racing winnings, that he had kept in a back room somewhere.'

I am speechless. I have a sense that Constable Murray is a pivotal part of this whole series of events — a policewoman, at that.

'He asked my mother if she could hang on to it, and give it to you in ten years' time. Of course, he paid her to do it.'

'The money was from Dad?'

'Yes. And for the record, I never approved of it. I'm guessing it came from a fixed race, and I'm certain the tax department knows nothing about it. Sadly, my mother got sick, so it was left to me to carry out his wishes.'

'Why didn't he tell me?'

'You didn't find the letter?' The sigh again. 'Mum said there's a letter that explains it all. Have another look.'

A sob rises up out of my throat, unexpected and uncontained.

She takes the sob I'm trying to suck back in as confirmation.

'I'm sorry things didn't turn out so great for you. Nevertheless, I think your father wanted you to enjoy the money. I'll leave you with that.'

She hangs up the phone, which I don't really notice. My father's selfishness . . . my memories of him . . . the thousand thoughts I've had about the contents of that box and why I received them, and now what it means, all smash into each other in my head, creating confusion and even a little joy. When did my father win $250,000? It must have taken him years. Or did he have one big win in the later years? Why didn't he tell me? I lie on the floor, letting the new facts wash over me. I realise I didn't tell her about the other boxes, and now it's the last thing I'm worrying about.

I drag myself to the meat room and uncover the box of money. I take it inside, pull out all the cash and throw it on the floor. I feel through all the seams in the box, pull open the bottom, and run my fingers through any gap I can find. Nothing. It is becoming less real. For a moment, I think I've imagined my phone call with Constable Murray, or I've misunderstood what she was trying to tell me. Was it in some sort of code that I should have understood? Is there an undercurrent that I have completely missed? I upend the box and shake it in fury, but nothing comes out. In my frustration, I tear at the corner of the box, and it comes away in my hands. I see a mess of writing across one of the panels. It looks a lot like my father's handwriting, scrawled in blue-ink pen. I sit on the floor, and rip at the crease so I can see the writing clearly. It is a letter, written directly onto the cardboard inside of the box, that starts 'Dear Son', but I can hardly read it, because my hands are shaky and out of control. It continues:

I know this is going to seem very strange to you. A box of money coming to you from your dead father. I'm aware money doesn't buy happiness or love, but it can surely help. I know how hard it can be on the land, and I thought a lump sum coming out of the blue at a time when all your lump sums (probably) were gone would be a blessing for you and Sarah. Marriage is hard. Your

235

mother and I struggled at times. At least the way we did it: for better or for worse. But I always loved her.

I knew she wasn't right for a long time before I admitted it to myself. When she finally went into the hospital, I was so worried there would never be enough money to keep paying her medical bills. Doctors kept telling me patients with dementia could live healthy lives for years, even if they couldn't remember where they were and the people around them. The only things I could think of to do were to sell the farm or take a huge punt. You know what I did.

I know you always disapproved of my hobby, and I did lose my share of bets in the early days. But at the end I had three good wins. Let's just say I had some good tips from a bloke I'd bumped into a few times over the years. I took the chance and won big. My plan was to leave the box in your mother's room in the nursing home as a personal possession to be opened in case of emergency. But then your mother died. It was so unexpected. I was going to put the money in the bank, but then I knew it would become a part of the estate and somehow Henry would get his hands on it. I decided the money should go to you. It is a gift, son. From me and your mother. I asked Gemima Murray to pass it on after enough time for Henry to have passed too.

Whatever has happened to you since we

went, I hope there has been joy. If not, I hope you have the fortitude to not let it destroy you. James is a terrific kid. You're so lucky in the friendship you have.

With all my love, Dad.

I am howling as if I hope someone will hear and come to help me. The money is from my father, not the Vasilievs, or Tito, or some other family of crooks — my self-serving, coat-and-tie father. That he would have given any thought to the personal stuff in my future is impossible to believe. I read it again and again, and see the word 'friendship' when he talks about James, and take it to mean he was envious of our link. I never thought he would have wanted friendship with me.

Weirdly, the word sticking in my head amongst all those bombshells is 'love'. It wasn't a word my father or his generation ever really got the hang of. When I think of the word and the concept, I think of James, Sarah, and Mum. I do not think of him. Maybe I do now. Not because of the money, but because there was more fear and loneliness in him than I ever realised. It must be terrible to have the person you love not remember you, and then be afraid you cannot afford to look after her. I think I am grieving for him, for everybody, and I might even be grieving for me.

I pick the cash up again and take it out to its place in the meat room. Then I walk down to James's area. I lie down on my back on the long grass at the edge. I talk to myself, babbling about the money, the bad guys, Tito, Shiflon, Ben, and the father I lost who had more to him than I ever realised. I feel like I've lost him all over again. Eventually, the words come back to Elaine. I am trying to suppress the anger I am feeling towards her. Why did she do all this to me? If she had just told me, I could have helped. I wonder if she knew the money came from Dad, because she never seemed that interested when I told her. But all the other stuff I know tells me it is time to confront her.

But first, I have a question for Constable Murray. I know I should be telling her things, but a question keeps bubbling up through the black mud of my brain. When I call, somebody else in the station answers, but I am quickly put through to Murray. There aren't many people in the station.

'Spent the money yet?'

'No, but thank you for everything you did.'

'I did it for my mother as much as anyone.'

This is going to be a brief call, because Constable Murray seems to have decided that her job gives her state sanction to dump on me.

'I was wondering if I could ask a question about the investigation into the stolen crockery?'

'Haven't we done this?' The sigh is back in her voice.

'It's a different question.'

'One question. I'll do what I can to help.'

'Why did they test the crockery for 'everything I could think of'?'

'I don't know. I'm not a detective.' The sigh is replaced by a lilt. Is it the money that makes her

238

dislike me? It's more than that. She enjoys my discomfort. I am the light in her day. At least I'm that for someone. But then she says, 'My understanding, and this is only from office hearsay, is that they have a hunch about something unusual going on in our district. Specifically in your area. I don't think they know what. The only person I can think of who behaves 'unusually' is you.'

I suppose people tell the police to go and fuck themselves, but it's not really in my armoury. She may be goading me.

Her goad having failed, she continues, 'The rumour mill has it that they've traced a link from somebody bad in the city to our little oasis. They haven't shared with us yet.'

'Well, thank you very much. You've been very helpful.'

'Perish the thought.'

I am about to give her something, maybe even everything I have, but then that last comment pulls the shutters down.

'And we still have your bag with your gun, and your pyjamas. You can pick them up whenever you want to.'

'Thanks.' End of conversation.

I tell myself I will ring her back and explain it all, and deliver the ashes and the powder, and maybe give her a leg-up with the detectives. But I am also thinking about loyalty — skewed, unjustifiable loyalty to Elaine. She is involved, and there is no way that her involvement is good. She knows about the boxes, and she's been trying to get them back ever since we became friends. Which means we're not friends, and that she only wanted to sleep with me for other purposes. Mucking about with ashes of the murdered people is a nasty business that she hasn't managed to report to the police. But still I feel loyalty. Tom's comment that maybe she doesn't know how bad this all is has stuck with me. The weeks we've been seeing each other, even though they've turned out to be false, have mattered to me; they've helped me take a few steps forward, and I can't stop myself being thankful for that. So my heart carries the day against my head, and I decide not to spill the beans on Elaine to the police.

But the police think something is stinky, and I am not quite as insane as I thought I was. Good news for a change. It means I have to follow up on what the boxes started, answer the questions, and maybe even right a wrong — any wrong that I can find.

★ ★ ★

Elaine is on Wilson Road, walking in gym gear, stepping out, swinging her arms. I've seen her on walks before, and never paid any attention except to swing my vehicle wide so the stones don't kick up at her. From the back, she looks tight and shapely. Nothing moves when it shouldn't, and I note the fact that I have registered this. I slow down, but she doesn't. I open a window, and keep pace with her. She keeps her face to the front. I say hello, but she ignores me. I have the surprising sensation of an adolescent crush unrequited. This fits, because

Elaine has become the sixteen-year-old who doesn't just reject you, but makes sure you know you're not worth consideration.

I am about to wind the window up, and 'man up' with it when she says, without turning around, 'How did your visit from the phantom bad guy, Vasily whatever he was, go?' The sneer is in full flight.

'He hasn't turned up yet.'

'Surprise, surprise.' Gravel is being punished beneath her pounding, brightly coloured joggers. 'So when is he supposed to arrive?'

'I don't know. Maybe he won't. We just guessed that when the Vasiliev family found out where the Costello remains came from, they would be pretty upset at us.'

'We? Us?'

'Me and my friends.'

'Your friends?'

'Yep.'

'If you have any friends, then they're as mad as you are.'

'Maybe. But someone was supplying the bones, and bones don't come without bodies. So either Tito was stripping the flesh off, or someone else was. A pottery kiln would be the perfect thing to deal with the problem.'

It stops her, and she swivels towards me, hands on hips, head forward. I push on the brakes.

'You're just going to persist with your ghoulish fantasies, aren't you?'

'I am.'

'No matter what I say. Did I do something bad

to you, or have you just let all this craziness get the better of you?'

'Why did you use me?'

'Use you? Please.'

She turns, and drops her hands.

'I could have helped, but instead you sacrificed me.'

'Fuck off.' She walks away without talking, interview over.

'You'd better make sure you've got that bodyguard on duty.' I call this out to her ramrod back as I pull over to the side of the road. I turn the vehicle off, and sit slumped backwards. Despite the way she is carrying on, she knows she has used me at least a little bit. What Shiflon said about Tito sending boxes to me must play on her mind. And what I've said, maybe.

16

And then Shiflon Vasser is in my house, lying on the floor behind the couch. I don't know how he got here, but I guess he snuck in when I was out. I have not seen his car. I don't see him at first, either. I hear him breathing, but I don't realise what it is. In the kitchen, I pick up a strange huffing sound in the next room that doesn't fit in with anything I'm used to. The sound is low and soft. I may be hearing things. Then I guess it is a lizard or something caught under the couch trying to wriggle its way out. I walk over to investigate, and I come across a body flat on the floor, face down, hands and arms up under the chest like a small child playing hide and seek: *I can't see you. That means you can't see me.*

'Shiflon?'

'Dave?' He doesn't lift his head, or acknowledge the stupidity of his situation.

'What are you doing here?'

'Um.'

'Have you got a gun?'

'No.'

'Well, get up. Talk to me.' For no good reason, I'm not scared of him.

He gets up slowly and stiffly, like he has been lying on my carpet for hours.

'What the hell are you doing here? You said you decided you couldn't trust me. You shot at me. Not just once, either.'

243

The whinny returns, slightly self-consciously. 'Sorry about that. I get demons.' He points to his head. 'They said you were one of the bad guys, but after you went and I cooled down, I realised you weren't. You got any coffee?'

'Instant.'

'Okay. Four spoonfuls please.' I go to make the coffee that I didn't offer to make, and he stretches indulgently and then plonks down into the couch.

I make the coffee, and return with it. 'So you're here to apologise?'

'Me?' He sips at the coffee. 'No. You should. This is awful.' I go to take the coffee back, but he hangs on tighter to the mug and says, 'But it'll do.'

I keep standing, watching him drink. 'What are you doing here, Shiflon? What's this about?'

'Oh.' He holds a finger up, and then uses it to dive into one of the deep pockets of his colourful, stripy pants. He extracts a smooth piece of very white porcelain, and offers it to me. It is flat with one edge that curls upwards. On the flat bit are some blurred colours that look like part of a photo printed somehow onto the porcelain.

'Be very careful with it, please.'

'What is it?'

'It's not so much what it is, but what it does.'

He doesn't say anything else, and we both look at the shard of porcelain.

'So what does it do?' I'm exasperated with the game.

'Tito gave it to me. He said I needed to give it

to you to protect you.'

This is too far-out for me, even after all I've been through.

'It's from the seventh box. I didn't tell you, because you said you already got seven.'

I remember the conversation, and how, at the time, I didn't realise the box of money wasn't part of the others. I remind myself that I only have six boxes now because Frank Costello took his.

'I meant to give it to you that time when you turned up at my place. I really did. But it had so much power, I could feel it protecting me. Like scary powerful. I told myself I needed the protection more than you did. Then I realised it didn't protect me from you, and I felt its powers waning. I knew it was because it was in the wrong hands. I had to make sure it got into the right hands. And now I have.' He looks pleased and relaxed. He sits back and does his best to enjoy my coffee. I put the shard on the sideboard, and sit on the arm of a chair, watching him.

He makes loud drinking noises, and seems fascinated with the contents of his mug.

'So what now?'

He takes one last drink, and stands. 'Now' — he hands me the mug — 'I have friends to visit.' He shakes my hand. 'Please don't serve that coffee to anyone you actually like. Look after the talisman and its mighty power. Adieu.'

He waves a hand in the air and then leaves the room, and I hear him go out the front door. I watch him walk out my driveway, and across to the box trees, where he retrieves a small motorbike. He straps on an ancient helmet, kick-starts the bike, and disappears, blue smoke blowing out behind him.

I take the piece of porcelain to the office, and leave it there.

17

A day later, I am at my sheds, picking things up and putting them down. I think I am attempting to tidy up, but it is a haphazard and aimless attempt. I am thinking about my mother. She was always tidying up, always moving, always setting things straight. I hear the sound of a ute drawing in close behind me. I turn, and see the yellow machine that is becoming the vehicle in my nightmares: Ben Ruder's ute. He steps out, adjusts his hat, shuts the door, and takes several steps towards me. I guess he sees me tense and brace myself, because he puts a hand in the air, and says, 'I'm not here for a fight.'

He lets the hand drop, and stands still, looking at me. 'I know we've had our differences, but I want to get past that.'

I always forget how short he is — something to do with the force of him. But now he looks small and maybe even sad in his tired boots and dirty shirt, the greasy hat pulled down too far. I feel like I might even have the upper hand.

'I heard you've been getting a hard time from crooks or something. As a neighbour, I wanted you to know I'd like to help out anyway I can.' His face is grim, and I think he might be genuine. When I don't respond, he adds, 'I know some pretty tough people. They could probably fix the situation.'

I almost laugh. Fix the situation? This is the

solution of one gangster against another.

'I can handle it,' I say. 'But thanks.'

He is quiet, and he looks away down towards where James rests. Then he says, 'Elaine has told me a lot of what has happened. Someone put you in hospital, others came here and threatened you. No one can handle that sort of stuff on their own. It's the time when you call on your community for help. Like when there's a bushfire or a flood. We all get together to help each other out, no matter whether we like each other or not. That's the way it's always been.'

I believe him, because what he says is true. We don't have to like each other to help each other. But I don't want his help, and I don't understand his relationship with Elaine.

'Thank you, Ben, for the offer, but I will be fine.'

He scrapes a foot back and forth in the dirt, and stops it as if that foot will betray him. I realise he is barely controlling his irritation at me.

'Don't be so pigheaded, Dave. Don't take it as an offer from me. We all need to work together.' He forces the word 'together' out, pauses, and then swallows something that I think might be rage. The attempt to be friends has not gone the way he hoped. 'These people are a threat to our community. We need to be united.'

It is possible he is concerned for his own farm and business. Maybe he thinks Buzzcut will target him next, or maybe he already has. 'I certainly appreciate your concern, Ben, but I can assure you I can handle the situation.' He clenches his jaw, and I think he might be gritting his teeth.

'Have they visited you?' I ask.

He is confused by the question. 'Me? No. I can handle this sort of stuff. I'm here to support you.'

'Or do they work under your orders? I know you want the boxes. I know you're mixed up in this, so don't try to pretend you're suddenly a good guy.'

His back stiffens, and he says without emotion: 'Suit yourself.' He swivels, and walks to his ute. I watch him go, but as I turn away I hear him say, 'I picked up something for you. It was under your mailbox as I came in.' He has a large box, the same size as all the others in his arms. He offers it to me, and I take it. It is not as heavy as the other boxes, but it looks the same.

'See you.' He raises a hand in farewell, and leaves me as if we've just had a friendly chat. Maybe we have.

I put the box in my ute. I'm not curious about the contents. Whatever is in there cannot be good. I go on strolling around my sheds absent-mindedly, picking up sticks and a bucket that the wind has blown out of place, and a piece of a beer carton pushed against the wall. I don't know what Ben is up to, but I'm guessing I will find out soon enough. I don't think he has the slightest desire to help me, so something else is going on.

In the evening, I put the new box on the kitchen bench, fatigued with the game. I consider throwing it in the rubbish tip, and forgetting about it. With a knife, I rip at the top of the box. It does not hold ash, or anything like it. I pull out the packaging, and reach in for a large, round, flattish object. What emerges is a big, smooth plate — a platter, I guess. As it comes out, I can only see its back, which is speckled in a blue-and-white web. It is large and solid, but light. I guess that's a craftsmanship thing. Even I know it has a particular beauty.

I turn it over, and hold it in my outstretched palms, admiring it. But I don't admire for long, because the platter has a photo stuck to the centre of it. It has been hastily and inexpertly done. The photo is not quite centred, and one edge curls upwards, away from the surface. I look closely at the photo, and recognise Tito Slade in a suit and tie, smiling, holding some sort of award. It is pleasant enough. Innocuous even, but underneath the photo in a dark felt-tip pen are the words, 'If you don't want him in a plate, give back the boxes.' I have to hold the platter tightly to stop it slipping from my hands. Why would they use Tito to threaten me? Do they think we were that close? Who would dig Tito's body up to prove a point?

I have to tell Elaine.

'Dave?' There is no annoyance in her voice.

'I've got something I need to show you. Will you be at home for a while?'

'I will. I've got something for you, too.'

'I'm coming right now.'

She is waiting for me at that front-garden gate near where I found her. Her face is wet with tears. The security guard is standing off to the side with his arms crossed. When I get near her, she puts an arm around me, but I keep the box between us. She guides me into her kitchen, and I put my box on her bench. Elaine is very quiet, and I think she might be shaking. I'm not asking myself why.

'I just got it. It's a platter, and it has a photo on it.'

She lets out a small cry, and covers her mouth.

I pull open the flaps of the box, and she puts her hands inside. 'It's a picture of Tito.'

She nods at me, and sobs. She takes the platter out, looks at it, and gasps once. It is a gasp of pain, but not surprise — simply an acknowledgement of something she already knew. She puts the platter down, and walks over to a small table against the wall. She picks up an object wrapped in tissue paper, and brings it to me. I unwrap it, and see that it is a platter, very similar to the one I brought here.

I am afraid of what I am supposed to be looking at. This platter also has a photo stuck to its centre. I know the photo. It is one that was in the local papers: a head shot of James at a football competition, smiling shyly after he was presented with a trophy for 'most improved'. My heart is trying to vomit itself out of my body as I attempt to read the words scribbled in marker pen beneath his shining face: 'Your son would look good in a plate. Don't push your luck.' I hug the plate to my chest, and slump to the ground. I am not crying. I am red-faced, snorting like a threatened bull. I could kill over this. I could do the worst things. Now I really

251

hope they come. Let them come. No one will survive. I sit steaming, soundlessly repeating phrases of revenge. These bastards don't know what they've come up against.

Eventually I stand, remove the photo as best as I can, go outside, put the platter in the back of my ute, get a hammer from the toolbox, and smash it until it is only fine grains of porcelain.

Then I lean back against the ute, and weep for James and for myself. How many times does he have to die? Every night in my head, and now again at the hands of these people. Elaine appears. She puts her arms around me, and her head against my chest. I hug her, but I can't register her pain; only mine.

She mumbles: 'I didn't know. I thought it was just the pieces they wanted. How could I believe he was cremating bodies in our backyard? I thought there was something strange, bad, about the pieces they forced him to make, but he wouldn't tell me what. He said he was protecting me.' She is pushing her forehead hard into my chest, and I don't know whether she is talking to me or herself. 'I thought, if you received the boxes, you would go straight to the police. Then the people who were blackmailing Tito would get angry at me and never leave me alone. So I had to do anything I could to get those boxes. But I didn't know why the pottery was so important. I thought it was because they were expensive pieces.'

I get into my vehicle, and she says, with a sudden strength to her voice, 'I'm really sorry.'

My hand is on the key, but I do not turn it.

'Don't do anything stupid, will you? It's just another threat. They're not going to kill anybody.'

I turn the key, and don't say, *But I might.*

I drive away. Maybe she didn't know. Maybe she really thought Ben was 'kinda cute'. I don't think so. For all I know, she masterminded the whole thing and is now trying to save herself. I drive slowly and methodically, turn at my mailbox, and wind my way to my decrepit house. But as I get close I see something is different in the garden. It is in James's area. There is soil heaped around the edges of the plot. Stupidly, I think someone has dropped off fresh topsoil for me, and then I understand that the soil has not been deposited — it has been dug up. I leap out of my ute and run to the gravesite, knowing they have dug up his bones and taken them, just so I know they're serious. On the edge, my foot catches on the pile of dirt, and I fall headlong into the hole they have dug, my hands stretched out in front of me, and I land with a thud on the coffin, my son's coffin. I rest my head on it, knowing it hasn't been opened and that what remains of him is still there in this little box. I hold the box and whimper, unable to face anything more.

At dawn, after waking up and lying in bed for maybe an hour, I get up, grab my shovel and rake, and head to where James's coffin still waits. I check again that it hasn't been tampered with, and then I begin pushing the soil over it, filling the hole, tamping some of the grass runners back in, and then raking the area smooth. When I'm finished, I crouch beside the grave and talk to James. I tell him I could take all my guns and my ammunition, and hunt them all down, Ben included. Kill these people for doing this to me. Let them know they cannot use my son or my son's death against me. For some minutes, I think this is the right action. I actually look forward to it, and I can picture myself shooting them all multiple times. I am nodding uncontrollably, agreeing with myself that this is the only course to take. Kill them all. And then I think I hear myself saying, *No. No one wants this. No one wants you to do this. Not James. No one.* I yell back that no one else knows what they are talking about; everyone left, taking the easy option, and I am the one who has to deal with all this terrible stuff, and I'm the one who has to protect James. My breathing is thick, and I am banging my fist down into the soft earth. And then I stop.

I look around to see if I've been yelling at anyone real. But it is just me and what is left of my son. The way it will always be. I need to protect him. I need to make him safe, like I didn't when he was alive. Not by killing, and not by shooting, but by giving them what they want.

18

I eat breakfast then pack the five ash boxes into the back of the ute, throw a tarp over them, and strap them down loosely. I'm going to put them in Ben's mailbox, return home, and wash my hands of the whole thing. No more shooting, no more violence, no more death. I pull away from the house and onto the road, and I see Ben's ute rattle past, going towards town or Elaine's or somewhere. I try to wave him down, but he does not look at me, does not stop.

The drive feels much longer than I know it is, but I reach his front ramp and barely noticeable property sign. I cannot remember when I have been to his place. Possibly as a child, before Ben bought the place. I have no real mental picture of his house or any other part of his operation.

I stop and sit, looking at the mailbox, thinking about what I know and what I'm about to do. It is a small mailbox. The boxes will not fit inside it. One box will not fit. I take a box out and put it on the ground, and look at it. It is a plain brown box that has been taped and re-taped. I have handled it so many times it probably has my sweat, the smell of my breath, and the imprint of my memories on it. If someone comes along and sees six boxes sitting in the weather, they might pick them up. They might even check inside them. I don't want that to happen. I put the box back in the ute, and turn into Ben's long driveway.

On a flat area close to the road, a white-faced heron stands, neck extended, looking at me. I slow down, because I know they sometimes like to feed on the recently dead. Maybe an animal has died on the side of the road. But then it spreads its wings and beats them downwards, pushing its great body into the air. Nothing happens quickly, but the bird is soon gone. There is no dead animal, and I wonder why I was even concerned.

The country flattens out in a broad plain all of its own. When Ben chose this farm, he chose well. It is soft country, with deep soils and little rock. I could be jealous if I cared about such things any more. I pass lush paddocks of oats and wheat, with faultless fencing that meets shiny ramps. I'd forgotten the kind of hard-driven perfectionist he is. The road winds its way across a creek, past a huge set of cattle yards and up onto a slight rise where Ben's house and the main sheds sit. His wife, Glenda, spends most of her time in the city. No one knows or probably cares whether they still are a genuine couple. I am certain she will not be at the house. I would not have seen her, even in the distance, for years.

I drive slowly towards the sheds, watching for vehicles parked nearby, where men might be fixing machinery in the sheds, or in the distance, where men could be returning to pick something up or swap machines. There are no vehicles. Nobody about. I don't even know why I'm here. Except that I need to get rid of these boxes, and I know Ben is a bad guy and there is bad stuff going on that he is somehow involved in. I take a run past the front of the large open sheds, and see nothing unusual: tractors, trucks, spray rigs, generators, and gear associated with planting and grain moving. There is nothing to see here, and I wonder what I thought I might find. Bodies hanging from a tree? Buzzcut and his mates having morning tea?

I turn the ute around, and loop back towards the house, keeping an eye out for anyone who might have seen me. But no one is around. I am keen to be out of here now. This could easily be the farm of a good person, a community stalwart, a successful farmer. The garden gate is at the far end of the fence, so I head towards it, thinking it is best to leave the boxes on his verandah.

When I am past the house, I see two foxes just outside the garden, sitting and watching me, cautious. Their ears are up, and they slowly crouch down, watching what I might do. I stop, trying to see what has brought them so close to the house. Perhaps there are fruit trees, a veggie garden, or even dog food to steal. Then I see another fox, sleek and dark-red shiny, cross the flat to join them. It looks back at me momentarily, and then trots towards the others, sniffing the ground here and there, pointedly displaying no sense of urgency. I look back to where he came from, and see behind the house a squat, rounded brick structure with a chimney almost obscured by a line of trees. I swing the ute towards it, and know that it is a kiln — a pottery kiln, if ever I have seen one. The bricks are dark-red and weathered, or maybe coloured by use. It's a construction that has been there for some time. I want to go and inspect it, to see if it has been used recently. Perhaps it has been there for decades, and never fired up. Maybe Ben's wife did pottery, too. But I don't have time to be snooping around. Someone is bound to turn up at any time. And then I think if I don't go and check it out, I will be stuck in another loop of 'maybe'. If it hasn't been used in years, then that line of wondering can be shut down. I look back towards the shed and down the road to the mailbox. Nobody is about, and I cannot hear a tractor or a ute.

I drive round the back of the house, and park where I think I can't be seen from the entrance. I walk through the back-garden gate to the front door, and knock. There is no answer, and I yell out quite loudly, asking if anyone is home. The house is silent. So I sprint through the garden and out the back gate. Then I run across the couple of hundred metres of grassy paddock to the front of the kiln. There is a car track: not a road, but a recently used line of wheel ruts. The grass has not been allowed to grow over the bare dirt. Neither has it been able to grow in the small area at the front of the kiln. I can see before I step that there is a faint remnant of a footprint. A large-tread work boot maybe.

The kiln has a cast-iron door at the front. I heave it open, noticing that it is not covered in dirt or cobwebs, or anything else that might suggest this thing is a never-used relic. Inside, the surface is clean, and swept clean. I can't tell if it has been used in the past few weeks, but it is certainly in use. And then I hear the sound of a motor — distant, and then suddenly close. I run to the side of the kiln, away from the noise. I look around, madly trying to locate it. I don't know what I'm going to say if it is Ben. I might even accuse him outright. But then the vehicle sound moves on towards the sheds and beyond, and I see a white farm ute bump its way to the paddocks on the other side. I try to steady my breathing, and I walk bent double, instinct telling me this is what you do when you are hoping not to be seen.

I start my ute, turn back, and speed up, leaving the house behind me, all the time checking mirrors for a sign of the ute or any other. Near the sheds there is a bloke standing next to his ute talking on a phone, watching me go. I pass the bright crops, and then pull up at Ben's mailbox. All I have to do is put the boxes in his mailbox, and then the problem is over. That was why I came up here. Except I am now certain that Ben was cremating the bodies, and that he was manipulating Tito and maybe Elaine. I should go to the police, but it would be so much easier to leave the problem here. The police might not even believe me.

I get out and reach for one of the boxes, but as I grab hold of it and feel the weathered cardboard, and the weight of the ash, I know that I am hoping if I give the boxes back, all the badness in the world will go away. In this scenario, Ben turns out to be a bastard, but not an evil bastard. James does not die, Sarah does not leave, Elaine does not get bashed, and I do not trash my life. Everything will be sweet. But badness never goes away. I'm the only person I know who could believe it would. I have to go to the police, no matter how messy it turns out to be.

I hear a vehicle approaching, and see Ben in the distance, the dust thick behind him. I shove the box away, across the back of the ute, jump into the driver's seat, and push the ute to reach a high speed as quickly as possible. He won't be able to stop me if I have enough momentum. We are heading straight for each other on this narrow road. I jam my foot to the floor. Maybe he suspects nothing, but I can't take the risk.

As we get closer, I realise a ramp marks the halfway point between us. If I can't get through that ramp before he gets to me, I'll be blocked — the only way round will be to smash through the fences on either side. But I am confident I am gaining on him and should make it through before he gets there. I sit down a little in my seat, and hang on to the steering wheel. I feel like I am beating him, and surely if I get past I'll be able to outrun his old machine. And then, when I am under a hundred metres from the ramp, I realise he has somehow increased his speed and that I am not going to make it as easily as I thought. He seems to be getting faster. As I reach the approaches to the ramp, he is on me, but I am still ahead. I cross the ramp, thinking I'll make it, but in that time he somehow gets to me, and power-slides his ute sideways across the ramp, hitting hard against the ramp side panels. The next sound is the noise of my bullbar crunching into his passenger door, and my head smashing into the windscreen. I try to restart the ute so I can back out, but it will not fire. I try again and again, but nothing happens.

The blood is starting to run down my forehead into my eyes as I get out, my feet unsteady on the bars of the ramp. I wipe the blood away, and feel my way along the bonnet. Ben is standing on the other side of his ute, watching me.

'What do you think you're doing?'

'What the fuck are you doing?' I ask, standing as still and straight as I can.

'I want my boxes.'

'They're not yours.'

'Yes, they are. There's a lot of money tied up in those boxes.'

I can't think clearly enough to come up with a strategy. I should just give him what he wants. I will give him what he wants.

'They're in the back. They're all yours.'

'Walk back over the ramp, and get away from the vehicle.' He motions to the paddock. I do as he says and make my way, hand-over-hand, back across the ramp and down the road. I turn, and slump down into the gravel. My head hurts something fierce, and my eyesight is a bit blurry, but I can clearly still see him begin to lift the boxes out, one by one, and put them in the back of his car. My aching head is saying, *Let it go, let it go. It's not your fight. When he lets you go, you can head straight to the police.* But still I lean back on one arm, and let my hand find the largest stone I can. Then I stand up, and when he turns to ask, 'Where's the seventh box?' I pelt the rock at him. It catches him just below the eye, and he staggers, one leg giving way for a moment. He pulls himself back up, and begins a loud, crazy roar, and runs at me, stumbling across the bars and then sprinting over the gravel at me. I wait for him. I am stronger and younger. I know that I can take him. But he hits me hard with his shoulder, and as I pull him away, we go down. He is hard-muscled and I am soft-headed, and we wrestle onto the grass, flailing at each other. I try to choke him, and then punch him with as much force as I can in the stomach. It doesn't stop him finding the rock, which he brings up and smashes into the side of my head.

19

I wake on what feels like a concrete floor, my head pounding and my eyes aching. My ribs are sore, and my stomach is tender. I open my eyes slowly, see I have been sick more than once, and then I smell it. I am in a single square room with white walls. It has no windows or cupboards or furniture. There is a door in the corner that is sealed into its frame. The only other things I can see are a water bottle and a piece of rope. There is something dried and flaky on my face, which I guess must be blood. When I look up, I see a rail with stainless-steel hooks on it for hanging carcasses. I vomit again, and it hurts so much I feel like my eyes are going to pop out of their sockets. I look around again at the walls and the door, and guess that this is a cool room. But the room is not cold. The cooling must be turned right up. I remember crashing into Ben at the ramp, and not much else, but I don't need to. I'm pretty sure I'm at his place, locked in his cool room. Locked away, for whatever reason. He must be piping air in somewhere, because you can suffocate in a room like this. I feel for my phone, but it is gone.

I drag myself across the floor and sit up, my back against the wall, and close my eyes. I force myself to breathe even, regular breaths. Someone will notice I'm missing. Maybe not. Probably not. I don't stay in contact with anyone, and I don't have anyone waiting for me. But Ben will have to get rid of my ute somehow, and explain a big dent in his own vehicle. Neither of those things would be easy. He's probably just keeping me here until he does what he has to with the ashes. When the evidence is removed, he'll let me go. Who would believe my story anyway? Not Constable Murray. It would only be my preposterous word against Ben's.

I sleep, and wake. I feel like I have been here for days, but maybe I haven't. I have no concept of time, and I am starting to lose the concept of me. I think I hear voices outside: Marko; Elaine; Tom; Ian threatening Ben, and demanding my release. They have come to my rescue just in time. But even my foggy brain knows this can't be true. The insulation in the cool room makes it soundproofed. I could never hear any voices except my own.

The next time I rouse, there is a sandwich on a plate on the floor not far from me. My head, and everything about me, hurts, and eating is something I feel I'll never do again. But I make myself lean across and grab the plate — ham, tomato, and cheese on white bread. I can't taste it, but I manage to eat it. At least he's not trying to starve me to death.

And then Sarah is sitting on the floor beside me, legs crossed, rubbing her hands on her knees. I ignore her, because it's impossible that she is here. She says over and over that she doesn't blame me, and it wasn't my fault. Accidents happen. I believe her, but it doesn't matter. It's all finished for me now. I tell her I love her, and she disappears. Then all the people that matter to me visit: Mum, Dad, Marko and Helen, Ian and Mandy, Ralph and Reedy, Tom Little, the fire brigade boys, distant relatives, and people I've known all my life. All of them encourage me, telling me not to give up. I just smile at them and nod, accepting their goodwill, but refusing to point out that there is no future for me, and nothing to be positive about. Even Elaine turns up, apologising and swearing she never knew a thing. At one point she takes off her clothes, but I turn away. I should never have had anything to do with her.

Then I'm alone. I stand for the first time in what seems weeks. My head doesn't hurt as much, and my sight is clearer. I piss in the corner, and the stench fills the room. I drink some water, and slump back down on the floor. Across from me is a rope. I pick it up, and run it through my hands. It is a good piece, fairly new, and maybe ten metres long. Why a rope? I look up at the rail bolted to the ceiling, and suddenly I know what Ben's plan is. He thinks I'm only a little push off finishing myself. Already mad as. A couple of days in solitary confinement, and I'm as good as gone. He's right. He's more astute than I ever gave him credit for.

I make the loop for a noose, and begin to tie the simple knot. I get it wrong, and try again, remembering how my father taught me. He told me it uses a lot of rope, but it doesn't jam and doesn't loosen too easily. On the second try, I get it right. I hang it up in front of my face. And then James is in the room on his motorbike — at least I think it's him, but I can't actually tell, because he is wearing a helmet that conceals his head. He rides around the room getting low on the corners, and flattening it out on the straights. Eventually, he stops and takes his helmet off. He is smiling that brilliant, bloody smile, and then he disappears.

I pick up the noose again, and my father says, *You'll be doing what he wants you to do.* He nods towards the noose. *When you're done, he might even hang you up in a tree at our place. No one would be surprised.*

No, they wouldn't.

It will take you weeks to die in here if you don't hang yourself. He'll have to kill you. Make him kill you, my father says. *The longer you're here, the better chance that someone will come looking.*

Who? I ask, and he is gone, right when I needed him. I undo the noose, and throw the rope across the room, then lie down flat on the floor, and sleep.

I am woken by Ben at the door. He has a bottle of water, another sandwich in a bag, and a plastic bucket, all in one hand. With the other hand, he points a revolver at me and says, 'Move to the other end of the room.' I shuffle my way over, and sit with my legs up, my forearms resting on my knees. He puts the food and drink down, watching me the whole time, then picks up the plate and the empty bottle, places the bucket in the corner, and says, 'Shit in this.'

'What are you going to do with me?'

He ignores me.

266

'People will come looking pretty soon. You know that.'

'No one is going to come looking. You buggered all that up, and you know it. No one gives a fuck about you.'

I want to say, 'Yes they do,' but I can't find the conviction.

'You still owe me a box.' He says it in hard, flat tones so I don't mistake him for a human being.

'It had money in it. I spent it,' I tell him.

He leaves, and I feel my brain begin to work like it should. If he wants to kill me, why hasn't he done it? Because killing a person, even if you hate them, is hard unless you're a psychopath. Is he really hoping I'll kill myself? It's possible. It even makes sense — no blood. He really could hang me from a tree, and by the time someone finds me, the birds will have pulled me apart. Or he could say the foxes dragged me in — I know there are plenty of foxes around here. But it seems obvious that he doesn't want to shoot me. Perhaps he's keeping me alive for someone else — someone who wants revenge, or just wants to ask me questions. But he's also got a logic problem. If I really think I'm going to die in here, which I have been thinking, what's to stop me from jumping him? All he can do is kill me.

I stand up and walk across the room, flexing and stretching my legs. They are stiff and uncertain, but the movement helps. I reach for the sandwich, and keep walking across the diagonal, then around the edges. My head still aches, but only in the places where it was hit. I stop at the door, and try to kick it out. The impact of my foot on the door does nothing except make my head hurt more. The only way out is through that door past Ben. But he knows that. He must think I'm too frightened of being shot to chance it, or he is only prepared to keep me alive for as long as it doesn't get too difficult. So if I rush him, he'll just murder me. Simple as that.

Is this what he did with all the victims? Kidnapped them from somewhere, drove them to the farm, and kept them in here until they killed themselves or were executed? Is it the bodies the foxes come for? I am exhausting myself with questions, and that is not a bad thing. I know it's pretty hard to hit anything with a handgun unless you take a steady, supported stance. If I'm quick and lucky, he might only hit me in the leg — which can kill, of course, but I feel like it gives me a chance. So the next time he comes through the door, I will attack him, and steal his revolver. That is my plan.

But he doesn't come. An ocean of time passes while I ready myself for his arrival and my move. I walk as much as I can stand it, and then I sleep fitfully, worried that he will come and go like the first time, and I won't even get a crack at him.

And then, finally, I hear a noise at the door, and it opens slightly. There is bright daylight in a thin line across the floor. I brace myself, but try to look half-asleep and pathetic. I groan as if still in pain. The light is too bright.

Ben's voice says, 'You can go.'

I think I've heard it wrong, but he says it again to make sure: 'You can go, leave, go home.'

The door swings wide open, but no one shows themselves. I walk out, shielding my eyes, looking around to see what is going on. I guess the evidence has disappeared, and all I can try for is kidnapping or something. Deprivation of liberty? Isn't that a thing?

Outside, Ben is watching, standing well back with a rifle casually hanging over one arm. Behind him is a guy who might be 'Sergei' from the races, but I am in no condition to tell. Ben tosses me my phone, and I drop it and then pick it up. The screen tells me it is Wednesday, 10.00 a.m. I have been here for something like forty-eight hours. There is a message from Marko, and two missed calls from him, and one from Ralph.

Ben waves the barrel at my ute, and says, 'It's working. The radiator was pushed onto the fan. We fixed it.'

I walk towards my ute. My head is fuzzy, but still a question makes its way through: *Isn't he concerned I'll run him down? Or is that what he wants?*

I get into my ute, and fire it up. He watches me, but doesn't move or talk or gesture. I drive away through the paddocks, and out through the front ramp. I can't feel anything, and I can hardly hold the road. It takes a lifetime to get home.

James's plot is neat, and the grass has hardly grown. I'm relieved. But the windows in my house are all broken. Inside, no one waits for me. Again, the furniture is all overturned, the cupboards pulled out, the carpets ripped up. I right my couch, flop down onto it, and sit like a genuine zombie, with nothing happening in either my head or my heart. Then I wake myself, and try to check if I am alive. Did I die in that cool room, but just don't know it yet? I go to the sink and turn on the hot water, and wait for it to be scalding hot. Then I stick my arm in the stream to see what happens. What happens is I feel a powerful burning sensation on my skin. I withdraw my arm, and leap around the room cursing before I get back to the tap, where I run cold water over the burn. Nobody said you couldn't feel pain in heaven, and everybody says you suffer pain in hell, so my test is inconclusive. I could be in hell. It's kind of a dopey realisation. This place has been hell long before I ended up in Ben's cool room.

I listen to the messages on my landline. Mick and Marko are wondering where I am. They've both got something they need to give to me. The messages on my mobile from Marko and Ralph are the same. I don't care what they want or what they have.

I sit back down on the couch, and fall asleep. In a while, I get up, not sure where I am or what has happened. The blood still caked on my face reminds me. I take a long shower, have a drink of water, return to the couch, and close my eyes. I have a nightmare about Ted and Special and wake remembering they have not been fed or thought of or cared for. I drive to the kennels where they sit waiting with their pure expectant hearts. I return to my house, but before I lie down again I walk to the meat room to see if the money has been taken. I'm not sure if I care, but I lift the cloth covering the box anyway. The money is still there. As usual, Ben's men weren't as thorough as they should have been. I find my way back to the couch and pass out.

20

There is a light knock on the frame of the door that I didn't bother to close when I came in.

'Dave?'

It rouses me, but I ignore it. I never need to have another visitor. I will never move from this couch. I am done. But the rapping is persistent, and I hear slow, soft footsteps making their way through the house.

'Dave.'

It is Elaine. She is cautious, and quietly spoken. It takes me a while to lift my head, and by then she has already walked into the room and is staring at me. 'God. What happened here?'

'Ben. Go away.'

She scans the room. It's not that much worse than it was before. 'We didn't know where you were. Marko said you were probably just camping or something.'

She sits down next to me. I do not look at her, and I'm not even sure she is real. 'I was too frightened to ring, because I knew you'd made a decision about me. But then Marko called, wondering where you were, and I started to worry that you'd done something to yourself. I've been ringing and ringing.'

I don't talk, hoping she'll realise I want her to go away, but she doesn't take the hint, so I say, 'Ben kidnapped me.'

'He what?'

'Held me hostage in his cool room.'

'No he didn't.'

'Yes he did. Your friend. He just let me out.'

Elaine jumps up. 'He can't do that. We've got to tell the police'.

'What do I tell them?'

'The truth.'

She takes out a phone, and begins talking to someone. I think she has called the police, but then I hear it is Marko. She ends the conversation by saying, 'Yeah, tell everyone.'

I close my eyes, and wish they would all just go away.

'You need to tell the police,' she says again.

'I haven't got any evidence. Just my accusation.'

'We'll find some evidence.'

'I don't think I can trust you.'

'You can trust me. I did the wrong thing, but I didn't know what I was involved in.'

We sit still and silently. I don't have the strength or the energy to work out if she is telling the truth. Ben will do whatever he wants to, and there is nothing I can do about it. I can hear her breathing, and I don't want to. No one can go back. Nothing can be taken back.

Then I hear her leave the house through the front door. My body relaxes, and I can feel my face flatten. I am alone.

But she soon returns.

'This arrived for you in a small box.'

'Of course it did.' I can't look at her or hear the mention of another box. It is more evidence that my existence is just repetition, and new ways

273

to experience pain. I'm sure that at any moment Buzzcut and his friends will be at my door, demanding to know where the crockery is.

'Look at it, Dave, please.'

I bury my head in my hands, and then sit up and begin to slap myself hard, suddenly grasping the possibility that this is all just a hallucination brought on by alcohol withdrawal. But nothing changes.

Elaine kneels down next to me. 'Please. I'm sure it was made by Tito. It's from a bowl or something, but it's not a broken piece — it's been cut. I'm sure it means something. See?'

I look at the thing in her hand. It is a pottery shard, bright-white and shiny. Elaine rolls it over in her hands. The flat part has colour on it, and I remember the 'magic' piece that Shiflon gave me when he was here. It is the same.

I put my hand out, and she looks encouraged, wrapping my fingers around the shard. It is smooth and weighty in my hand. The colour is on the flat part of the piece. It looks like a section of a photo somehow incorporated in the glaze. *God, no.* It must be another photo of James. Why would she bring me this?

And then, of course, a car pulls up outside. Mick comes through the front door, carrying something in one hand, and saying, 'Where the fuck have you been? I've been trying to reach you. Had to drive all the fucking way up here.'

He sees the room, and Elaine, and stops, checks her out, sticks out a hand, and says, 'Mick. Brother-in-law. Ex.'

They shake hands, and he walks over to me,

274

puts a palm on my shoulder, and asks, 'Are you all right? You look like shit.' And then, as if to deflect attention from his comment, he says, 'Redecorated, I see.'

'I'm okay.'

'I got this in the mail. The note said it must get to you. I figured it was from one of your gangster mates. I thought it might blow up. I went into the scrub with a bike helmet and leathers on, and opened it. Nothing happened. It's just a piece of pottery. You people and pottery. Fuck.'

He extracts a piece just like the others, and I take it and put it alongside Elaine's, and hold them up. He seems impressed. They click neatly together: pieces of a pie. They have been cut like timber lap joints, one overlapping the other. It has been done so precisely that when I join them and hold them out, you can't tell there was ever a join. Elaine and Mick watch, entranced. I put the pieces down, and stand up, thinking I need to get my piece when another vehicle stops outside my house. I brace myself. When does this end? Does it only stop if I do?

Marko and Ralph blunder through the door. 'Hey, what's going on? Bloody hell, this room.' Marko says, standing just past the doorway, with Ralph at his shoulder. 'Are you sick?'

'No, I'm fine.'

'You don't look it,' Ralph says.

'We've got stuff we're supposed to give to you,' Marko says.

In the palm of his large hand, Marko has another box. He pushes it at me. Ralph does the same. 'It came in the mail, but we couldn't get hold of you. Elaine said just bring it over.'

From each box I take a piece just like the one Mick has brought in. I take them over to the table, my legs like wet noodles beneath me, and, holding on, click them together. Then I go to my office and retrieve the section that Shiflon gave me, and go back to the table. They watch me, unable to decide what to do with me. My shard clicks in, and I now have five parts of a six-piece puzzle. They show a photo taken from an unusual angle, maybe from someone's pocket. It is of a man alongside a brick kiln. It shows the bare-dirt area in front of the kiln. The photo is clear and crisp. The man is Ben, and he is reaching over something that looks like a body, but without the sixth part I cannot tell.

'Shit. That's Ben,' says Ralph. 'What's he doing?'

Marko is quick to explain. 'I reckon he's putting a body in a kiln to burn it. We need that sixth piece.'

'Who would have the sixth piece?' Mick asks.

The rest of them immediately say, 'Ian.'

I shake my head. 'If Tito made this to protect me, he wouldn't have thought of Ian as someone close to me.'

'He wouldn't have thought I was, either.' Elaine might be about to break into tears.

'Yes, but if he thought I might get into trouble, then he would have assumed you'd be involved.'

And then she asks the question that I wouldn't, 'What if it's made with human ash?'

I almost knock the made-up bowl onto the

276

floor. If Tito did this as a final attempt at providing protection, then of course it is made from the remains of someone murdered. As I think about this, another car arrives. This time I'm sure it is Ben, come to threaten or kill me. Maybe he knows about the bowl. Maybe that's what he and his goons have been looking for the whole time.

I tell everyone to hide, and they move to go, but then stop. Marko says, 'Nope. We're not hiding.'

But the face that pokes through the front door and says 'Hello?' is Tom Little's, unmarked and innocent. 'Am I interrupting something?' he says. I can hear my friends relax.

'No. Please come in.' I know immediately why he is here. I remember I told Tito about Tom — how much I liked him.

He sidles through the door, carrying another small, brown box in two hands.

I take the piece out of his box, and slot it into its place. Everyone crowds around to see the photo of Ben pushing a body into his kiln. The man's face is undistinguishable, and all I know about him is that he is dead. There are actually gasps around me. It is a gruesome picture, even if you don't know what it represents.

This is the reason Ben let me go. He couldn't find the seventh box, so he chose to let me go and lead him to it.

Elaine breaks into our private thoughts. 'Tito took this photo, didn't he? He was there, helping Ben put the bodies in the kiln. He was part of this. He cooked these poor people.'

Everyone looks at her, thinking that she is right and unable to say anything to comfort her.

'Can everyone take a photo of this, and send it somewhere safe?' I ask. Elaine's pain and remorse are not my current problem. They respond and pull out their phones, and frame the bowl and the photo.

'Marko, would you ring the police and tell them we've got important evidence in a murder case, and we're bringing it in right now?'

He steps away and puts his phone to his ear.

And then we are in the vehicles in convoy: Ralph and Marko at the front, then Tom, me, Elaine, and Mick in the rear. We take it steady. I have told them not to let anyone pass, no matter who they are or how angry they get. The guys at the front and the back spread out from the middle three, hoping they can handle any problem that comes along before it reaches me. I have divided the pieces of the bowl between Tom and myself. If Ben or one of his men gets to one of us, hopefully the other one can make it.

We take the turn out of Wilson Road, and see no one. If so much hadn't happened in the past forty-eight hours, I would think we were being melodramatic. Surely one of us can just whizz over to town with the evidence? But nothing is beyond Ben, so we have to do the safest thing. We pass the mailman going the other way, and his face says he'd like to know what we're up to. He will tell Ben what he has seen.

We continue on the road to town with no other traffic.

And then I see a ute in the distance behind us.

It could be anyone, but whoever they are, they are really setting a pace. I see the ute come up behind Mick, hardly slowing. It tries to pass, but Mick takes the middle of the road. The ute slows, and I hear it honk its horn, and it tries again. Mick snakes from side to side, blocking the way. Then the ute veers off into the table drain and out into the long grass. Mick gives chase, but he can't match the craziness of the ute driver, who is tearing along the uneven terrain on the side of the road. Mick loses speed and falls back. Elaine, now last in the convoy and the only vehicle between Ben and me, has not moved position, and the ute is coming up to overtake her. My blood turns cold, and I realise that I've been soft in the head. She is in on this with Ben — of course she is — she must have alerted him that we were on our way to hand over the evidence.

Ben gains on us. Marko and Ralph and Tom pull back, in case they can help. I am slamming my hands against the steering wheel, screaming at Elaine, but she doesn't hear me or see me. Her face is blank in my rear-view mirror. She is lost to something I don't understand, and I realise I have to put distance between me and her, and fast. On the two-way on Marko's channel, I say, 'Got to make a run for it, Marko. It's all we can do.' I hear, 'Roger,' and see his vehicle immediately speed up. Tom gets the message, and increases his pace.

But now Ben is almost equal with Elaine, bumping and jumping through the rough ground and over the tall tussocks. I am cursing Elaine and her trickery, and my endless stupidity, and I push my foot to the floor as Ben gets level with Elaine's taillights.

And then, as Ben begins to move in towards the road, aiming at me, I see Elaine spin her wheels. Her car turns sharply and peels off, spearing over the drain, through the grass and headlong into the front point of Ben's ute. There's a tremendous crunching sound and I can see the look of shock and rage on Ben's face as the impact sends him spinning off across the grass. Elaine chases alongside him until he comes to a stop. She spins and rams her bullbar against his passenger door, forcing his machine across the paddock until it hits hard up against a fence.

I cheer, and shake my fist with triumph, and leave them behind, hoping Mick will soon be there to support her. Before I can radio Marko to help, he has thrown a sliding U-turn, and headed back towards where Elaine is waiting. I wave at Tom to go forward, and we continue to the station in safety.

21

I am at my mailbox. The air is warmer than it has been for months. The European trees are in full bud, impatient for spring to step forward. It is mail day, but I am not going to check the mailbox. Whatever is in it can wait until I return. For now, I am on my way to lunch at Marko's in his back courtyard with the fire pit going, if needed. There will be good food and drinks, and favourite old stories. It won't be the same as it used to be, but it will be something like it. Friendship long held, I guess. I am giving Elaine a lift. We're friends, too, and we might stay just that. There is no rush. We can take it as it comes.

After we dropped off the pieces of the bowl, Constable Murray called the detectives in, and they were apparently very happy with what we had delivered. A DNA test showed the bowl was made with human remains, probably from the man in the picture. They had a whole lot of stuff on Ben, the fake Vasilievs, and significant underworld people who had disappeared without a trace, but they hadn't been able to make the links between them. We did that for them.

Constable Murray told me the detectives now believe that Ben invented the Vasiliev family some years ago out of a small group of thugs that included one assassin. It was an attempt to divert attention from himself and his money-making operation. They suspect that, at the time, Ben was feeding the bodies of his victims to his pigs, but they think this will be difficult to prove.

So Tom got the story of a lifetime. A city newspaper picked it up, published it nationwide, and then hired him. He was even a celebrity for a few days, and did the rounds of morning television. This week, he moves to the city to start the new job, and I wish he wouldn't. It's a selfish wish I keep to myself.

Ben was arrested, and is awaiting trial. He denies everything. He says the idea that he would threaten me, or lock me in his cool room, or force Tito to make pottery from human bones is just a delusion made up by someone who everyone in the district knows is off his head. I think that's his main defence: the whole thing is a ridiculous fantasy made up by a lunatic who hates him. It won't go well.

But I don't care. I've given the police as much as I can. I would rather forget it all, because I need to begin again.

I went to James's grave this morning, and talked to him for a long time. It was the first time for over a week. I tried to explain what happened. I know he can't hear me, but I needed to do it, and there is some comfort in it. I don't miss him any less, but I notice I'm liking me more.

Sarah is getting married when we get the divorce organised, and she says I'll be invited to the wedding. I'd rather she stayed married to me, but that's a stupid thing to feel, so I'll settle with being happy for her. I plan to give her what is left of the cash, and ask for some time to get the farm productive again so I can pay out her share. We'll see how that goes.

I asked Lenny and Trevor if they could work for me three days a week to start to get things into shape. They agreed to. I've also cleaned up my house, used some of the money to get the windows repaired, and spent longs days digging, weeding, and rehabilitating Mum's garden. I think it is a good place for James to rest. And for me to go forward from.

I sometimes wonder what would have happened if I had known, in the beginning, that that first box was from Dad: if Constable Murray had brought the box to me herself, or I had seen Dad's note on the inside of the box on the day the money arrived. If I knew then that the cash was a gift from my father, maybe none of this would have happened. When those boxes of ash arrived, I would have taken them straight to the police. There'd be no story to tell. No one would have been shot at, threatened, bashed, knocked out, or hurt, and Tom wouldn't be leaving.

I know Tom is so excited with the possibilities of his new life that I need to stop wishing he'd stay. I will soon.

I leave my mailbox behind, and drive towards Elaine's. She'll be waiting at her front gate, because she is always on time.

Elaine has told me she didn't know anything about Ben's underworld life. She's still having trouble accepting that Buzzcut and his mates were working for him. Apparently, Ben had never shown his nasty side until he started demanding she produce the boxes. He claimed the family who the pottery was for were threatening to hurt him if he didn't find the boxes. I suppose that's all true. I don't know what else I'm supposed to believe.

An echidna waddles along the side of the road, all spines and snout, and I slow down in case he decides to cross. But he turns unhurriedly into the long grass, and I am amazed, again, at how he manages to be bizarre and perfect all at the same time. It gives me a sense of peace, and I realise I'm happy enough to be me, to be Dave Martin. I'm pretty sure I couldn't say that if all this crazy stuff hadn't happened.

We do hope that you have enjoyed reading
this large print book.

Did you know that all of our titles
are available for purchase?

We publish a wide range of high quality
large print books including:
Romances, Mysteries, Classics
General Fiction
Non Fiction and Westerns

Special interest titles available in
large print are:
The Little Oxford Dictionary
Music Book
Song Book
Hymn Book
Service Book

Also available from us courtesy of
Oxford University Press:
Young Readers' Dictionary
(large print edition)
Young Readers' Thesaurus
(large print edition)

For further information or a free
brochure, please contact us at:
Ulverscroft Large Print Books Ltd.,
The Green, Bradgate Road, Anstey,
Leicester, LE7 7FU, England.
Tel: (00 44) 0116 236 4325
Fax: (00 44) 0116 234 0205

Other titles published by Ulverscroft:

RETRIBUTION

Richard Anderson

Early one Christmas morning, in a small town deep in rural Australia, Graeme Sweetapple is heading home with a truck full of stolen steers when he comes across an upended ute that has hit a tree. He is about to get involved with Luke, an environmental protestor who isn't what he seems; a washed-up local politician, Caroline Statham, who is searching for a sense of purpose, but whose businessman husband seems to be sliding into corruption; and Carson, who is wild, bound to no one, and determined to escape her circumstances. Into their midst comes Retribution, a legendary horse worth a fortune. Her disappearance triggers a cycle of violence and retaliation that threatens the whole community. As tensions build, they must answer one question: is true retribution ever possible — or even desirable?